# Contents

*Dedication*

*To Sue and Big Dan*

# Chapter 1

# Black Mountain

All over Belfast the blistering Sunday afternoon sun drew young and old alike outdoors.

Some people had small front gardens in which to sit and relax. Others had gardens, back and front. But most working-class people, apart from those who had moved out to the new Housing Trust estates, sat at the doors of their brown terrace houses or in their backyards to be sunned.

There were elderly people on chairs and next door neighbours chatting to each other, resting on cool, creamy-coloured window sills, the sharp edges of which had been rounded by annual coats of paint. A little girl in a dry bathing suit crosses the road clattering in her mother's high heels. A budgerigar in its cage is hung from a cup-hook in one door: a gurgling baby tos and froes in its swing hung from another door. A few sparrows, tippling on melting tarmac, enjoy a dust-bath in a small pot-hole.

In the Falls there was nothing contradictory about music from the BBC's *Two-way Family Favourites* for British forces in Germany playing in a side street from noon to one o'clock only to be followed two hours later by the live broadcast of a Gaelic football match on the Dublin station, Radio Éireann.

Children aged four and five years went venturing into the next street. Young and older children, who had assembled into gangs and who had thoroughly rooted out their own districts, made sorties into new lands — from the Falls across to the embankments of the River Lagan or into the leafy sereneness of the University, Stranmillis and Malone residential areas to admire the palatial houses and villas and their luxuriant gardens.

Those teenagers not off to the parks (where their mothers believed them to be) were away discovering by train or bicycle the delights of Helen's Bay or Bangor on Belfast Lough. In other parts of the city working-class children sneaked off to the hills which skirt West and North Belfast.

From Antrim Town direction, Black Mountain and Divis Mountain have little shape or form. But from Holywood in County Down they are clearly visible and most striking against a milky skyline at sunset. People look at them, too, from the southern suburbs of the city with perhaps no more interest than for a sign of the weather, of how low the clouds are.

On this day in July 1963 five boys and one little girl were resting before they continued their climb of the mountain.

The youngest of the gang, eight-year-old Jimmy O'Neill was here with his cousin Tony and was not a close neighbour of the others. He listened intently to their conversation.

'Shoosh! Listen,' ordered Tommy, the smartest dressed of them all, as the boys sat in their Sunday-best tee shirts and shorts and absorbed the majestic view of Belfast city. Sure enough there was a peaceful silence as the noise of life below fell short of their altitude. Only a low breeze occasionally rustled in their ears and a turn of the head neutralised the sound.

'Hey Tommy,' Seán McCann asked. 'Where do things come from? Like all this and the sun?'

'From God, of course,' he replied. 'Everything comes from God. Your mammy and daddy comes from God.'

'Our Angela comes from God,' chirped in Seán's sister, Mary Ann, as children often do, whose convictions are strengthened through repetition.

The sun shone from behind her and splinters of light poured around her auburn hair which was tied with a skinny yellow ribbon in a bun on top. Little red wisps in masses escaped the discipline of the bow and added to the halo effect.

'Hey. Where does our dog Cocker come from?' Jimmy asked.

'Everything comes from God,' muttered Tommy. He quickly added: 'Stevie. Where do trolley buses come from?'

Before the eleven-year-old had time to blunder, Tommy couldn't restrain himself and declared: 'The back of the City Hall!' They all laughed as the trick question and its answer sank in.

Big Stevie Donnelly was chubby but well made. It was his task to trample down nettles, test the ground and help the others up any steep elevations. His head of thick, black hair and round face and his natural reticence disguised a fearlessness when roused. He lived in the street next to Tommy, Seán, and Tony who were aged nine or ten, and who were all classmates when school had broken up for the summer holidays a few weeks previously.

Stevie had come down a weight, so to speak, by playing with these three particular friends. Even though he was their elder, he wasn't quite ready to leave behind forever cowboys and Indians

# WEST BELFAST

## A Novel
by

# Danny Morrison

THE MERCIER PRESS
CORK AND DUBLIN

The Mercier Press, 4 Bridge Street, Cork
24 Lower Abbey Street, Dublin 1

© Danny Morrison 1989

British Library Cataloguing in Publication Data
Morrison, Danny
    West Belfast
    I. Title
    823'.914 [F]

    ISBN 0–85342–910–3

*West Belfast* is a work of fiction. With the exception of historical
personages and situations all characters and events in this book are
entirely imaginary and bear no relation to any living person or event.

### Buíochas

*I would like to thank Mary Hughes for her painstaking work in
typing the manuscript and for her suggestions: those who read the
first draft and also suggested improvements; and all my many friends
and comrades for their unfailing encouragement.*

Printed by Litho Press, Midleton, Co. Cork.

and other games which gave him such pleasure. He enjoyed the respect which his brawn earned him. Without him there was no way they would have crossed foreign territory — the Whiterock and Ballymurphy housing estates where their very welfare was in peril.

Though the oldest boy led, the navigator remained Tommy. Standing four feet tall, with one hand covering his puffy eyes from the dazzle of the sky, he had been arguing for some time with Stevie that whilst from the ground the summit might appear to rise from this part of the mountain — and they even argued whether this was Black Mountain or Divis — the highest point was actually on the next hill.

Struggling uncomplainingly behind Stevie, Seán, Tommy, Tony, and even Mary Ann, came Jimmy, armed with a bow and a quiver full of arrows. He lived in the next district to the others, but just far enough away to sever it off with clear lines of demarcation, even from the adult's perspective of grocery shops, the butchers' and pubs most frequented, from which the distinctive notion of *their* locals was derived. Opting for these friends of his cousin Tony, Jimmy showed a streak of apparent independence and some mettle. But it belied an innocence which found expression within the privacy of his home where he loved to sit on his mother's lap, in jealous competition with his younger sister, Sheila, and be cuddled, or carried to bed in his father's arms after a long day.

When deep in happy thoughts he normally walked with a determined stride-and-a-half in hopping movements, his brown longish hair bouncing up and down. Now his legs were sore and his forehead and armpits exuded an odourless, puppy sweat. He could have gone on but was glad to have heard the call to halt.

'Your daddy doesn't own ya, ya know.'

'Whad you say?'

Seán repeated his claim.

'Whadya mean?' Tony asked Seán, whose dimples deepened as he struggled to explain himself.

'Your daddy doesn't own ya, 'cos ya came from yer mammy.'

'But he helped put ya there,' speculated Tony, who had picked up that notion from various innuendoes.

'How'd he do that, Tommy?' inquired Seán, turning towards their mentor.

Tommy appeared stumped.

'Eh? Ach I can't remember. . . Is yer daddy old, Jimmy?' he asked.
'Naw.'
'What age is he?'
'Fifty, I think.'
'Gee! Fifty and he's not old?'
'Naw. He can still run. He can run faster than me. You wanna
see him the other night,' he added in his defence.
'See that cut, Stevie?' Tommy interrupted and pointed to his
knee. 'I got that fixing a puncture when a big chisel this size sprung
from a spoke. Did ya ever see a scar like that? Did ya? Did ya
now?'
Stevie admired it.
Tony said: 'Ya wanna see our Phelim's head. He fell and hit it
against the hearth.'
'What age is he?' queried Tommy again.
'He's none, but he's okay now.'
'Whadya call a German bank robber?' challenged Jimmy.
'Dunno.'
'Hans Up!' he zestfully bellowed and they all laughed, concluding that Jimmy was good fun, okay.
Seán called to his sister to be careful and there was a pause in
their incessant chatter as brains were plundered for meaningful
submissions. Seán and Stevie kept responsible eyes on the little
girl who lifted high her pleated frock in nipped puckers with
either hand to avoid getting it caught in the undergrowth. They
moved on and encountered small white rocks which soon changed
to smooth grey stones. They found themselves on a path on one
side of which the thistle-covered ground fell in one sheer drop
from the sky. On the other side was a small rampart covered with
throbbing green moss. A brood of primroses sheltered in soft soil
under the belly of a bush and there was the sweet smell of wild
woodbine.
A thick briar, larger than any of them, released by Stevie's shirt,
shot out from the embankment like the tentacle of an octopus, its
thorns like suckers, frightening Seán and causing some nervous
laughter.
The path led them past the Hatchet Field — so called because
of its shape. In one corner stood an old single storey house. A few
chickens pecked around the yard but the occupant was not about.
They moved on up the path and came down to the gulley and a
small stream, six inches of crystal cool water at its deepest. With

his bow and arrows Jimmy hunted for fish the way Lok and Shan did in his reading book.

'Be careful!' shouted Mary Ann. 'If you fall in you'll catch ammonia and yer mammy'll kill you.'

'It's okay . . . I'm learnin' to swim,' he said, bluffing.

The other four split into British soldiers and Germans and fought each other until they were exhausted. Then they fell to the ground in a heap. Tony poked and picked in the grass, checking for earwigs before he rested his head. Stevie wondered what the time was.

'Stevie, Kipper Kelly whacked Tony with a stone yesterday,' recalled Seán.

'It wasn't a stone, it was a brick,' corrected the victim.

'And he and his brother hit you with a hurley, didn't they?'

'It wasn't a hurley it was just an ordinary tennis bat,' he added casually.

'Tell our teacher; they go to our school,' Seán compromised when Stevie remained unstirred.

'Ya should have told Big Stevie when it happened,' added Tommy, and he continued maliciously: 'Kipper's da's got one leg longer than the other.'

'Howdja know?' the others asked, crowding around him, even though it was common knowledge and they had seen Johnny Kelly's limp. Seán had heard there was a food shortage during the war and he had caught rickets when they had to eat mice and rats.

'Howdja know?' they asked Tommy again.

'Kipper told me 'imself. His da comes in drunk and falls into the chair like King Kong,' and he flumped into a soft cavity in the ground which acted as an armchair.

'And Kipper has to pull off his da's socks. The first one's easy but then he has to put his hand way, way up into his trouser leg to find his other foot.'

'Geee.'

'Yea. Johnny Long Legs.' They all mischievously giggled and set aside the traces of guilt in their young minds. The conversation turned to handball and football. Tommy, with his mind's eye surveying what he thought was their street a mile or two below was a bit pensive about the previous subject, so he added: 'Kipper's always chasin' and makin' fun of Mickey Boyle.' Mickey Boyle was a Mongol child although they were not quite sure how to define his handicap.

Jimmy lay on his belly staring into a pool of still water whose smooth surface kept being upset by little whirling abrasions. Seán scratched his head, trying to pull out midge flies.

'What's the difference between fizcley handikep and mently handikep?' Seán asked. There was pondering.

'I know,' butted in Jimmy. 'When you're mently handikept you're really, really handikept,' and they all shook their heads in agreement.

Tony passed around a lemonade bottle which contained diluted orange juice. They all took a swig at the warm drink and vied with each other in identifying landmarks such as the trolley-bus terminal at the top of the Whiterock Road; the Falls Park; Milltown Cemetery; the M1 Motorway, which opened the year before; the King's Hall; the large spire of Broadway Presbyterian Church on the Falls Road; and the derricks of the shipyard.

Jimmy was rigidly attentive and was mesmerised at the extent of their knowledge. The city and its geography was beginning to take shape in his mind.

On the horizon was the sea; then on the coast were the cranes and oil terminals of Sydenham. He studied the city centre buildings, their boxed and rectangular and dome-like shapes; the church spires; the factories and houses — mills, brown terraces giving way to white gable ends; bright unmossed roofs; patches of green and the swoosh of trees rising out of the ground. The realness of it all, the Sundayness of it all gave the picture a quality which could only have been appreciated from this height and at this distance. It was breathtaking.

*    *    *

Seán and Mary Ann were supposed to be in the custody of their fourteen-year-old sister Angela. After an early Sunday dinner her parents, Mary and Frank, had left their eldest daughter with clear instructions: she was to wash the pots and dishes, tidy up the kitchen and keep house generally. Paul, who was twelve, had to stay within two or three streets, and Angela had to keep a special eye on the youngest two. There was salad for tea but they would be back anyway no later than six or half-six. She could have one or two friends in the house but that was all. They were off to the christening of the baby of Mary's younger sister, Maureen.

Having a daughter old enough to mind the others was one of the first rewards for all the years of worrying and sacrificing. However, Angela did not settle comfortably into the role of nanny: Mrs McCann didn't feel she could always trust her; and she detected a frustrating rebellious streak which often tested her own composure and tolerance. A few weeks before, Mrs McCann had beaten her around the room with a feather duster when she learnt from a neighbour that 'the eyes of the whole chapel were on your Angela yesterday when she went to Mass without a mantilla or anything on her head!'

Tempered by such incidents Angela had learnt to deceive her parents into believing that she had moderated her behaviour and was over such phases. And why shouldn't they have believed her! She had been the apple of her father's eye and was said to have strongly resembled his side of the family. No other couple's daughter was as original as their very own Shirley Temple. When she was younger she would dance and sing for visitors and make adults laugh when she dropped the threepenny bits they gave her down the front of her dress. She hadn't been a bit coy, was more than forward and it was only as she grew up that the development of her own character, her individual self, began to occasionally infuriate her parents.

Mary and Frank were realising that they had also to learn to live with a maturing person, whose presence could stifle their conjugal life and the freedom they had enjoyed together in the evenings when the children were put to bed. Although she could exasperate her parents she also gave them much satisfaction. Mary drew much mirth out of her emerging personality. She and Frank often had joked about whom she took after.

On this day Angela's job was to mind her sister and brothers, but within half an hour of her parents' departure and of completing the washing-up she had bribed Paul to stay in the vicinity of the house and she would favourably see to him over the next week. He had been obliging but shortly after she took off the two youngest also had disappeared and he was conducting a search, not too frantically, but with some concern.

So here was Angela lying on her back in the Falls Park, her young brothers and sister the farthest things from her mind. She was dreamily carried away by the attentions paid to her by the teenage boys, all two or three years her elders, gathered around her and her best friend Patricia. Her physical maturity and risque conversation terrified and thrilled them. Among themselves the boys ridiculed her character and unjustly attributed to her a sexual promiscuity of their own imagination. True, she was heading towards danger, but her reputation was propelled by gossip ahead of her actual experience. To ensure that they got the right message, however, she regularly cast off her shoes and Bobby socks and on would go nylons, garters, high-heels and make-up — 'Care of Mary senior,' she would boast — as she took a long drag on a cigarette pilfered out of 'Frank's packet'.

Carefree as ever, she was lying under one of the many beech trees, whose silver-grey bark was russet-stained as if the rain-water had rusted it in streaks. While carrying on a conversation she could see in its entwined boughs the figures of naked, embracing lovers.

The park's lawn had been mown perhaps a week before but shooting through its close-pile growth were marginally taller daisies which established themselves in clusters. Angela flicked the ash from her cigarette into the grass and egged on one of the lads: 'Go on; tell us what he said.'

The teenager, who had finished his schooling in June, blushed and involuntarily squeezed the yellow sponges in the centre of the daisies. He was embarrassed at being cornered and pinned down on the specifics of the sex education he had received from an equally uncomfortable Christian Brother. He was sorry he had begun the story and now his mates were punching him in the kidneys and throwing him backwards.

She revelled in entertaining the others who were falling back in laughter as Patricia kept biting her lower lip, rolling her eyes and giggling.

'We're gonna get nowhere with you, young man,' Angela said dismissively, matron-like, already feeling boredom coming on. Her ears picked up with the sound of music. She dragged Patricia to her feet.

'Quickly, that big hunk has a wireless . . . Must go men. See youse.' And linked to her friend's arm they followed behind an athletic-looking figure. They broke into a rock'n'roll routine which provoked scowls from the old people on the benches around the bowling green, including one disapproving grey-haired gent, hands resting on a blackthorn walking stick, who nudged his petite wife. She was more preoccupied with nibbling at a salad sandwich, staunching the flow of mayonnaise from her mouth with her little finger, and keeping her teeth in. Her old lips simply took up a secret smile at the youngsters.

\*    \*    \*

They had crossed the stream and waded through dense bracken, gorse and the acres of heather which seemed to have a stranglehold over half the hillside. The more they struggled the more the barbs and stems would stick to and exhaust them. Once or twice, Mary Ann and Jimmy disappeared, their cries alerting the others who then rescued them. Finally they reached the flat top of the mountain. The boggy soil was black. On a broken concrete base stood a concrete plinth, like an ancient sundial, possibly to mark the altitude but the markings were indecipherable. Belfast was gone from view but through the haze to the west they could see the faint shimmering of Lough Neagh. The back of the mountain was eerie and deserted. There wasn't even a cyclist or stroller on the Tornaroy Road.

Only the magnificence of Ulster Television's aerial now held the attention of the gang.

'It's big, but it's not that big,' pronounced Tommy, ending five years of juvenile speculation that every Viscount and DC 3 out of Nutts Corner airport was about to crash into the towering mast.

'Whaddle we do now?' asked Tony, wearily.

'We go down again.' And everybody looked to Big Stevie who had just spoken.

\*    \*    \*

The two girls followed the music from the BBC's Light Programme blaring out of the transistor radio which belonged to the bronze body in the shorts.

Angela was in two minds about her attitude to 'Mr Muscles', as she had christened him, and he knew he was being followed by the two. Her shoulder-length auburn hair she had to keep fixing behind her ears as it fell loose everytime she and Patricia bent with laughter at each new ribald comment they could think up to describe Muscle's physique. By the swagger of his walk he obviously had a high regard for himself. They followed him through the shade of the avenue of chestnut trees and the great oak on the tarred and pot-holed path from the bowling green to the small, brick-bridge, and up the path to where the noise of cheering and splashing rose from the open-air swimming pool, the Cooler.

The afternoon session was well under way. A minority of people paid in at the turnstile. These were women with their children and young men with their girlfriends, whether in slacks or skirts, indisposed to scaling the six foot fence or scrambling through the earthen hollow dug below the iron railings from the City Cemetery side.

'Are youse going for a swim?' Ricky said to Angela and Patricia, having introduced himself. It was obvious that they were only out for a walk.

'Do you work or are you still at school?' His eyes were on the freckles of Angela's face.

'I'm a secretary, though Josie here, my sister, is going back to St Dominic's in September to do her . . .' she almost said 'Junior', ' . . . Senior. What do you work at?'

'Do you know the shop on the Andersonstown Road?' They had heard of the shop.

'Yeh my . . . my father owns it and I'm the manager, or I will be soon.' He waved to several other teenagers who were in swimming shorts, excused himself and said he would be back in a few minutes if they would still be around.

'I think yer man fancies you,' said Patricia. She was just as attractive as her friend but Angela's extrovert personality and drive gave her the advantage. Ricky spoke to his friends and they all shared a joke, he winking at Angela. She brushed out the hem of her dress along the grass where they sat and stared closely at a buttercup amid a colony of buttercups. Its five petals were stretched before the sun in exultation and radiated a dazzling allure to insect life. The incessant splashing laced the air with a coolness which could be smelt. She looked to the sky and loved everything: this earth, the air still and then breezy, the canopy of trees and the rustling, the heat beating down on them, her youthfulness, the little game she and Patricia were playing. She felt a burst of elation within — a surge, an accelerated rush of blood and serenity, and she was suddenly intoxicated with the drug of life and had to restrain herself from screaming aloud her happiness.

She came back to the teasing game with Ricky who was entering into his routine. With a panache he knelt on his hunkers, dipped his hand into the pool as if it was a font and blessed himself before cutting a neat hole in the water with a dive which ended with his re-emergence three-quarters way up the pool. Small lads admired this ostentation which few of them would have had the nerve to copy just yet. He returned a number of times and spoke through the railings to the girls, showing off his radio which lay on a pile of clothes. Angela was fascinated with the toy but she couldn't pinpoint what she now disliked about its owner.

To one side he probed Patricia: 'Would yer, your mate go out with me to St Theresa's tonight if I asked her?'

'God I don't know. She's an awful lot of typing to do — from work, I mean. She brings it home, you know.'

Using his hand as a squeegee he wiped the excess water off his hairy legs. This Angela looked very young, he thought; but when he looked at her figure it was a woman he saw.

'Ask her for me.' The sleek otter was gone again.

'Well, whadda ye wanna do?'

'I don't like him.'

'You're crazy. He's gorgeous.'

She felt that Ricky was a cocksure bore, three or four years her senior and yet really immature. When he returned he was pleased to see the two girls conferring.

'Okay,' smiled Angela. 'But pick me up at a quarter to eight and be nice to my ma.'

He was uneasy about this arrangement, preferring instead to see his dates either outside the dance hall or at the corner of their street if there was no bus journey involved.

'Right,' he declared. 'St James Road it is, seven forty-five sharp.' He was proud of himself for that last touch of finesse, making the conversion in a second. He repeated the door number.

'Seven forty-five, now don't forget,' confirmed Angela.

'How could I!' he joked, and apologised for not being able to borrow his father's car as he ran off to challenge the water again.

'Jeepers, we'd better be going. My ma and da will be back from the christening soon. Let's go, 'Trish.'

Even the desultory talk had gone out of the gang's conversation and they didn't undertake the downward trek with the same enthusiasm as their climb, though the journey was now much easier.

'How long do ya 'hink it'll take?' was the general moan.

Behind some bushes, close to where the Whiterock lonan, or lane, met the end of the Ballygomartin Road, grey smoke came belching out. The gang climbed into the field and Stevie lifted Mary Ann over a gate which had been securely tied.

'Aw, awwww!' gasped Stevie as they found themselves confronted by three hard-looking boys who, it was obvious, owned the fire.

'They could be Orangemen,' whispered Stevie, bewildering Jimmy and Mary Ann; but making Tommy, Tony and Seán nervous. They knew that people called Protestants lived in New Barnsley, even had heard of a neighbour or two referred to as Protestants or 'converts', but had no social intercourse or contact with them and so they were a little afraid.

'Let's get out of here,' declared Tommy, his voice slightly trembling. His whole abdomen tightened as he attempted to put some spine into his crumbling composure. He told God that he hoped Kipper Kelly's father's leg would grow some more (he just knew he shouldn't have said that about Mr Kelly), and took a deep breath, bracing himself.

The gang was going nowhere. They were surrounded.

'Hey boy. Let's see your bow and arrow,' declared a tall fellow.

One shot wouldn't harm anybody, thought Tommy, but he wasn't prepared to express that view.

'Nehh,' Stevie's answer was definitive and Jimmy began to wish that he too was elsewhere. His mother would be angry to discover that he had been up the mountain and had had the recent birthday present she had lovingly bestowed on him stolen. Mary Ann was more curious than frightened. She knew convention. She would not be required to do any fighting. It would be resolved between Stevie and the ugliest and biggest of the other gang.

'Hey Scobie. You lost a bow and arrow just like that-un,' lied Tall Fellow, who was about thirteen, to his companion who had a cast eye. He was in long trousers, noted Seán. It was almost men they were up against! he thought.

'Yeh,' said Scobie. 'That's mine; gimme it.'

He moved to take it off Jimmy, whose heart now sank, but Stevie said loudly:

'Push off and leave 'im alone.'

'Where do youse come from?' Tall Fellow was still sizing up the situation.

'Why?' Stevie wasn't giving an inch.

'Whadda ya call the pope?' he sneered.

Stevie was expecting a denigrating remark though Tommy suddenly read the situation and realised that they were Catholics, they were all Catholics. What was his name? What *was* his name? He had learnt it so that he could show off on some occasion and it had been recently on the news, though over what, he wasn't entirely sure.

'Pope John the Twenty-third!' he blurted out with a smile.

'Wrong! *He* died three weeks ago.' And with that Stevie and Tall Fellow were engaged in hand-to-hand fighting, like Sumo wrestlers, trying to bring the other to the ground. Once the atmosphere was smashed things were not so bad and Tommy felt better joining in with the shouting. Most fights were clean and there was no 'jumpin' on'.

'Go on Big Stevie, punch him!'

Stevie was doing too well and Tommy's heart came to his throat when the third, much smaller member of the other gang began pushing him, asking him who he was shouting for. He was mortified at being afraid of a dwarf and the next minute he was hurled into the fight. Within seconds there was a mêlée as Scobie dived in with a terrifying, confident scream pulling Tony in with him. Jimmy and Mary Ann, however, remained uninvolved. Tony's head was covered with his arms. He was on the ground, hardly being touched though bodies were getting pushed and shoved around him and he was seeing stars in the tight darkness of pinched eyes. While members of Stevie's team became exhausted and retired the three strangers pushed furiously and captured Stevie in a head-lock, screaming at him:

'Do ya give up! Do ya give up!'

Stevie choked but didn't give up and his companions felt sick with shame as they licked their wounds, afraid for themselves of going to his aid. Something in Jimmy snapped and he let a yell out and dived into the scrum, adding a few pounds to Stevie's efforts and surprising everyone.

Tall Fellow momentarily released Stevie from the grip and grabbed Jimmy by the buttocks to hurt him and throw him off.

'I farted in your hands,' Jimmy shouted into his face.

'What!'

'I've just farted again!'

'Ughhh!'

He immediately let go of Jimmy, disgusted. Stevie winded Scobie and with a scowl frightened off the small member. Then, in the first critical act of violence he followed up by punching Tall Fellow, shattering his prestige. His nose began to bleed and hostilities were ended as abruptly as they had begun. 'I'll get my big brother for you, ya pig. He's a hard man and will fix you,' he threatened, as the two sides slowly parted: the three former attackers hurling abuse from a safe distance. The gang made their way on down the lonan. They were in marching mood again. Jimmy had saved the day.

'Me a fart bomb,' said Jimmy and the rest of the gang shook their heads as they triumphantly marched home singing:

'Barney Hughes' bread,
'Sticks to yur belly like lead.
'Not a bit a' wonder, farts are like thunder,
'Barney Hughes' bread!'

\*　\*　\*

Angela had arrived home just in time to mollify Paul who was shouting at Seán and Mary Ann. She washed their hands and faces, gave them salad and severely chastised them for being up the mountain. But she forgave them, she said, for confiding in her and they weren't to tell their mother or father.

When Mr and Mrs McCann arrived home they were happy to see the house in order. They always knew if there had been a party in progress when they were away as the house was tidier than when they went out. The house was in home-condition: the *Sunday Post* was scattered about the sofa, the comics page below a chair, and the bathroom towel was lying on the bathroom floor.

They had enjoyed themselves at the christening and the beer and Babycham had whetted their appetite. They had returned home to see to their children before going out to a local club. Unusually, without any protest, Angela said she would keep house. She merely asked what time they were leaving at, which was not too early — they had to stretch the purse.

\*　\*　\*

It was half-seven. Ricky turned off the Falls Road and into St James Road, humming to himself. He had the number of the house firmly implanted in his head. He was quite looking forward to seeing Angela although he couldn't understand the formality. Instinctively his eyes worked ahead of him and he saw a dilapidated house. The curtains were unwashed, paint was peeling off the door, the windows were grimy and the small, weed-grown garden was full of papers which the wind had blown in. The place looked shabby. His heart went out to Angela. He began whistling as he walked past the house just to check the next consecutive number. Secretary, my foot, he thought.

He walked up the path and knocked on the door. There was a hollow echo, no sign of life. A boy pulled up on a bike.

'Hey mister. Nobody's lived there for two years. The oul doll's dead.'

Across the street in Patricia's house, Patricia, Angela and another girl, Rose, were hiding behind parlour curtains, screaming with laughter. Angela had her hands between her legs: 'Oh mammy, I'm gonna wet myself!'

Ricky carefully looked from side to side to see if anybody spotted or overheard the wee bastard on the bike talking to him, before he shuffled out of the path and out of the street.

\* \* \*

In Sandy Row, on the Shankill, in the Falls, in Short Strand, the children were called in in shifts, depending on their ages. From hundreds of yards away a mother's voice could be heard calling 'Jimmy! Jimmy!' or some other name and a faint voice would reply: 'Wha'?'

'Come on. It's time to come in.'

The streets would slowly empty of the very young. Often hoaxers would reply with a deluge of abuse aimed at getting the hailed one a box on the ears.

Another child in some other street is called and replies: 'Wha'? Whadda you want?'

'Time to come in.'

'Ach mammy, Rhonda Smith's still out!'

'All right then, five more minutes.'

'Ten more!'

'Get in here right now!'

In another street a girl informs a woman: 'Mrs McMahon your Gerard's hiding behind that car . . . Mrs McMahon your Gerard's only after throwing a stone at me . . .'

'Gerard, I know you're behind that car. Get in before I brain ya!'

'Mrs McMahon your Gerard's only after giving me the fingers. . .'

Clout!

'Mammy, mammy, mammy! I got blempt in the wrong!'

\* \* \*

Jimmy and Sheila begged their father to stay a few moments longer. The bedspread was light, the bed spacious. They were in their pyjamas, they had had their supper and were being tucked in by their daddy: it was a comfortable existence and the world was very peaceful, the world was very good.

'Ach daddy, tell us a wee story. Go on,' implored Jimmy.

'Okay then. Tom Thumb. Now night night and go asleep.'

'Daaaady!' bemoaned Sheila, feeling cheated. 'Ach daddy, tell us another wee story.'

'Okay. Tom Thumb's wee brother. Now there, away youse go asleep,' he chuckled but the kids weren't for letting him leave.

'Now if I tell youse a story do you promise to be quiet and go asleep?'

'Yip.'

'Yippee.'

'Once upon a time, a long, long, time ago the wee boys and wee girls didn't go to school and just played all day long beside the river or fed the chickens or climbed trees. Their mammies made baskets or sewed clothes and their daddies went fishing or else they planted corn for bread.

'Anyway, they were all very happy and now and again they had parties and everybody sang and danced all night long . . . '

'Did the wee girls have to go to bed, daddy?' queried Sheila.

'Don't interrupt me now or I'll not tell youse it.'

'Shut up Sheila. Go on daddy, go ahead,' said Jimmy attentively.

'One day when the daddies were out working the bad men came and they burnt down the huts and killed the animals and stole whatever they could. They shouted and roared and chased everybody away . . . '

'Geee. Is this true, daddy?'

'Shut up Jimmy. Tell us what happened next.'

'The women ran into the forest and the bad men went looking for them. To stop the babies from crying and giving their hidey-holes away the mammies put their hands over their wee mouths. Everybody was terrified and then the daddies came home and chased the baddies away.

'Everybody went back and built their huts and got something to eat.'

'I don't like that story, daddy,' Sheila said.

'I'm not finished.'

'After a few months all the mammies noticed that the babies had no teeth — they just weren't growing . . . '

'Flip me!'

'They didn't know what to do and the mammies were crying and blaming themselves. But then one day a wee boy and his sister were out playing near a white hawthorn tree when they heard someone calling them.

'"Psst!"

'They looked around but could see nothing.

'"Psst! Over here! Are youse blind or sumpin'. Open yer eyes!" It was a little Leprechaun and although the kids were afraid they peeked into the bush.

'"Don't be letting her get too close!" said the Leprechaun who had no clothes on and was covering himself with his hands.

'"What's wrong?" said the boy. "Why have you got no clothes on?"

'"Do ya think I always go around like this! Catch yerself on. I went for a dip and a bloody big rabbit stole my magic jerkin and britches. If you find them and bring them back to me I'll grant the pair of ye a wish. One wish mind ye, I'm not a bloody millionaire."

'The boy and girl searched all the rabbit holes and found a big rabbit lying on its back, unable to get up.

'"Help me! Help me! Can't you see I'm stuck! Pull these things off before I die!"

'They pulled the britches and jerkin off the rabbit who was very grateful and they brought them back to the hawthorn bush.

'"Turn yer head away, wee girl, or you'll not get a wish."

'When the Leprechaun got his clothes back on he leaped into the air with joy and landed at the top of the tree, He somersaulted and danced and shouted: "Fooled you! Didn't I?"

'The wee boy said: "You can't go back on your word, you promised us."

'"No, I suppose I can't. But I drive a hard bargain."

'"You're a cheat!" the wee girl said.

'"Okay, okay!" said the Leprechaun. "I'm only kiddin'. So here's what we'll do." He told them his plan and the boy and girl smiled and grinned and danced with him around the hawthorn tree.

'Now wasn't that a nice story. Now, go asleep,' Peter ordered them as he rose from the side of the bed.

'Ach daddy. What was the plan?' demanded Jimmy.

'If you don't tell us, I'm gonna cry,' announced Sheila.

'Jeese, I almost forgot to tell you!' Peter pretended, apologetically.

'The Leprechaun told them to go back to the village and to secretly meet all the other wee boys and girls who were five and six and seven years of age. When their baby teeth fell out they were to hide them under their pillows. He would send fairies around to collect them and put money in their place. The fairies would collect the best teeth and polish them brand new and give them to the wee babies.

'Sure enough within a few weeks all the wee babies' mouths were full and they were able to chew sweets and talk and their mammies cried with joy at the miracle.'

'That was a nice story.'

'I liked that story,' said Jimmy, who checked for loose teeth when his daddy went downstairs. He then sat up, pulled the curtains aside, looked up at the mountain and wondered if his friends Big Stevie and Mary Ann were in bed and asleep.

\*   \*   \*

Ironically, at sunset, the more the night fell the more the ageing day flared in the western sky behind Black Mountain. The creeping darkness eventually prevailed, but even when the sun disappeared there was still a comfortable coolness about the grass and daisies and the ground was now redolent with fragrances that had been suppressed by the day's heat.

From below garden thickets came a reserved moistness and an earthiness. From nettlebeds rose an alluring sweetness.

From underground, latent spirits crept through tiny, matted roots, into the souls of wildflower, grass and bush, spilling out into the open where the light wind carried them off into the new atmosphere. The rich earth was giving off night.

# Chapter 2

# The O'Neills

John O'Neill awoke to the familiarity of his bedroom ceiling slowly defining before his eyes. He once or twice gently chewed over the iron taste between his teeth and gums. A yawn broke the sleep seal on his lips and prised open his mouth to the full. He inhaled a large draught of fresh air from a seam of ventilation which floated through the open window. Raymond lay next to him, undisturbed.

By the side of their bed John Buchan's novel *Greenmantle* which John had read until two or three lay. He looked across the landing and saw the face of Jimmy who seemed to instantly awaken. His youngest brother took a breath and stretched his curled-up body like the petals of a flower bursting out of their bud. Sheila was fast asleep beside him.

'You make me my breakfast?' he asked.

'In a few minutes,' said John, smiling. He surveyed the latticed ceiling which he imagined went through seasonal changes, the dulled, original white, emulsion paint with its hair cracks now taking on a sharp, creeping depth in the summer's heat.

How many times have I woken to this view, he thought, as he stretched his limbs. He spent the time before rising in personal reflection, attempting to make sense of himself, and tried to poke a mental finger into the blank future to scrutinise what it held. He was sixteen and he was impatient to get out in the world. Peter, his father, was annoyed that he had not made a go of schooling and the opportunities, rarely available in his day, for an education. It was the inclination rather than the aptitude which his son lacked. Idle, he was a drain on the family's resources and Catherine, his mother, was obviously dipping into her purse to support him. Unknown to him John returned to his mother some shillings — he had earned a little money through delivering leaflets in the suburbs around Belfast announcing carpet sales, and supplemented repayments of his debts through his takings from gambling at which he was very lucky. While he loved the thrill of small betting at the greyhound tracks and enjoyed the company of some older companions, and was accepted and fairly well-known at the pitch and toss schools beside the bookmakers, this extrovert face was the street side of his nature.

There was another side to him, however: a conscience he couldn't lie to; the inner self whom he couldn't fool, which saw through the bluffing, the bravado, the acting, the show-off. He was just beginning to appreciate that there was nothing simple about the process of maturing. He was discovering increasingly that he was more naive than he thought and that there was a lot of badness in people that he never imagined.

Staring up at a curled lip of hard paint above the picture rail he recalled a bitter lesson, a shameful episode, from three years previously about which no one but he and his teacher knew. Waiting on the landing to be dismissed for the lunch-break he saw a fellow pupil, a minor bully but still more than his match, lean over the balcony and spit down onto a group of first years. The spittle hit a well-known weakling, a frail youngster who instantly burst into tears and some minutes later became sick. The form master from below ran upstairs to consult with his colleague. John's class were marched back into the room and each was threatened with six strokes of the cane from the teacher. He said he would give them the opportunity to escape punishment: it was impossible that no one out of a class of thirty-two had seen the culprit, and indeed John knew it was more likely true that half a dozen others witnessed the incident. He distributed pieces of paper to each boy. They were to write down the name of the boy they saw spit or whom they thought had done it: it was to be completely anonymous.

John was in a dilemma. He despised the bully and didn't want him to get off scot-free. The teacher was capable of carrying out the mass punishment, he had done so before over trivial infractions. There were bound to be other witnesses. Why leave it to one of them to shoulder the sole responsibility of naming the guilty one? He might feel better for not having personally fingered the bully, who was so cowardly at heart that he wouldn't even own up to save the rest of the class. But John, by not showing solidarity with those prepared to name the rogue, was also acting in a cowardly fashion. There was also the chance of someone maliciously naming an innocent class mate, though not even the teacher had considered that possibility.

John wrote down the bully's name, Paul McShane, and folded the paper which, along with the others, was collected by the smug teacher. The class was released and he hurriedly ran off to his lunch, the boys expressing relief among themselves that they hadn't been caned.

Passing subsequently through the corridor beside the lockers the teacher, who had suddenly appeared in the frame of an open door, beckoned John to him.

'This is your writing, isn't it?' he pressed him. 'Well, isn't it?'

The boy was trembling, close to tears, afraid of someone seeing him in the compromising company of the teacher. He was being overtaken by the speed and gravity of the ramifications of his action and never in his naivety did he believe that his disguised handwriting would be recognised. Worse still, it slowly dawned on him that he must have been the only one who had written anything down.

'You're sure he did it? Are you sure?'

'Yes!' he gasped at last, convicting the bully to a dozen strokes of the bamboo cane one end of which was thickened with inches of cellotape to inflict extra pain.

'Good boy. Away you go.'

John skulked out of the room and in class couldn't look the bully in the eye. He took no joy from McShane's ill-founded cockiness which arose from his mistaken belief that the teacher had drawn a blank.

There was a knock on the door and the headmaster, accompanied by the teacher, took McShane out. He came back into the room, minutes later, his face writhen.

'I've been expelled,' he moped to one of his friends as he filled his schoolbag. Head down, he seemed to drag himself out of the room.

John was ashamed and felt close to tears. There was nobody he could turn to without the risk of putting his treachery into the record. That night he was depressed and it took him hours to fall asleep. The whole talk in the class the next day was speculation about who was the squealer. Then, on their way out to the yard for the ten-minute break, McShane was spotted with his mother outside the principal's office. Forty minutes later the principal brought him into the geography class and spoke to the teacher.

John was so relieved he was overjoyed and felt obliged to patronise McShane for months afterwards.

Lying now on his bed he winced at his collaboration with the teacher. He had never really considered the phenomenon of the solidarity of the classroom though from that moment onwards to him it was stark. Looking back on the whole incident he now admitted to himself that he had grafted noble intentions onto what was really an act of self-preservation. His concern had been really to avoid sore fingers and palms and even though the class had been spared a heavy caning, and even though the shock of expulsion apparently contributed to the reform of McShane, John still regretted and was ashamed of his action, his and the teacher's secret. That hypocritical gyte, he said to himself, as he watched the erratic flight of a buzzing bluebottle around the ceiling.

'Right! Jimmy, let's go!' he said, coming back to the present.

When they got downstairs John looked at the clock on the mantlepiece: it was twenty-five to nine and the house was still quiet. This was the start of his father's two weeks holidays and it was the first day in perhaps a year that his mother wasn't the first up. She was always downstairs, even in the dark winter mornings lighting the fire, and it seemed it was nine or ten o'clock at night before she actually took off her apron as if signalling her day was done. Raymond was still asleep and Monica was staying in their Granny Stewart's, Catherine's mother.

John opened the front door to lift the four milk bottles. A stout boy, not from the locality, stood on the step, just about to knock.

'Is your Jimmy coming out?' asked Big Stevie.

'He hasn't got his breakfast yet. He'll call for you.'

'Ach it's okay, I'll wait here,' he said, making John feel awkward and inhospitable.

'Can I stand at the door until my corn flakes are ready?' pleaded Jimmy.

'No. I don't know where your clothes are and it's too early to be out running the streets. He'll see you later, okay?' said John, directing his concluding comment at the caller.

He poured out the cereal but didn't shake the milk bottle as Jimmy liked the cream.

'Want some toast?'

'Na. Just corn flakes. Do you hink the wevver's going to be good for the Fifteenth?'

'How do I know. Why? You're not collecting for the bonfire so soon are you?'

'Yeh. Me collecting for two. One here and one wiff Tony O'Neill's gang. We're gonna have the biggest on the Road!' he declared enthusiastically.

There was a stirring upstairs and a few minutes later Catherine came down: 'Morning everybody.'

'Hiya!'

'Mornin'.'

'Go on in and I'll finish off,' she said to John as she donned her apron. Catherine be'' ved in doing as much for her children as was possible. It ' ld have been mistaken for spoiling them, or a possessiver but she believed it was just straight-forward loving y were entitled to be not quite spoiled but certainly se well, to be able when they were older to look back at a .appy childhood and to be inclined to perform the same function for their own family. Life becomes hard enough the older you get, she thought, without being burdened and disciplined from the very beginning. Her husband had a different, stricter view. However, because he went out to work at seven each morning and returned home at around half-five and wasn't in the house when the kids had to be got ready for school, when they came home for lunch, when they were off sick, he wasn't able to enforce his regimen. She also knew him intimately and knew that for all the facade of a disciplinarian beneath it he was really quite good and kind. What was causing her particular concern at this time was the increasing gulf between John and Peter, the son misreading the father, the father having some undefined resentment of the son. She couldn't exactly pinpoint when she first realised that the usual words of disagreement parried between the adolescent and her normally equable husband were more like serious friction between two strangers.

'Would you do the yard sometime today?' Catherine asked John.

'I'll do it this morning because I want to head downtown later,' he replied.

John loved going downtown: going from large shop to small shop; the smells of new, expensive furniture in the big stores; the clothes and food sections; and then the cafeterias where he and his friends had chips and milkshakes before wandering through the same places Saturday after Saturday. In particular they loitered at the record shops to hear the latest music from Britain and America, and could spend another hour browsing through the dark, enclosed fusty alley-ways of Smithfield where almost anything could be bought or sold in the best second-hand shops in Ireland.

He could trace his fondness for Royal Avenue, High Street and
Castle Place back to the times, regular occasions, when Catherine
would arrange to meet him after primary school. Despite his
dexter overcoat belted tight at his waist by Miss Ryan, his teacher,
and his schoolbag slung over his shoulder to ensure he didn't
leave it behind anywhere, he felt like a big boy boarding the
trolley-bus, paying the conductor as if out of his own pocket, and
travelling into Castle Street all by himself, undoubtedly much to
the admiration of seasoned travellers. There, he was met and
taken by the hand around Sawyers, Robbs and the Co-op, and
then treated to coffee and a pastry with real fresh cream. His
Granny Stewart saw to Monica and Raymond on those days,
before Jimmy and Sheila were born, and as they and the others
grew up they too were feted in kind.

The rest of Catherine's brood slowly arrived downstairs.

'Would someone lift in the bread, please,' she asked, and
Raymond, wearing just the bottoms of his pyjamas stepped out
the door and lifted a loaf off the window sill.

'Ask your daddy does he want this in bed,' she said to Jimmy,
indicating breakfast.

'Daddy!'

'What? What is it?'

'Eh . . . Eh . . . Mammy? What am I shouting for?'

'Ask him . . . Never mind. Peter! Do you want your egg up
there or are you coming down for it?'

'No. I'll be down.'

She put out the breakfasts and sat Jimmy on the sofa to help
dress him. He gently put his small forefinger at the corner of her
eye without smarting it: 'You've some sleep in it. Me get it. There!
It's away now.'

She thanked him with a kiss but he was lost in humming to
himself the seven catchy bars of 'Seventy-Seven Sunset Strip'
which he had now almost mastered.

Peter came and sat at the small table, saw John switch on the
radio and impatiently adjust the tuning dial.

'Will you wait until it warms up. You've only put it on. What
are you after anyway?'

'Some music.'

'Just leave it on the Home Service, I never get to hear the radio.
How are you fixed for money?'

'Okay, why?'

'Maybe you could lend your oul lad a few bob?' he added, mellowing.

'Well, when will ya give it back to me?'

'Ah, I'm only kiddin'. Sure it's the holidays, isn't it,' he said, making his meaning no clearer, but Catherine needed just the intonation of a few words to detect that he was in a good mood.

\* \* \*

Before noon, the house was clear of family. John had gone into town, Monica would return at her own pace, and Raymond, Jimmy and Sheila were playing about locally.

After his breakfast Peter finished reading the newspaper and had announced his plans for the day.

'If you don't mind, Kate, I think I'll nip over to my mother's to see how my da's back is. I promised her I'd fix the clothes line so I'll be about an hour and a half. Is there anything you want?'

'Maybe you could take some of the kids with you. They haven't seen your mammy or daddy either in about a fortnight.'

'Okay, that's okay. I'll ask them but they probably won't want to go.'

The children were too anxious to get out into the streets with their own generation so Peter left on his own.

Catherine began scrubbing the hall tiles and then the front of the house including a good portion of the neighbours' footpaths on either side. She enjoyed the early afternoon sun. Passing neighbours bid her the time of day and some stopped to gossip.

Everyone thought that thirty-eight-year-old Mrs O'Neill was a very pleasant and friendly woman who ridiculed no one. She would, uncomplainingly, take nonsense from some of the nui-sances and nosey-parkers for hours outside shops or at their front doors. In short, she was a good listener and her only comments would be judicious and supportive. In the course of receipt of really private matters from a wife worried about her husband's behaviour she would act as a mediator, gently hinting, and perhaps ever so dishonestly, that she had been through a similar tribulation for which there turned out to be a perfectly reasonable or innocent explanation.

She was resting on the staff of her tough scrubbing brush, waiting on Mrs Clark, an active middle-aged woman, who was clearly in a bubbly mood: 'Suppose you heard!'

'Heard what?'

'I won one hundred pounds at Bingo last night up in the Holy Child school in Andersonstown. I was sweatin' on number nine for ages and I could hardly shout when it was called.'

'Good for you.'

'You should come out with us. You'd enjoy yourself.'

'Ah, you know me, I'm a homer . . . Hello Peggy, how's the wee lad? I heard he needed four stitches.'

Peggy Carson joined them.

'God, I was up to a hundred. You know when somebody tells you, you think the worst. He's running around now, showing off to his mates. It's me that's got the worry. Here, did you see the polis out at Conlon's . . . '

'When?'

'Two of them, walkin'. I couldn't help seeing them.'

'What's that about, sure they're not in any trouble are they?'

'Well I was talkin' to Rosie,' interjected Peggy. 'And she goes in and out of Conlon's. Says I, "I saw two peelers at Eileen's door." Says she, "I was there in the house when they came and didn't Tommy near fall off the chair, he didn't know what to say." Says she, "After they left he came in and said that the RUC had received a complaint about their Seamus playing handball and was warning them to keep him under control." Says I, "That's not what I heard." Says I, "I heard he sent a letter to the RUC luckin' to join and they were out to interview him." I wouldn't be a bit surprised either 'cause an uncle on his mother's side was an oul peeler.'

'Here, did any of you know Tommy Conlon's brother, Martin? Well, he's back from England.'

'His wife's looking better,' said Catherine responding to Peggy. 'She used to look awful failed. It must be ten years since I saw her, a wee girl from Lisburn, isn't that right?'

'Lookin' better! No wonder! that's not his real wife. That's his fancy woman. His natural wife still lives in England. The oul blirt left her . . . '

'God save us! That's awful,' said Mrs Clark.

'Now, you never know,' cautioned Catherine.

'I hear you won money last night,' said Peggy.

'News travels fast.'

'How much did you tell him you won?'

'All of it, of course.'

'Well my mother always taught me, never let a man know how

much money you have in your purse. Keep two purses, one always empty. Do you know it's Frank's anniversary this coming Friday,' she recalled of her dead husband.

'He'll be dead four years if God spares him.'

'Gee, you wouldn't think it was four years. He was a good man.'

'One of the best,' she added.

Mrs Clark shuffled at Peggy's hypocrisy and changed the subject.

'The Murrays are leavin', did you know?'

'No, where are they going? Up the road?'

'A wee bit further than that,' said Mrs Clark. 'They're headin' to England, though I heard they were trying to get into Australia.'

'They'll be no great loss, she's always out shouting at the kids or tellin' him to go back to his mother's, throwing suitcases out the window and then the next minute they're walkin' up the street, arm and arm, like Romeo and Juliet, big smiles on their faces. It's a wonder they've any cases left to pack,' added Peggy.

'Ach no. She's a nice wee woman, she just suffers from her nerves, that's all,' Catherine responded.

'I wouldn't live in England, you know. What with all that killin' and sexual attacks. Every week some woman is strangled with her own nylons. It's gettin' as bad as America,' said Peggy.

'I know, isn't it awful,' Catherine added. 'There's that wee girl last month, just outside Manchester, sixteen years of age, left home to go to a local dance and never arrived. She hasn't been found since.'

'Well,' said Mrs Clark, 'I'm sure you're busy Catherine' — she shot a look at Peggy — 'so I'll leave you to get on with it. I'll see you.'

'Cheerio now.'

Peggy also bid her goodbye and then said: 'I believe she suffers from her varicose veins. I hope I'm not gettin' them. Must go and get myself a cup a tea and sit down for a while.

'Here, before I go, what do you think of them?' She showed off a new pair of brown shoes. 'Got them in Sandy Row. I'll not tell you the price but they were a real bargain. Toodleloo.'

\* \* \*

Catherine lifted her handbag and Peter went out to the yard to use the toilet. She looked into John and Raymond and told John not to be reading too long as it would be sore on his eyes. Peter then came up and ordered him to put the light out as it was late. John protested and felt like rising up against his father when he stepped into the room and switched off the lamp. I can't take much more of this, thought John.

'Daddy, it's only one o'clock!' and he switched back on the lamp in what almost amounted to a challenge. His father relented but was surprisingly agitated as he shut all the doors.

'You're in the wrong and you'll have to lay off him, Peter. I don't know what's getting into you.'

'I know, I know, I just can't help it. I don't think I'm ready for old age,' he said, turning to her with a half smile.

'For God's sake, catch yourself on, granda. You're forty-three. Maybe you're right! I'll have to get myself somebody younger!'

They smiled at each other and turned out the light.

Catherine was warm and kicked off the sheet into the middle. It must have been half an hour before the thoughts in her mind began losing the constraints of consciousness and became slipping images. Each time she turned over brought her back from the border of shallow sleep until she eventually crossed the line and ended another day. Suddenly Peter said something and his words fell like stones from the sky breaking the peaceful silence, striking the skin of her mind, not quite penetrating, but disturbing her. He repeated himself and she awoke cross: 'I was sleeping and you woke me.'

'Well, I didn't know. Your head's only hit the pilla'.'

Her temper though quickly subsided.

'Do you think is he asleep?'

'I heard him switch his light out about fifteen minutes ago,' she said.

Peter looked but could see no bright strip at the door saddle in John's room and he closed their door.

'That's nice perfume you're wearin'.'

It was only some face cream and she responded by saying: 'Aye, I'm sure it is. It's the lard from the frying pan you smell.'

'You know how to really turn a man off!'

She rolled over to him and he gently stroked her hair. She warmed to his affection and kissed him on the lips, the wee lad she had known for twenty years and been married to for seventeen. No matter the difficulties they had, the rows, the disappointments (and there had been many early in the marriage), nothing could shake the faithfulness between them. Marriage was sacred, a sacrament bestowed from on-high. She may have preferred a more romantic man — though those few who had been amorous and articulate were usually after one thing. She certainly would have liked a more prosperous life. But she got on with things and made do, which was what her mother had encouraged her to do.

So down the years she had grown closer and closer to Peter in affection and had invested her life in the miracle of their children, her beautiful family. To bring them into the world, to see them grow up, strong and healthy, well-fed, good-mannered, to witness their personalities emerge, was an immensely emotional, and sometimes spiritual experience. The process of life never failed to enthral her. She prayed upon waking every morning and she just couldn't imagine what she would do without her religion and faith nor how any person could say they didn't believe in God. To her it was impossible not to believe in God and Jesus Christ. God was the explanation for everything. She was certainly too humble to allow her faith be shaken by the challenges to God's universal goodness from the phenomena of wickedness and evil, natural disasters and poverty, deprivation, famine, poor black children the ages of her own starving to death in Africa and India. But all these imponderables only added to the mystery of life, made her grateful that they had been spared such calamities, and placed a duty on everyone to pray for God's intercession for such poor people and for a resolution of their extreme and grave position.

She was a devoted Catholic and she derived from her religion an inexplicable internal satisfaction and contentment. On such occasions as the Easter ceremonies or Christmas midnight Mass or at the Retreats the overwhelming numbers of devotees all in communion with God filled her with pride. But she also loved to be in the chapel alone in the presence of the Eucharist with only the flickering candles. It was at these times that she felt what she could only describe as a form of melancholia. It was a feeling not really of loneliness and certainly not of dejection but one of enhanced communication with her soul even though she sought no answers to the bewildering questions posed beyond the chapel gates.

So she got on with life, learnt a little every day about human relations and believed thoroughly in the idea that all the good you gave out would one day, and maybe not in this life, be returned in kind. There was nothing to lose by being nice, by being patient, considerate and helpful.

'Are we okay?' Peter asked as he ran his hand up and down her arm, soothingly.

'Yes, I know my days. We're okay.'

'That's good,' he said. 'That's good.'

\* \* \*

From mid-August onwards mothers spoke ominously more often about school and the need for new clothes. Days, which to the children in early July lasted *all day long*, were in the week just before the start of September startlingly shorter and shorter until the last weekend was gulped up by some mean monster which, on one dark leaden night, even put a bitter nip in the air.

Suddenly, the Lollipop men were back.

From half-eight until just past nine o'clock the footpaths were bulging with little, and larger, brains (on feet shod in new shoes) — none of which had volunteered for scholarship. The younger ones would have been quite piqued to have learned that their mothers, who walked them to the very classroom door because it seemed they couldn't bear to be separated from their babies, actually were *glad* they were at school again and that a routine had at long last returned.

And with such a routine the days quickly turned into weeks.

\* \* \*

'I see in the paper that the gas lamps are to go.'

'Where's that? I didn't see that,' said Catherine, standing at the kitchen door in her apron.

'Right here. We're getting electric lamps.' Peter handed her the paper.

'Does that mean I'll have nowhere to swing,' piped in Jimmy.

'No, it doesn't. Just you get on with doing your homework,' ordered his father. 'And never you mind.'

'Mammy, he's stole my rubber,' complained Sheila.

'Naw, I didn't. That's mine!'

Catherine looked at the rubber.

'That is Jimmy's. Where's yours?'

'I can't find it.'

'Well I'm fed up buying you rubbers. You can do without. Jimmy lend her yours. Move out of the way so I can put a shovel of coal on.'

The two youngest children, lying on the mat, pushed aside their homework books to make a path to the fireplace. Their father was engrossed in the newspaper, his shoes by his side, twiddling his toes, waiting on his stew.

'Where's John?' he asked.

'He's not home yet.'

'Where's Monica?'

'I don't know where she is. She's got domestic science, but should've been in before this.'

'Where's Raymond?'

'Are you quite finished your roll call! You might have put on some coal. I'm stuck out here making your grub and all you can do is sit there with your feet up!'

Raymond's footsteps could be heard on the stairs and he came into the living room.

'Where were you?'

'I was upstairs, where did you think I was?'

'Don't give me cheek.'

'Well, I was upstairs doing my homework.'

'That's okay, why didn't you just say that.'

'I bloody well don't know what's wrong with you today. You're like a beaten bear and you're driving me and the kids mad,' said Catherine as she slammed his plate of stew onto the table.

'Thanking you,' he said, sheepishly. What was wrong with Peter was that he had been informed earlier that day that he was possibly facing being laid off at work. He was working with a squad of men for a building contractor who had run into financial trouble and was cutting back in the number of houses originally scheduled. Although employment was seasonally affected by the weather he still expected that he would have had work indoors until February. Now, Christmas was only nine weeks off and he hated the prospect of not being able to hand his wife the money to see to presents and clothes. Furthermore, he had placed his last five shillings on a race in a wild flutter and that too he had lost. Tomorrow he would have to ask Catherine for the bus fare to work and she would ask questions. He had been determined not to bring his mood home but it kept rising to the surface until it intemperately came out.

He scattered a whirl of brown sauce over his dinner, dipping his bread and butter into the mince and carrots. He second eldest child, Monica, arrived home.

'Hiya daddy, Hiya mammy,' she greeted her parents. She went out to the kitchen where her mother exchanged sign language about the state of play.

'The heat in here would kill you,' the girl remarked.

'Here, before you get changed, give him his tea.'

'And this is for you,' said Monica, handing her mother a dish in which from a few ingredients she had brought to school, she had made apple crumble pie.

'Oh, very nice! He'll think this is the Grand Central Hotel,' laughed Catherine.

They had their dinner: Jimmy and Sheila at the table where they could cause the least damage; Raymond and Monica on their knees on the settee; and, lastly, Catherine, at the table when Jimmy finished. The dishes were cleared away, Catherine washing, Monica drying. Peter told the kids to keep quiet during the news but even before it was over he draped his head with the paper and fell asleep in the chair, with Sheila giggling at his snoring behind the vibrating pages.

Jimmy stole over to his father's chair in the corner and urged on by his sister he lifted the paper. His close presence awoke his father.

'For God's sake!'

'She told me to see if you were asleep.'

'I didn't.'

'Yes, you did.'

'Have youse got your homework finished? No. Well then do it.'

'Daddy, help me do me spellings.'

'Come here and I'll do them,' said Catherine, sitting down.

'No, it's okay. I'll do them.' Peter took the book and asked him questions. He shuffled his feet, scratched his hair, put his finger in his mouth and rolled his eyes at the inscrutability of the letters B and D.

Catherine was going through Jimmy's schoolbag. He had several books — a blue jotter, an exercise book for homework, both of which were stamped Northern Educational Company, and a stapled catechism backed in brown paper and covered in RAF logos. At the bottom of the small canvas bag was a pencil which was sharpened at both ends and a haemorrhaging blue biro. Outnumbering his academic possessions were three folded, empty, cellophane Smiths crisps bags, a marble, two whelk shells, a wooden ruler with John's name on it and which was chipped so badly as to be of no academic use (it was actually used as a catapult), and a rich mixture of serrated pencil shavings and several hundred crumbs. Catherine could appreciate why Jimmy was the only person who felt really safe about putting his hand into the bag.

She removed the homework-book and shook her head disapprovingly.

'Have a look at that,' she said. 'Read what the teacher has written at the bottom.'

Peter opened the page at the sums. Jimmy had six sums out of twenty marked correct but underneath the teacher had written with his red pen: 'This is copied from Joe Montgomery!'

Peter had to smile.

'I suppose wee Joe had the same fourteen wrong with the same wrong answers?'

His son put on a bashful look.

'If you're gonna cog at least make sure you're coggin' off someone good.'

'Peter!' Catherine called out. 'Don't be teaching him to cheat.'

'Naw, daddy. It was Joe Montgomery who copied off me. I got those six right meself,' he declared proudly.

The front door, swollen by autumn dampness, rubbed at the jamb and after a few seconds John entered the living room, closing the hall door behind him.

'And what kept you?' said his father, not growling but expressing mere curiosity.

'Ach, I walked it up. Didn't fancy the queues in Wellington Place, and Castle Street was just as bad.'

'Where's my grub? In the oven? It's okay, I'll get it.'

'No, go and wash your hands and face,' said Catherine, handing Jimmy his book back. 'I'll put it out.'

John ate his dinner in silence and felt fairly tired. Through a friend of his father he had found work in early September and had started in a mechanical engineering firm in the Markets district, close to the city centre. The boss told him he was now an apprentice but John wasn't totally convinced, even though he had recently begun to attend a technical college two nights a week. His work day began at 8.30 am: he filled the pot-bellied stove with coke and lit the fire, brushed the floors and then he rode a messanger-boy bicycle around the town to collect crankshafts, pistons, bearings or camshafts. The basket had been removed and replaced with a larger box which added to the bike's instability. He cycled into most parts of Belfast but once had to go as far as Lisburn which was eight miles away. Some of the journeys were short: to the railway stations at Queens Quay, Great Victoria Street and York Road. His most routine lengthy journey was up to a garage on the Antrim Road.

That day he had had to make the journey three times, including two pick-ups in the Shankill Road. He was feeling fairly jaded and was convinced that at least one of the journeys was deliberately created for him by one of the older mechanics, Bronco McIvor, whose thick arms were tattooed with Loyalist slogans. He was grim looking and rarely spoke to John but when he did address him it was never by his Christian name. It was, 'Go over to Simpsons' or 'give-is a rag,' or 'go and get milk'. John soon became accustomed to the hostility and the resentment. The boss knew it was happening but said nothing as McIvor was too valuable a worker. John was also aware of a coolness in his boss towards him which he couldn't fathom because, after all, he didn't have to employ him, a Catholic, in a firm where the majority of the workers were Protestant. It was as if his boss couldn't come to terms with his own patronage which had followed a word from one of his longest serving employees, Harry McPeake, the acquaintance of Peter.

When John had tried to discuss his frustration with his father, Peter began to lose his temper. He may not think he was learning anything but he was, Peter insisted. He was told to stick at it. 'You have to have a trade,' he said. 'Otherwise you're going nowhere.'

So John stuck at it though he hated it. As soon as he turned into the Markets the red brick building with the grimy windows came into sight. He would take a deep sigh and grit his teeth.

The floor in work was permanently covered with a dark slime of grease and oil which John attempted to keep clean. On the wall was an ancient electric clock whose glass was cracked. The hour hand, black and tipped like the nib of a large fountain pen, slowly governed the day when McIvor wasn't ordering John about. Even when he brewed the tea for the burly engineer and the others there was no gratitude from him. He would go off and sit with two or three workers of his own persuasion whilst John ate his sandwiches from his lunchpack either on his own or with Harry who, although a Catholic, seemed, John thought, to have no real problem communicating with the others. It was all fairly confusing at first though the rules of the game began to fall into place.

He could have shirked his work and taken his time in returning from a collection but he was too proud and defiant and saw himself in some imprecise role as a representative of his section of the community, the Nationalists. So when he picked up a parcel he sped back to work, not to win favour but to show that he could do his job just as well as the next man and to give no man an excuse to ridicule him. He kept the concrete floor sawdusted and swept and made sure that there were always rags in stock and paraffin in the tub at the sink for washing hands. He scrubbed the toilet and removed a sludge which had lain for years in the four corners of the small closet. He regularly checked that cut newspapers were in supply from the cord nailed to the back of the ill-fitting door. He found two screws which righted the door so that it shut flush and offered some privacy.

He made work tolerable but he still loved to see the minute hand strike 5.30 pm. And he loved Friday afternoon when they finished at 4.45 pm. The men went off drinking and he, with his overall under his arm, headed for home up May Street and round past the City Hall to catch a trolley-bus. Inside his pocket was his wage packet, of £3.12s 6d which he gave unopened to his mother. She gave him back £1.2s and when he rolled the two 10/– notes in his pocket he felt on top of the world, even though next week's bus fares had to come out of it. Furthermore, he gave Monica and Raymond 6d each and Jimmy and Sheila 3d each and rose in their estimation in the small hierarchy of adulthood.

John finished his dinner and squeezed on to the sofa beside Monica who was engrossed in some homework and Raymond who was watching television. His father lit up a pipe and thought about his financial problems.

There was a knock on the door which Catherine answered. One of John's older friends, Felix, was looking for him. He came into the hall and both boys sat on the stairs, clearly somewhat excited.

'I had to queue for ages,' said Felix. 'But I got them!'

They examined and re-examined the tickets for the Ritz Cinema. John was thrilled. His friend was prepared to accept the money in instalments. They cost 10/6 each. When John came in and sat down his father asked him what had Felix wanted.

'We're gonna see the Beatles on 9 November! We've actually got tickets!'

'The Beatles, huh! In my day entertainers were real musicians, Beatles. What a name! How much is it costing you?'

John resented the question and ignored it and something else distracted Peter's attention.

Catherine remembered that Raymond needed a shirt ironed for school the next day, rose from the table and went out to the kitchen which was by now quite cold. Jimmy was under the sofa with a toy car. The onset of dark nights, especially when the clock went forward, meant he couldn't go out to the street after half-five. Sheila, who sat to the side of their black and white television, asked her teddy bear what it was getting for Christmas and heard it reply in a squeaky voice that it was getting a small doll dressed in a white wedding dress.

Peter looked at the flames being swallowed by the black chimney. He mustered himself, pulled on his shoes and went past Catherine and out to the yard for a shovel of slack. Pins and needles of frost stung his nose. He worked quickly. Sitting by the fire again he used the poker to break up some coals which had fused together. The fine slack fell into the crevices, flared and sparkled for a few minutes then an even, yellow and orange glow radiated heat into the O'Neill's small living room.

# Chapter 3

# Divis Street

The winter nights had been lonely ones for Catherine. Peter had been the last one laid off work and the family had just about managed Christmas. He told her of his decision on Boxing Day and by the second day in January he was in his cousin's in Birmingham. By the end of his second week he was sending her home 'good' money. By the third week the homesickness which he had experienced on his five previous occasions in the 1950s working away from home struck him like a permanent headache but he had to persevere. When, through a phone-call, his brother in Belfast informed him that he had work for him he was thrilled. She too was thrilled when he telephoned her to a neighbour's house. She had missed him on those cold nights, missed him in bed, missed cooking his meals, washing his clothes, missed having a husband around and a father for the children.

She met him coming off the boat. She was so glad to see him that she threw her arms around him and cried so publicly that she was embarrassed.

'Hey now,' he said. 'You'd think I was coming back from the war!' Jimmy and Sheila had been kept off school for the occasion and they tugged at his coat. They took a taxi home — 'We're rich,' Jimmy had whispered to his sister — and the father told them about his life and work in England since he had left Belfast three months previously. He was loaded with suitcases, more full of presents than articles of his own clothing. Raymond and Monica ran home at lunch-time to see their father. When John came in from work his father stood up from his chair and put out his hand. It was the first time that John had ever made a serious handshake and he was surprised that it felt so natural an expression of goodwill. They then hugged and John was again surprised by his father's affection and the brown eyes which seemed to fill with tears which were just contained by a sniffle. Out in the kitchen John thought about how long it had been since he had touched his father. Not since he was a child when he had sat on his knee, or kissed him goodnight had he been really close to him. He still kissed his mother in greeting, almost as a natural reflex, but the

43

sensation he had just now experienced made him consider the nature of the bond between father and son and how it could supersede rancour.

That night the family had a celebration with visitors and relations calling in for drinks. Jimmy later collected the tin tops from bottles of Wee Willie, Double Diamond, Monk, Blue Bass, Piper, Carlings and Guinness for currency to do exchanges in the street.

They had enjoyed the night's revelry which, for the adults, had gone on until almost 3 am. As Peter lay on in bed for a well earned rest Catherine rose with John, who was late for work, and the children.

'Monica, make sure that child is well hopped up,' she said, tucking the scarf in around Jimmy's neck and buttoning up his duffle coat.

'Comb his hair, it's sticking up.'

'It is combed.'

'Then pat it down.'

Monica licked the palm of her hand and patted Jimmy's spiked hair as he squirmed and resisted.

'Gonna be sick! Gonna be sick!' he shouted.

'Don't be such a pockill!' Catherine chided him. 'Stand still! Stand still!'

She gave Jimmy a note so that the teacher would release him early for a dental appointment and after she got them all out she went back to bed.

March was coming to an end. The afternoon sky was clear and a strong, cold wind was peppered with street dust which made Jimmy's eyes run. He met his mother at the corner and later Sheila asked him what it was like to get a tooth out.

'Ya think you're in bed.

'When you wake up it's bleedin'.

'And then you yap, 'cos it's very, very sore.'

The next day Jimmy took ill at school and was sent home early. It was a Friday and when John came in his youngest brother lying on the sofa, a bucket on the floor, gave him a wan smile.

'Me sick.'

John gave him some pennies, then got washed and went to his bedroom to change. He heard a retching and then Jimmy shouted up: 'I was sick there now again. Wasn't I mammy? Do you want to see it John?' he called out as if the world doubted him.

John came, sat beside him and felt his forehead which was cold but sweaty.

'Me like that smell. What is it?'

John winked at him. He was wearing some aftershave lotion that his father had brought back as a present.

The winter nights had been lonely ones for John also. He and his mates who had nowhere else to go on week nights, stood at the corner, talking, arguing about Gaelic football, soccer, music, attempting to detain the girls who were out for walks because they too were lonely. Some of his friends were extremely successful and after a snatch of a conversation with a passing group of girls would declare, 'See youse later, I'm leaving what's-her-name home.'

John had poor luck. He was shy and lacked enterprise. He had left home one or two girls but always felt awkward and couldn't strike the right note. He now paid more attention to his dress and spruced himself up.

'Where you going?' asked Jimmy from his bed.

'To a dance,' John replied.

'Can you dance?'

'No.'

'Then why are you going?'

John ruffled Jimmy's hair with his hand and laughed.

'A very good question!' he said and left.

At the dance John out of the corner of his eye caught a glimpse of someone who immediately attracted him. A ghost of *deja vu* shivered over him. Then he remembered that perhaps five or six months before, he had seen this girl. He couldn't be sure when it was but he was convinced it had been on a Saturday. Two people, perhaps sisters because of their likeness, stood in front of him at the bus stop. The younger one turned around and after a long glance smiled at him. Because of the angle of the autumn sun he hadn't even been sure she was looking at him and he was taken by surprise by the tenderness of her gesture. She had inspired, or provoked, or supported, the inchoate romantic within him. He now recalled that it *had* been a Saturday. She had made such a deep impression on him that the following Saturday he had walked, out of his way, to that same bus stop hoping to see her. He was disappointed but it was a disappointment tempered with the belief that if she was for him then fate would, no doubt, throw them together again.

Now there she was, out on the floor, jiving like an expert, moving and turning, occasionally clapping her hands. When Angela nodded hello to him he felt really glad that they had decided to come to this particular dance. He smiled back at her. In between every two or three numbers performed by the showband, the Master of Ceremonies, Big Al, would take the microphone and make some inane remark which would send everyone laughing, regardless of its absurdity.

'Here, I fancy her,' said Felix to John and another friend, Gerard, pointing to Angela. She heard him and replied: 'Well I don't fancy you!'

The two boys sneered at Felix and slapped him on the back of the head. John was relieved at this rejection but as the night wore on Gerard was up dancing with Angela two or three times. His concern and jealousy were fully justified when Gerard came back: 'I'm leaving her home! John, would you walk her mate Patricia up the road. Angela says there's no problem and that her mate really fancies you. Well?'

At dances there was about a half-hour before the end of the night when — for those who came with no firm arrangements — the wooing went into its last and serious phase. Usually during the evening a girl had a fair idea, from who got her up to dance most, who would be proposing to leave her home. Similarly, a boy knew from the enthusiastic or lukewarm responses he had received who were the girls most approachable. Of course, negotiations could often be critical and misjudgements could be made which could lead to humiliation. Arrogant girls with too high an appreciation of themselves could find themselves spin-stered if they got the arithmetic wrong on contending suitors. The reason why offers were delayed being put and decisions not taken until this half-hour was quite simple: the possibility that someone better would become available and show themselves. And so by a quarter of an hour before the end perhaps almost two-thirds of the crowd had been paired off. Out of desperation some later offers were made en route to the cloakroom or in the street. And, of course, there were those who weren't asked and those who hadn't got the nerve to ask. John had seen several exceptionally pretty girls none of whom attracted him, even were he in with a chance and able to overcome his retreating bashfulness. He had also seen many not so pretty but very attractive girls. Patricia was attractive but her friend Angela was incomparable. There was only one word to describe her, and this was the first time its meaning dawned on him. She was beautiful. Her long, reddish-brown hair was striking as she had danced.

'Well?' asked Gerard again. 'Will you walk Patricia home?'

'Okay,' he replied, but his main purpose was to find out more about Angela.

They bought three chips from a vendor, Angela stating that she would share Gerard's and this gave her the opportunity of linking his arm. John and Patricia walked behind them, talking about work and school exams.

When the couples split up the two young men arranged to meet back in twenty minutes. John was there first.

'How did you get on?' he anxiously asked his friend.

'Fine,' he answered. 'She told me she wants to see me again. She's a passionate little girl,' he laughed. 'How about Patricia?'

He shook his head and pushed his lower lip up into his face indicating that they had found little rapport.

At least once a week John was in the company of Angela and Gerard and he became secretly infatuated with her. Felix had asked his honest opinion of her but John expressed antipathy and disinterest. Felix said he didn't like Angela and the thought that someone would have a bad opinion of her pained him. She was the epitome of life and soul; her confidence towered above theirs; she was articulate and intelligent and each time he saw her he identified some extra enhancing feature which he had failed to notice before. He discovered which Mass she attended, found a pretext for being in that chapel, and then made sure they bumped into each other afterwards.

'Hello John, what has you over this way?'

'Doing a message for my da. It was simpler to go to Mass here. I think I'm going in your direction. Mind if I walk?'

'No, no, come ahead.'

She lived in the same street as his uncle Harry whose son Tony often called for Jimmy.

She enjoyed their conversation and his ability to make a drama out of the seemingly uneventful episodes in his work. He was, however, more interested in her views about life and wanted to know what she had been studying and did she think she would do well in her exams.

'And what would you like to do?' she asked him, changing the subject.

'What I'd really like to do is travel and see the world. Sometimes, living the way we do, we have a very narrow view of things. I'd like to see how other people live, how they cope with their problems.'

She had given him an audience and he realised he had got carried away. He blushed.

'Are you talking about earning a fortune . . . coming back rich?'

'No. Not at all!' he said. 'Naturally, I would like to have money but I'm talking about broadening my horizons. In fact, I've put in for the Merchant Navy and have been waiting on a reply for some time. I've heard so much about the sea.'

'What I would love,' she said, 'is to be famous or married to someone famous, or powerful, or wealthy. I can't stand poverty . . . In fact, these streets sometimes drive me crazy, they are so dense and dirty. Look at the dogs, they're everywhere. At night there's cats fighting on our toilet roof.'

John tried to empathise with her views which he felt she undoubtedly held in good faith.

'Would you not like to travel? See London, Paris or New York . . ?' These three particular cities he mentioned as a concession to what he imagined was her concept of cosmopolitan life beyond Belfast.

'Why, do you know any millionaires who would take me away,' she jested. 'Honestly, I'm not quite sure what I want out of life but it has to be splendid and unique. I haven't got into tackling the problems of the world, the way you appear to have. Is it worth it? Who cares?'

John felt slightly dismayed. 'But if you don't have a view of the world,' he argued, 'the only thing you have a view of is yourself. . . '

'That's correct!' she shouted into the summer sun. She said it so disarmingly that he also laughed. He was left with the abiding impression, however, that her views could be altered through time.

\*   \*   \*

'There's crowds gatherin' in Divis Street!' Gerard said to John as soon as he came to the door. His friend was agitated: 'Quick, get your coat! Felix's meeting us at the corner.'

John grabbed his jacket and shouted to his mother that he was going up the road for a walk. They met Felix and the three of them proceeded at a quick pace towards Percy Street. Up until then none of them had any interest in the October 1964 election which was due to take place the following month. In Divis Street was the election headquarters of Sinn Féin, the political organisation which had close links with the underground Irish Republican Army, the IRA. On Sunday, the day before, a Mr Ian Paisley, self-styled Moderator of the Free Presbyterian Church, had addressed a meeting of his followers in the Ulster Hall. He threatened to invade Divis Street, which was in the predominantly Nationalist Falls area, unless the Irish national flag, the Tricolour, was removed from the window of the Sinn Féin office where it was on display.

In work that day John had had to listen to Bronco boasting that he would fulfil Paisley's promise unless the Unionist government took action.

Many men had planned to be on the streets that night just in case the Loyalists did enter the area which had been the scene of clashes between state forces and their supporters, on the one hand, and Nationalists, on the other, in the 1920s and 1930s, and, indeed, periodically throughout the century before the six-county state was created by the 1920 Government of Ireland Act.

That day the Minister of Home Affairs met his top advisors. He also met Paisley and appealed to him to call off his march and he agreed to a rally at the City Hall instead.

John and his friends arrived at Percy Street/Divis Street corner about a quarter-past nine. The sky was dark but the weather was mild. A crowd of several hundred had gathered and were standing, mostly on the footpaths, close to the election head-quarters. Some were gathered at Raffo's shop eating fish and chips or penny scallops. A large contingent of RUC men came on the scene, some in cars which pulled up close to the offices. The people made a passage for the senior officer and three others.

When they discovered the door locked two crow-bars were produced from the boot of the car. The crowd hissed and booed as the door was smashed in. The RUC seized the flag under two orders which banned the public display of the Tricolour. Although the people were hostile no one dared take any action.

As they drove off the shouted abuse reached a pathetic crescendo, showing just how cowed the people were. Dormant feelings of Nationalist identity and a hitherto unexperienced anger stirred within John. News of the flag seizure spread rapidly and the numbers now swelled to about 500. A small section of the crowd then began to hurl abuse at the Sinn Féin office, expecting direction and leadership.

'We want our flag! We want our flag!'

'Could we have some calm please!' someone in the office appealed through a loudspeaker. They were heckled. A man next to John jabbed the air with his finger and shouted, 'We want our freedom!'

'We want our flag! We want our freedom!' the crowd chanted as they spilled out over the road. Further down the street the RUC had to redirect traffic. There was much cat-calling and the air was tense. Just *being* on the road, in such numbers, in defiance of the law, gave the people a tremendous sense of strength and acted as a channel for their frustrations. The loudspeaker crackled again: 'The seizure of the flag by the RUC was an abject surrender to mob law . . . But let's not forget that behind Paisley, behind the Stormont government lies the hand of British imperialism . . . '

Felix rolled his eyes in boredom at the dissertation: Nationalists could see the Loyalists, they couldn't see British imperialism. But there was a cheer when it was announced that the Republican Election Directorate had issued an ultimatum to the RUC that unless the flag was returned by noon on Thursday it would be replaced. The crowd then sang the Irish National Anthem before dispersing.

At work on Tuesday Bronco was jubilant.

'Billy? Any of youse see that oul flag knockin' about! I've nothing to wipe my hands on!' Then he laughed loudly and the other workers smiled.

On Tuesday night Paisley held another rally outside the City Hall and demanded that those responsible for the display of the Irish flag be prosecuted. In Divis Street crowds again gathered outside the election headquarters. John watched as two twenty-strong rows of RUC men pushed people back on to the footpaths and made sure there was no repeat of the previous night's road blocking. It occurred to John that the police were obsessed with even the most minor infraction of the law. Keeping open the road had become an excuse: allegedly for the free movement of the citizenry when in actual fact it was the assertion of authority and supremacy: keeping the citizenry on the footpath, or, as all of those present interpreted it, keeping them on their knees. Most of those ordered back on to the footpath obeyed the police. There was some pushing and shoving and a few coca cola bottles came flying from the back and smashed harmlessly in the middle of the road. The older RUC man in charge remained unflappable but a few younger ones became agitated and began making threats: 'Hey you, I know your face. Move back!' 'What's your name?' demanded one uncouth RUC man of a middle-aged Republican.

'Fuck off, you Orange bastard or I'll knock your teeth in.'

One of the RUC sergeants overheard the exchange. He had been around for a long time, was a seasoned participant in such confrontations and he and the Republican had each other's measure. He ordered the young policeman down the row and told people to take it easy. The road was successfully re-opened and much of the crowd felt cheated. Many of the teenagers had some experience of RUC harassment: stopped in the street for carrying a hurley, which was considered an 'offensive weapon'; chased for playing handball; or being ordered to move on, even from their own street corners.

As the tension rose Liam McMillan, the Sinn Féin candidate in West Belfast, announced that he had sent a telegram to the British Labour Leader, Harold Wilson. It read: '*ARMED POLICE USING CROWBARS SMASHED INTO REPUBLICAN HEADQUARTERS, BELFAST, WITHOUT WARNING, SEIZED IRISH FLAG. DEMAND YOU CLARIFY ATTITUDE TO THIS VIOLENCE AGAINST DEMOCRACY.*'

The word went around that they should disperse and come back the following night.

John, Gerard, and Felix, headed down to the Spanish Rooms for some pints of scrumpy cider and to discuss politics and women. The events had been unusual and a major change from the young men's normal routine. What they signified, though, was way beyond their understanding. They had always grudgingly accepted the circumstances in which they lived.

John's mother and father had asked him to give an account of his movements because of the trouble in Divis Street. He lied to them and said that he and his friends had been in St Paul's Hall playing snooker.

On Wednesday night Felix went into town with a girlfriend. John and Gerard again went down to the election headquarters. It was the place to be. The air was full of excitement and expectation. The RUC had still not handed back the flag.

There was a heavy RUC presence about 150 yards below the Sinn Féin offices and as the onlookers — men, women, youths — swelled in numbers they had to walk on the road to negotiate their way around those standing still. Inevitably some more gathered at these points and cars had to make their way through a narrowing passage. Trolley-buses, however, couldn't make large turns and each time one approached, the protestors — because this was what they had now become — had to move out of the way.

It was approaching 11.30 pm as the last trolley-buses of the night were waiting in Castle Street. People started singing rebel songs opposite the election offices. The singing infuriated the RUC and they moved in on a section of the crowd and pushed them about. Others at the front and side resisted the pressure to disperse and John realised what was happening — things were rapidly reaching a head.

'Come on,' he said, 'everybody's blocking the road.' They blocked the road in one mass which seemed to frighten the police who then withdrew. A number 13 trolley-bus approached the road-block but the crowd wouldn't let it through. There were altercations between some of the Glen Road passengers who complained that they had to get up for work in the morning.

'It's well for ya!' shouted a curly haired man in a reefer jacket.

Two tender loads of reserve policemen were rushed to the scene to support the original fifty on duty. There were now about 500 people involved in the protest. Their mood was defiant and they were in good humour. By blocking the road they had challenged the authorities and achieved a victory. It was notice to the government that it couldn't walk over the people.

The police drew batons.

'Jesus Christ!'

'Run!'

Without restraint a large force of RUC men ran into people, batons flailing, kicking and punching. People fell on the ground and were trampled over. Young people stayed and fought them but the violence of the batons became too much. Flocks of bottles came flying through the night sky and some took their toll on the police. But then fresh police made a second baton charge and chased the demonstrators up towards Albert Street or down into the side streets where the uniformed men were pelted with milk bottles, stones and vegetables and tins of fruit looted out of a shop.

John lost his friends in the confusion and took refuge in Lemon Street with about 50 or 60 people. Just as the first ones who fled stopped to rest, the RUC reached those at the back caught in retreat. There were more screams, women could be heard crying. An RUC man caught John by the back of the collar and crashed him into a doorway. Most of the blows fell on his crossed wrists and arms.

'Fenian scum!' he shouted, his mouth frothing, as he tried to arrest John. The policeman had outdistanced his colleagues who had realised they were too thinly spread. From nowhere Gerard appeared behind the RUC man and hit him over the head with a bottle which stunned him and caused him to release John. He staggered and both young men then fled into the side streets and made their way home. Gerard was full of nervous laughter and his conversation see-sawed between boasting of the incident — 'Did you see him fall! Did you see him!' — to deep dread — 'Oh God, John, you don't think I killed him, do ya?'

On Thursday after the Republican candidates for the Belfast constituencies arrived back from handing in nomination papers in Crumlin Road Courthouse they returned to their election office. They held a little ceremony which included the singing of the Irish National Anthem and then the Tricolour was once again placed in the window. They took no chances and locked the door.

Shortly after 2 p.m. a column of RUC men marched out of Hastings Street barracks and up into Divis Street. Those people who had been standing at street corners became excited and frightened, many chastened by the previous night's violence. The police, carrying batons, their holstered revolvers hanging from waist belts, ordered everyone off the street. Those who delayed were pushed and made move along. A tender appeared and drove up to the election headquarters. Eight RUC men tried to break down the door. Three of them used a pick-axe and two crow-bars but failed to gain entry. One with a crow-bar then smashed the large pane-glass window, stepped in and seized the Tricolour. Some women began struggling with the police. One girl was knocked to the ground. Her brother screamed: 'Let her go! Let her go!' He was beaten over the head and then arrested. The flag confiscated, the RUC then withdrew and marched back to their base. The crowds quickly reassembled and demanded that the stolen flag be again replaced. People, especially young people, were angry and were demanding more leadership than they were getting from the Republicans who were calling for restraint and for people to go home.

'What the hell is all this about?' shouted a Sinn Féin supporter who just wanted to get stuck into the RUC for previous humiliations.

'We don't want to get the blame for any trouble,' said one of the election officials. But his despondency was detectable. He had been involved in a small campaign by the IRA from 1956-62 which had collapsed for lack of support. He had spent three years interned without trial, reflecting on and analysing the situation. Despite resistance among the rank and file the Republican leadership had decided to change tactics.

Among some of them there was now an implicit acceptance of partition as being almost irremovable and so they were concentrating on a semi-constitutional approach. They hoped to break into the political mainstream and build a radical organisation which might later attract Protestants who were interested in sharing a common ideology in social and economic issues. And now, at their first attempt at playing the game within the government's rules, here was reaffirmation of the impossibility of reforming the state.

From 6 pm onwards as people finished their dinners and as the evening turned towards night the crowds had multiplied. Children were taken in and old people stayed at home. Several thousand had gathered across the width of Divis Street just above the bend in the road. Word reached them that around the corner the RUC riot squads, police tenders, water cannon and Shoreland armoured cars were lining up.

Over the loudspeaker an appeal was made for people to go home. As the appeal was being answered by a shower of stones thrown by their own supporters at the office the RUC charged.

The people scattered in every direction. The young fellahs split up into gangs, raided public houses for empty beer bottles and barrels for barricades. They ran into side streets and began siphoning petrol out of whatever cars they could find.

John and his friends fell in with a group of about 15 to 20 men who were lifting up the cast-iron metal gratings and smashing them for ammunition. A crowd of demonstrators had gathered at

Albert Street corner and jeered the police who surrounded the election office.

A group of rioters charged the RUC cordon and the police made a half-hearted charge but retreated under the withering fire of stones and bricks and metal shrapnel. A bus was hijacked and set on fire at Northumberland Street. The rioters tried to lure the armoured vehicles off the main road, into their terrain where they could escape into the rows of terraced housing. But the police weren't falling for it. The petrol bombs were then moved up to the front of the road. John had thrown his jacket into someone's house. The street fighters were panting and sweating but ironically the water cannon, further down the road, was being used on bystanders and anyone in the Durham Street and Townsend Street area who innocently opened their doors to the commotion.

Shoreland armoured cars raced up Divis Street and into the Falls Road scattering the people blocking the roads. Occasionally the cars would drive slowly and in their wake would be an RUC riot squad which charged a safe distance into side streets and made arrests. With nobody directing the fighting the police had a fairly easy task breaking up the groups.

'Follow me!' ordered a huge man in his late twenties. 'Quickly! Put the beer barrels across the road.' The gang which John had joined did as they were told. 'Get ready. As soon as I charge prepare to let them have it.' The hairbrained scheme became clear to all. An armoured car turned the bend and accelerated to crash through the makeshift barricade. Its underside got caught up in barbed wire debris and as it slowed down to stop and move into reverse the big fellah charged at it with a long bamboo pole — taken from the hijacked trolley-bus — which was normally used for connecting the booms to the overhead wires. The pole passed through the driver's slit, shuddered for a second and seemed to be swallowed up into the guts of the vehicle. Attached to the end of the pole was a bill hook. The big fellah pulled the pole backwards and forwards looking for heads to catch. The driver had been injured and there were screams from inside the armoured car as a shower of petrol bombs rained down around it. Suddenly the doors burst open and the steel-helmeted RUC men ran down Divis Street pursued by a cheering crowd. The abandoned vehicle then burned with a fierce yellow glow, and its reinforced tyres melted and exploded like muffled gunfire.

When John arrived home it was 1.30 in the morning. He had completely forgotten the time. The lights were lit in the living room. His father jumped up when he heard the key twisting in the door.

'Where the hell have you been! Your mother's been worried sick. I've been out looking for you. You were in Divis Street, weren't you? Look at you! Covered in dirt. Think it's great fun, do you? Have you nothing to say for yourself? What have you to say to your mother? Eh?'

'Da, I'm old enough to look after myself. I'm not stupid. I wasn't arrested. And I wasn't hurt. But the cops started it. You saw that for yourself on Monday night and again today ...'

Catherine sat weeping on the sofa.

'Mammy I'm sorry but they started it.' Catherine wept harder. Nothing could appease her. As the night had passed and news and rumours came in from neighbours she had pictured her son lying in the street, dead, killed by the *situation* rather than run over by an RUC vehicle or knocked fatally unconscious by a stray brick. She was still in the trauma of this irrational. Her lips were trembling and only slowly did she come around as Peter held her tight and stroked her hair back from her moist cheeks, wetted by small sheets of smudged tears.

'You should be ashamed of yourself,' his father repeated. 'Don't you ever, I mean ever, do this to us again ... Come on love. Come on and I'll put you to bed.'

John sat downstairs, feeling the constraints of family responsibilities bear down heavily on him, on his actions, on his freedom. He had no doubt that there was going to be more rioting the following night and he wanted to be in the thick of it. But to do that he was going to cause his mother and father immense worry and a lot of suffering. To bow to this parental disapproval meant staying at home, doing nothing.

In the past few days he had learnt more about the history of the Nationalists since partition, than in all other years. He thought about what partition had done to them. They had turned in on themselves, attacked their own Nationalism as obsolete, as a liability. They accepted defeat. And the peace of defeat, whatever its cost, seemed to be accepted and carried over into the psyche from one generation to the next. Then, whenever a person born free, stood up and dared say 'Let's fight', the people were more loyal to their submission: they were safe with the life they knew.

And this explained why they would rail against even a minor call to arms, why they rose up — some of them with paradoxical viciousness — against the minority who said, 'Unless we fight, our spirits are dead.'

These thoughts and the concluding conviction prowled through his mind. He was still sitting on the chair, biting his lip at the crisis that would occur in the house after dinner on Friday night, when his father came down the stairs. Peter's temper had cooled down but he was still angry. John was being used by people, his gullibility exploited.

'Da, would you catch yourself on? I'm over seventeen, I can see what's going on. Nobody's leading me astray.'

'But you saw what it's doing to your mother. You've been in Divis Street, you've thrown your stones and we're glad, really glad to have you back safe with us. I have seen all of this before and it changes nothing. Please don't be breaking our hearts,' he said, turned around and went back up to his bedroom.

That night and the following day John felt under immense moral pressure. Fortunately, McIvor, for some reason, was not at work.

On his way home he decided that he had to go out that night, whatever the consequences. In the living room the atmosphere was strange. Everyone seemed to know that a momentous clash was looming. The children hardly spoke and there wasn't the usual bickering between Sheila and Jimmy over the space they were occupying. John said hello to his father then his mother. Peter filled his pipe for his after dinner smoke. He had switched the television off so that the main story on the news — the Divis Street riots — didn't become a point for their attention.

Suddenly there was a crash in the kitchen and a squeal from Catherine. The handle from a pot of boiling peas had caught in her sleeve and spilled over the cooker. Her right leg was inflamed as she collapsed in agony. The kids wailed hysterically and Peter and John were panicking.

'Quick! Phone an ambulance!' said Peter, as he applied a cold face-cloth to her leg.

\* \* \*

As they waited in the casualty department of the Royal Victoria Hospital while Catherine was being attended the first injured civilians from the rioting were being brought in in ambulances.

The rioting had spread from Divis Street for three-quarters of a mile up the Falls to Dunville Park, only yards from the hospital.

Catherine was kept in for observation. At home that night John and Peter said little to each other. Out on the Falls Road the baton charges and petrol bombings lasted for several hours. Forty civilians and four RUC men were hospitalised. Scores of people were arrested. And in Dublin a 1,000 people marched to the British Embassy protesting against the actions of the RUC.

Saturday night was relatively quiet although five people were arrested during a baton charge after a plainclothes detective was struck with a milk bottle. Catherine had been released from hospital earlier that day. Her burns weren't as serious as at first thought and she was told to take a long rest. On Sunday over 5,000 people took part in a Republican march from Beechmount Avenue to Hamill Street where a Sinn Féin election meeting was held. John told his father that he was going to the march and Peter replied that he didn't give a damn.

The Tricolour was carried at the front of the march and the RUC — clearly under new instructions — were in such thin numbers on the ground that their presence was token. Some sort of a *quid pro quo* must have been worked out because although the Tricolour was triumphantly carried through the Falls and the police backed off — which some interpreted as a sign of victory — the flag was not again placed in the window of the election head-quarters.

Several hours after the peaceful march and rally Ian Paisley addressed 2,000 of his supporters in the Ulster Hall. He warned that Protestant leaders were showing weakness in the face of Republican pressure and that unless they stood firm their 'faith' would be in jeopardy.

# Chapter 4

# Courtship

After the Divis Street clashes life had returned to 'normal'. The Republican candidates fared badly in the election, most of them losing their deposits. The affair blew over but McIvor never let John forget it.

It was an incident, months later, on Ash Wednesday that finally decided the future for John. On that day, shortly after arriving at work, Bronco said to him, 'You've a bit of dirt on your forehead,' and smudged the ashes John had received earlier in chapel. He exploded and threw a punch which the older fellah combated and then they seriously went at each other. It lasted about half a minute and John was being pulverised before the other workers pulled them apart.

'Do that again, ya Fenian bastard, and I'll kill ya! ' promised Bronco. John ignored him but he was reprimanded by his boss and warned that if there was any similar occurrence, any more disruption, he was out. He was almost past the point of caring. At home there was still residual friction between him and his father. That night he mentioned that he was thinking of going to sea. Peter was immediately enthusiastic. Catherine couldn't believe what she was hearing from either of them though her husband eventually convinced her that it was what John needed. It would do him good. And besides they couldn't hang on to him for ever: he had to leave the nest at some stage. A few days later John went down to the Shipping Federation Offices — the pool — and signed papers. He had been expecting word almost immediately to go on a six week course to Sharpness, England, where novices were trained. But there was a lengthy delay and he began to despair. Some time later as he made his way through the town he met some seamen from his area who had disembarked from the Heysham ferry earlier and were now moving between pubs.

'Well Phil, how's it going? I'm still waiting . . .'

'Listen! Listen. You're the very man I'm looking for.' He told John to get around to the boat and speak to the Chief Steward if he was interested in getting a start as a galley-boy.

'Tell him you're the fellah I mentioned.' He saw the apprehension in John's eyes and said, 'Okay, okay, wait and I'll go around with you.'

Having spoken not to the Chief but to the Second Steward John was excited. If he wanted to work he had to start there and then. It was no time for indecisiveness. Work in the kitchen would start in a half-hour and the boat was sailing at 9.30 pm. He turned to Phil: 'Jesus I'm dying to go but I haven't been home yet . . . Would you tell my ma and da what happened?'

'No problem. Leave it with me.'

'Do I not need anything? Passport? Clothes?'

'No, you'll have no trouble. It's only for a few days.'

The vessel, the *Duke of Lancaster*, was packed with passengers and John worked in the kitchens which serviced the second class cafeteria. Fish and chips, bacon and eggs and sausage and chips were the most common orders. He worked at a huge stainless steel sink washing greasy plates which mounted beside him. Knives, forks and spoons lay over a foot deep in the hot, steaming water which had a rancid smell no matter how much soap he poured in. Between this smell and his queasy stomach, unused to the sensations of sailing, he had to run to the toilet regularly and retch. The cafeteria closed at 12.30 am and it was about 2 am before John, totally exhausted though still exhilarated, got to bed in a small hot cabin. It was so tiny that there was no room for anything but the two double-bunks and the one tall locker which it contained. The churning of the propeller and the engines' pistons vibrated throughout the ship and made the berth hum. He closed his eyes for what seemed to be about ten minutes when a cabin mate shook him and told him to get back up again. He had been asleep for three hours and it was time to go and prepare the tables for breakfast: the boat was due to dock in Heysham at 6 am.

By 10.30 am John had finished cleaning the dishes, washing the dining-room tables and scrubbing the floor. His stomach was like a burst football which had been pulled inside out. It felt exposed to the lashing of waves and was raw from the pain of retching. He still couldn't keep food down.

He went to his cabin, undressed and showered and intended resting for the remainder of the day before they set sail on the return journey that night. However, he was called again to the cafeteria to help lay out the tables for the crew's lunch between

12 pm and 2 pm and spent another hour cleaning up dishes for about a 100 people. At 5.30 pm he then had to help make the tea and sandwiches for the crew again. Trains from London, the Midlands and the North of England began arriving from 10 pm onwards and the cafeteria had to be again prepared for those passengers. It was the same routine except he worked until 4 am since the boat didn't leave until after midnight. On other occasions it would have to wait if a train was delayed. John got two hours sleep and was then up again.

It was about 11 am on Sunday before he, and the majority of the crew who were from Belfast, disembarked. He was so exhausted, so purged of the romantic notion he had of sailing that he positively looked forward to going back to work and seeing McIvor the following day.

When he arrived home there was uproar. His family didn't know where he was on Friday night. Phil had got drunk and only sent word to Peter on Saturday afternoon that John had got an offer of one sailing. An argument ensued and John, through pig-headedness, declared that he had loved it and was going to resume the offer he had for later that week.

On Monday he went into work. He planned to leave without making an announcement as the atmosphere up until he actually departed would then have been intolerable. But there was one thing which was on his mind and that was how to repay Bronco for all the torment he had inflicted. He racked his brain for schemes and finally settled for one which would rely on flattery. He saw Felix who enthusiastically agreed.

On Tuesday Bronco was called to the phone.

'Hello,' said the bellowing voice. 'I wish to speak to Mr William McIvor.'

'This is Bronco McIvor,' he replied, his heart pounding.

'This is the Reverend Ian Paisley ringing. Could I speak to William McIvor? Is William there?'

'Yes, yes Reverend Paisley, this is me. What can I do for you?'

'William, I wonder could you call up to my church on the Ravenhill Road this afternoon. I wish to make a proposal to you. I need a young Protestant man to drive my Rolls Royce and I've heard you're good at cars ... You can name your own wages ...'

'That's right Reverend, I know a lot about cars. I'm, I'm, I'm flabbergasted... I just can't take this in ...'

'That's because you're a silly fucking idiot!' Felix's voice screamed down the phone at him. 'What are you? An idiot . . .'

Bronco looked around and saw John laugh out loud. It was the heartiest laugh that John's lungs had ever bellowed. Bronco dropped the phone, grabbed a wrench and with murder in his eyes, came running at John. He slipped on a large patch of oil and grease, over which no sawdust has been scattered, and lost his balance. John grabbed his jacket, ran out the side door and up the street laughing aloud, tears streaming down his face. He was still laughing a half-hour later and people walking by wondered if he was quite sane.

\* \* \*

Reconciled to the idea of him going to sea, Catherine and Peter bought him new shirts, jeans and an extra pair of shoes.

At sea John was taught conduct and how to dress properly. Personal hygiene was emphasised. He was shown how to set a table, how to use forks and spoons to serve vegetables, from what side to serve, how to pour gravy, when to remove plates, how to run a kitchen with the exception of the cooking which was supervised by the chefs.

'Changing your shoes twice a day,' advised one head waiter, 'is a good way of looking after your feet.'

Back home he registered at the Pool and then signed on at Corporation Street Social Security Office for his weekly unemployment benefit. He was allocated to the *Buffalo*, a container boat, which sailed between Belfast and Preston. A few months later he was on a passenger ship between Southampton and New York.

It was at the end of his first trip back from New York when arriving in Belfast that he met Angela in the city centre. He hadn't seen her in months since Gerard split up with her. He had his kit bag full with presents. It was a Saturday morning. A lot of his bashfulness had worn off but he had still to become sexually involved with a woman, though most of his companions had raucous times when they 'hit port' abroad. He went drinking with them but usually preceded this with an expensive meal in some reputable restaurant.

He saw Angela in Castle Place. She was looking covetously through a shop window at a toiletry display. He walked up behind her.

'Booh!'

She jumped. 'Well look who it is! And how are you keeping? I see you've a bit of a tan.'

'Yes! High life on the high seas.'

They looked in each other's eyes, the delays between conversation causing a little awkwardness but nothing serious. John came straight to the point.

'Would you like to go out tonight?'

'Sttt, I can't. I've something else on.'

His response was, 'Fair enough, but remember. All you have to do is wink at me and I'll come running. Just like that . . .' and he winked at her, so uncharacteristically devilish, that she replied, 'Okay! what about tomorrow night?'

'Great!' he exclaimed. 'Hold on. Wait a minute.' He searched his bag and gave her a small bottle of perfume, Youth Dew by Estee Lauder, which his mother was eagerly expecting.

'Here. This is for you,' he said.

She admired it. 'Gosh, I couldn't. You got that for someone special.'

'No, I've another bottle,' he lied. She gladly accepted the gift and they arranged to see each other the following evening. Meanwhile, John felt a twinge of conscience. He had another present for his mother which she would just have easily been pleased with but he knew the only way he could rest his mind was through not disappointing her. He went into a shop and bought another bottle and was slightly taken aback at the retail price.

He saw Angela on Sunday night and arranged to see her late mid-week as she was busy preparing for exams.

A few butterflies rose in his stomach when he recognised her approaching, her step sure, a broad smile on her lips.

'How do I look?' was the first thing she said.

'Do you want me to really tell you?' he said, in an admiring tone. They went for a long walk. She gave him her hand as they strolled along the Lisburn Road, she picking some roses from the gardens. He made her laugh and now and again squeezed their entwined fingers. He felt happy and proud to be accompanied by such an attractive young woman. There was an immanent confidence about her which was almost palpable. She provided an emotional shelter which he had never had before.

At the dark end of her street she snuggled up to John, kissing. A few minutes later, John placed his right hand under her unbuttoned coat, across her stomach and then slowly worked it up the outside of her jumper and felt the supple bulge of her left breast. Angela gave him a wider and longer kiss. He was in heaven.

'Here, I have to go, it's getting late,' she said. They arranged another date.

Angela gently coaxed Mary Ann over towards the wall. The little girl resisted in her sleep the cold side of the bed. Angela warded off with silent ouches the creaks lest they wake her sister, and carefully climbed under the blankets. She heard her mother ask Frank how long would he be, she was going on up, and he said he would join her shortly.

Angela lay still. She was tired but couldn't rest. She had enjoyed John's company. She fell asleep but then awoke, not knowing the time.

She rose to go quietly downstairs and visit the lavatory. As she made the turn in the stairs, a few steps from the bottom, she discovered her father at the mirror above the mantlepiece man-oeuvring a hand mirror from all side angles and from above to examine his receding hairline. He almost dropped and broke the mirror when he detected her presence and threw a newspaper over it as she entered the living room.

He was a little flustered and she was ashamed for creeping up on him. On her way back to bed she gave him an unusually warm and protracted 'night, night' consoling kiss. He climbed onto the hearth again and rolled his forefinger around his balding pate, convincing himself that it was still quite small, hardly noticeable, about the size of an egg cup, and not as big as people actually saw it, about the circumference of a soup bowl.

\* \* \*

'So who are you going out with now?' asked Angela's Aunty Maureen who sat on a tall stool sipping at a cup of percolated coffee.

'A strange sort of fella,' she laughed. 'Quiet, a bit too serious, but good looking and kind.'

Maureen smiled. Her niece regularly called up to see her and have a chat. Angela also enjoyed Maureen's company. Although she was her mother Mary's younger sister, only nine years separated niece and aunt. Indeed they were often mistaken for sisters.

In many ways Angela reminded Maureen of her own wild youth. She saw this reflection and did nothing to discourage the streak of hedonism she recognised, though she was careful not to overindulge Angela nor undermine her mother's authority.

Angela picked up Maureen's baby boy, Gary, who was almost two years old. She wiped his mouth and grabbed the flab of his belly, squeezing him and making him gurgle and laugh.

'Anja, Anja!' he shouted to her, begging her to stop but enjoying it.

Maureen was prettier than Mary, and Angela supposed that she took some of her looks after her. Both had some light freckles below their eyes; they had the same protuberant lips with distinctive surface lines. Maureen, though, had a leaner frame and had recently acquired a slightly tired general mien in comparison to Angela's youthful vigour. Angela's mother saw more of a likeness in spirit. Her younger sister had given their mother the same type of problems. She had been rebellious and shameless. But time had worked it all out of her system and she had eventually settled down so there was no reason why Angela couldn't do the same.

The young girl often listened to Maureen talk about her past life which sounded so exciting and promising yet she was baffled by the final outcome. Her aunt and uncle Desmond were as alike as chalk and cheese. She was attractive and gregarious: he was eleven years older than her, portly and quiet but could talk insurance schemes and policies with an authority and a confidence which was attested by his growing prosperity — their semi-detached house in residential Coolnasilla was just one example. His face was bloodshot with broken veins and his black hair was sleek with cream. He wore blue suits which gave him a conservative look: she dressed in short and flashy skirts with bright coloured tops.

Angela couldn't fathom the attraction between them but it was there. As soon as he entered the house he would find her and kiss her and then go back to the hall to hang up his car keys and overcoat. She would have his slippers beside his chair. In the evenings they would rarely go out but would sit together on the settee and watch television. They had a full drinks cabinet but apart from special occasions would only take a brandy or a hot port as a night cap once or twice a week. Angela was struck by the boredom and routineness of it all, yet Maureen not only seemed, but was unquestionably happy and content. Desmond would regularly bring her presents — usually a record of some popular music which he loathed but she loved. Every summer for the past five years of their marriage, with the exception of 1963 when Gary was born, they had a fortnight's holiday in Ireland or England. When Angela called in to see Maureen, and the two disappeared into the kitchen from where howls of laughter would erupt, he would raise no objection but simply shake his head and smile. There was nothing for him to hear since he knew his wife's past and what Angela did was Angela's business.

'Do you see much of him?' asked Maureen.

'Actually, he's been away at sea quite a bit.'

'You know what they say about sailors — they've a girl in every port.'

'Possibly you're right, but I doubt it. He's a mate of Gerry's and when we first met he left Patricia home. All he did was ask about me. So she said.

'It's a strange feeling for me to be thinking so regularly and constantly about the one person.'

'Sounds as if you're smitten, if you ask me. You should lure him here some night in July when we're away. Pop open a bottle of wine, stick on one of my black lace negligees and scare the bloody pants off him!'

'Hey! You're supposed to be keeping an eye on me, not encouraging me to climb into bed.'

'It has to happen to you sometime. Make sure it's pleasant and not in the back of a plumber's van up some entry lying on top of a carry-out.'

'How do you know it hasn't happened already? Eh?'

'Because it hasn't. You've still got that girl look in your eyes and besides I'd be the third person to know.'

'That's right,' Angela replied.

\* \* \*

Angela and John went to the pictures and went dancing together when he was on leave, though he was bad on the floor and usually stayed on the sidelines. Sometimes they called up to Maureen's and spent the evening there. On occasion Maureen and Desmond would go out and leave them babysitting. John was home around the twelfth of July when the Orangemen had their traditional parades and on the thirteenth he took her on an Isle of Man excursion which she had thoroughly enjoyed. They had kissed passionately and he had made more forward suggestions but she had resisted him.

Leaving her home a few nights later they kissed at her corner in the shadows for what seemed a long time. She felt really suscep-tible but had to remain firm. He expressed no anger and laughed at her virtuous stance which also caused her to giggle.

'Do you know what Mark Twain said?' he asked.

'No, what did he say?'

'He said, "Be good and you will be lonesome!"'

She smiled at him, kissed him on the cheek and ran up to her door before turning and waving bye-bye.

John was going back to sea the following week, early August, and he wanted to break the news to Angela. The call of travelling and the fact that he was more or less penniless were what motivated him. He had enough common sense to know that she wouldn't be broken-hearted but there had been a whole fascination — which both of them shared — about getting acquainted. He walked over to her district and Jimmy asked could he go with him. Mr and Mrs Mc Cann knew that John was seeing their daughter but he wasn't exactly an invited guest in the house. Angela didn't want him subjected to a litany of questions concerning their whereabouts. So, generally when he called she was ready to go out. Jimmy called for his cousin Tony who lived nearby but he had gone downtown with his mother.

Angela had to pay some bills for Maureen who had gone on holiday. She suggested that they bring Jimmy into town with them. In the Wimpy Bar they had hamburgers and chips. Jimmy sat on the seat feeling important and mature. When Angela opened a packet of cigarettes the 10-year-old said, 'No thanks. I used to smoke, didn't I John? But I stopped about five or six weeks ago. I don't drink anymore either.' He giggled and Angela laughed.

'There's something your da could be doing with,' John joked to Angela, pointing to a man with an ill-fitted hair-piece.

'Jesus,' she whispered. 'It's like a golden hamster.'

'No it's not. It's a hair helmet!' shouted Jimmy, causing customers to stare at them. Fortunately, the man in question didn't realise he was being talked about.

Afterwards they brought Jimmy around to the Model Shop in Upper Queen Street and Angela bought him a balsa wood aeroplane. Later, John let Jimmy off the bus and they continued on up to the Glen Road. Maureen had forgotten to cancel the milk and her niece was to lift in the two pints and leave out a note.

John sat on the settee, one leg clasped between his joined hands, the back of his head just tipping the laced antimacassar which smelt of Brylcream or Morgan's Pomade. Her Aunty Maureen's living room was airy and bright. It had large windows at the front and the back with net drapes arranged in showy bows.

'Do you want a cup of tea? There's plenty of milk,' she said, indicating the bottles she held in either hand.

'No thanks.' He stood up and crossed the carpeted floor to a mahogany table where fruit was mounted on a silver dish shaped like a tropical leaf.

'I'll have one of these, okay?'

'Go ahead. Wait and I'll get you a knife.'

He followed her to the kitchen which, again, was very modern, spacious and flooded in light. When he split the orange, the juice immediately shot in a line across the bread board leaving a few dribbles at the tip of the knife. He popped the segments into his mouth and slowly chewed one after the other. The citrus gave off a powerful fragrance and every few minutes he would involuntarily sniff the tips of his fingers.

'Can I stick on the radio?'

'Aye if you want. She's got some new records.'

'Music is always in the background for our generation, don't you think?' he asked.

'I hadn't thought about it,' she replied.

The conversation was fairly stilted. They were alone and no one would be disturbing them. They went through the LPs and made fatuous comments. She wondered for a few moments and then dismissed the thought. No. This is not how it would be. I'm being silly. She glanced at John who had removed the record from its sleeve. Atmospheric dust sparkled and journeyed in a ray of sun and she dug the toes of her feet into the new carpet whose pile smelt rich.

'"Beatles for Sale"!' he exclaimed. 'I saw them in the Ritz. They were brilliant. Can I put it on? Do you like them?'

'I prefer the Rolling Stones, but go ahead. I like Paul McCartney but not John Lennon.'

She watched his actions as he re-rolled and tucked in his fallen sleeve and was lost in his own small excitement about the record.

That the sight of his bare arm or his backside in denims should stir in her almost provocative images amused her. He caught her looking at him and disarmingly smiled back. But he also felt a tiny twinge of apprehension.

However, as soon as he sat down he threw his arm over her shoulder and they both felt much more relaxed. She turned her face and they kissed for a few seconds, paused, and then kissed for what appeared to be a full minute. They explored the insides of each other's mouths, the soft, scored, pebbly cheek tissues, gliding over teeth, the tongues duelling, then rolling and pressing deep into the mouth, each little pleasure another layer of rising passion.

'I think this LP is absolutely brilliant,' he asserted during one of the momentary breaks.

She smiled.

'Shush! I know what you're gonna say,' he declared, almost disappointedly. 'You still prefer Mick Jagger.'

'Actually, what I was going to say was that the Beatles are becoming my favourite group, if you must know!'

He whistled wistfully.

Her top lip was like the hood of a pink orchid. And, in a completely unwitting impression, her bottom lip often appeared sensually swollen in a way which undermined her innocence. To self-deluders, the men who eyed her, it was almost a public display of pudenda aroused.

His hand fell accidentally on her bare foot and he kept it there when she didn't withdraw. There was no conversation, no embarrassment at the silence, just listening to the music, with momentary glances at each other and mutual smiles or a sigh of suppressed laughter at how potentially foolish they might look to a fly on the wall.

> Oooh I need your love babe,
> Guess you know it's true...
>
> Hold me, love me,
> I ain't got nothin' but love babe,
> Eight days a week ...

Hold me close and
Tell me how you feel,
Tell me love is real . . .

Let me hear you say,
The words I long to hear,
Darling when you're near . . .

Words of 'Love You',
Whispered soft and true,
Darling I love you . . .

Someday you'll know, I was the one,
But tomorrow may rain, so-oh I'll follow the sun . . .

From her little toe with his forefinger he traced the seam of an imaginary nylon stocking, along the side of her ankle, up the calf of her leg. There was a powerful thumping in his heart as he was allowed to continue. She felt her temples blink and her face flush. She felt the flush sensually creep across her breasts, tautening her nipples which then relaxed again when the area in suspense suddenly shifted to her loins. He swallowed hard. She had to catch her breath. Her thigh became indistinguishable from her goose-pimpling buttock. Their blood was shot with adrenalin. He had never before had his hand on a girl's leg and he wanted to savour the licence. She was conscious of being swamped in warmth between her legs and this was now her primary sensation.

'Come on, we're going upstairs!' she gasped.

She had held and studied babies with big, blue eyes and dimples. She knew intimately the back of the head and the shoulders of Mary Ann whom she slept with. She imagined she knew through familiarity every facial way and turn of all her family, could trace the origins of scars on her brothers' hands and count the hairs out her father's ears. But this was a different type of interest and fascination, this physical scrutiny. She found herself lightly massaging the contours of his shoulders with her finger tips, not knowing the source of the inspiration but intuitively motivated.

Momentarily breathtaken with her increasing audacity she exhaled a muted, tingling laugh and a giggle rang through the rings of her throat as John kissed and bit her neck. Her chin retreated in mock defence to her chest bone, like a snail into its shell, and he tickled her on the back so that she opened again but this time to his gentleness. She measured the fleshy lobes of his ears between her finger and thumb and they spent silent moments just exchanging long glances, transmitting thoughts, experimenting with the light and shadows, running fingers through hair, discovering curls, squeezing small imperfections, examining the quicks of nails, then pressing lips to lips and circumscribing each other's faces with soft kisses and young breath.

He looked into her eyes and saw little brown diamonds in tiny pools of milk.

His close-shaven face was the smoothest part of their bodies.

Their daring was tempered with patience, and a happy agreement was at work.

Angela felt strange, strange sensations. Though it was late afternoon and the sun filled the whole house she felt entranced. Nagging thoughts of her mother had vanished; so had the outside world. She was cocooned and in an abandoned frame of mind, her body enjoying the laziness and comfort the wide mattress offered, yet tuned intensely into responding to each caress, each tug and impassioned kiss.

She wiped the natural oil from John's forehead and beads of sweat like escaping sap rose immediately. She brought his forehead down and with the fine tip of her tongue licked the salt away, etching 'I love you' on his brow.

As they kissed, John's head slowly rocked from side to side, the pressure and pleasure waves giving his lips a sexual thrill. Their tongues were tingling, dancing, spelling explicit questions and positive replies, diving and flicking as their buds tasted excitement.

Throughout this exploration John's fingers had occasionally and deliberately brushed against her breasts but had concentrated on drawing lines from her ankle to a border on her right thigh with a desperate discipline which was now reaching exasperation. The tossing and turning had loosened her blouse at the waist and two buttons were undone. Within seconds he was playing with her flesh, along her spine and up to her pointed bra, gently digging his nails into her. He pulled some more of the blouse and stroked the dark hair of her armpits with his right thumb, and then slowly his forefinger rose up the nylon, feeling its way carefully, impressed and excited. He imagined his pulse shoot in spurts at the joint in his thumb. His other fingers took up the grope. Flesh shrivelled to a hard nipple which even through the fabric of the brassiere, he imagined, pierced the palm of his hand.

In the struggling his own trousers' zip had come undone and when she sat up on her elbows to uncuff her sleeves and begin undressing she laughed at the sight of his erection. His clothes had been strangling him for some time and despite their new-found intimacy he still preferred to throw the counterpane over them as they undressed.

She contracted her shoulders towards each other and the straps of her bra fell down her arms, its cups falling away to reveal magic flesh, free and ripe.

The sight of her lying flat, raising her behind and deftly removing her navy blue knickers with her thumbs at the side pleats and down her legs left him dazed as he longingly stared at her beauty. Within seconds they were entwined.

The kissing itself had almost shattered John's sexual composure, the pleasure had been so intense an experience. He fumbled, selfishly searching. They joined together at his bidding and within a short space of time he spent himself, but kept going until the look in Angela's eyes revealed his farce. She turned over and softly cried, the tears moistening her hair. John saw and smelt the teardrops. He was puzzled, confused and extremely and belatedly worried that perhaps he had made her pregnant and that it was that fear which had upset her. He felt desolate because a curtain had suddenly fallen between them.

He couldn't communicate without revealing how cheapened their love-making had been subsequently made by his twinges of hypocrisy and selfish concern, on top of his impetuousness.

Angela was crying because her person had just changed. The experience of her losing her virginity hadn't been earth-shattering but there was a quiet satisfaction — the thought of her mother for some reason raced from one corner of her mind, across the picture and out of the frame — and the tears were a spontaneous, affectionate adieu to childhood. She was five days over her last period and knew she could not become pregnant. She couldn't articulate the swarming in her mind and was slightly annoyed at

John's sudden change of affection. However, she turned to him and laughed and her brightening had a relaxing effect on him and he smiled.

'Are you okay? I didn't hurt you, did I? I'm sorry.'

'Why? What's happened? Have we done it yet?' she said with some conviction, bursting out laughing once again at the incredulity expressed in his startled and pained eyes. She cuddled up close to him and he held her: she staring across the width of the room, he at the ceiling. The silence was a form of communication. Their breathing became light and later he was never able to fully recall if they had slept, though he thought they had dozed for a while in the stillness. She would always remember, not whether they slept but the excitment of repeating to herself, you've done it, you've done it, girl you've finally done it! And because she had done it with John, she would always cherish the memory of his boyishness on what became known to her as *that afternoon.*

She put her forefinger into his belly-button, which was free of body hair, and screwed out some fluff, rolled it into a ball and flicked it over the side of the bed.

'Hey! That was mine.'

He forced her down and pinned her arms with his knees in horseplay as he sat across her breasts, irrepressible laughter shaking his rib cage. It was all with a familiarity beyond imagination just hours earlier.

'Ready for round two!' he demanded.

'Oh, I'm ready. But are you sure you are!' she said getting the last word.

In the evenings before Maureen and Desmond returned John would call up to the house to see Angela. They would potter about like a married couple and on one occasion she cooked him a meal. Before he went back to sea they spent some of the warm nights going on long walks. It was one of the periods when she had given up cigarettes on his encouragement. She was surprised at her frugality: normally she couldn't wait to spend a boyfriend's money and go on the town. But she enjoyed these strolls and the slow baring of her innermost thoughts to another individual whose attentiveness was not conscripted or merely courteous but was based on affection, awe and wonder.

One night after leaving Maureen's they were kissing below the trees at the corner of Coolnasilla and Glen Road. The sky was teeming in colour and light. He said: 'There's a shooting star . . . make a wish.'

'Where? I didn't see it.'

'Watch. You'll see more . . . There!' And to where he pointed she saw the faint trail just disappear.

'Yes! Yes! I saw it. There's another one . . . and another one.' She was excited at the sudden discovery. 'I never knew there was so many.'

'There aren't,' he replied. 'Well, to be correct, there are but we don't always see them. Those ones belong to the meteor Perseid. It passes over us every August and they're part of its shower.'

'You know. You're really clever.'

He smiled. 'Well, did you wish?'

'Of course, but I'm not allowed to tell you,' she said as she repeated the wish that these simple moments of happiness would last forever.

# Chapter 5

# Destinations

Over the next few months John was away on short trips between Belfast and England and on other occasions between Britain and Mediterranean ports. However, Angela's love for him never faltered, indeed it grew stronger. She considerably settled down. Although she still went out to an occasional dance she remained loyal to him. She had passed her exams and had decided to stay on at school rather than take a course in commerce and typing which had tempted her. John wrote regularly, even if he was only away for four or five days and she looked forward to receiving such mail. She sent him postcards care of the Seaman's Mission in whatever port he was arriving. He could see that they had not been picked at random but had been carefully chosen. They would contain romantic, esoteric messages and references to their intimacy which no stranger could ever guess at.

When in Belfast he regularly called into her house for her. Similarly, John brought Angela to his home where she was made welcome after Peter received confirmation that her parents knew that they were going out together. John disguised his true feelings for Angela when they were in front of his parents, partially out of pretence of modesty. To Catherine their relationship was respectable and she would have been shocked to have learned the truth. Monica, who was now working, had her boyfriend call at the house. It was better to know what they were up to rather than not to know, was Catherine's remark to Peter. Jimmy would sit at the edge of the sofa admiring his big brother's girl. He had a crush on her and wanted to show her his toys and books.

When Catherine went out to the kitchen to make tea Angela would follow her and help with the sandwiches. Catherine was convinced that despite the girl's physical maturity, intelligence and obvious fondness for her son there was something about her which was disturbing and she couldn't place her finger on it. In turn, Angela detected this suspicion which triggered off in her a disinclination to remain too long in the house or spend an evening there. John was upset, especially since she insisted, 'Your mother doesn't like me!'

'That's not true!' he replied, wounded at the thought that the two women closest to him had an antipathy towards each other.

In December the winter cruises to the Caribbean were beginning and John was anxious to get on one of the boats. Up until then he had been a casual seaman, but by now he had been on enough trips to 'earn' his seaman's book, and so he registered with the shipping federation. He would get a start on a ship much quicker and would get an extra weekly allowance in addition to his unemployment benefit, although this hardly mattered since he was regularly away. However, he could only turn down one offer of a ship — the companies wanted seamen they could rely upon and those on contract were deemed to be serious about their commitment.

Angela raised no objection — she could see that he was hesitant about going away for a longer period because of her. She also knew that there was something — possibly a thirst for wordly experience — drawing him out of his home town. Perhaps it was a taste for adventure. They had bickered from time to time: not over anything serious and especially not the life he led which meant that they saw each other intermittently though for passionate moments. The arguments were small matters over the choice of places they would go. Before he left he would usually take her downtown for a meal. His criticism of the cuisine, comparing it to somewhere abroad that he had eaten, irritated her. As soon as he detected a hint of tiresomeness he would panic and would seek assurances about their love which cracked her brittle composure all the more. But as soon as he was away she missed him. She settled down to compose a letter to which she would add a few more pages each night. She would then sprinkle the letter with some Youth Dew and when he arrived in New York and checked in with the Seaman's Mission the thick perfumed letter would be awaiting him and all his anxiety would disappear.

In January John reported to the federation in London to join an oil tanker which set sail for the Persian Gulf from where it would draw aviation fuel to South Africa, back and forth for six months. He had talked with Angela about the possibility of going on a much longer trip and she said she had no real objection. She enjoyed his letters but particularly their reunions. So with more than a little apprehension he left for England and told everyone he would see them in the summer.

Most of his friends, acquaintances from Belfast or those with whom he had worked on previous trips, had signed up on other vessels. On his very first day he had a row with the second steward, Chris Hutchinson, an ill-mannered Londoner, ten years his elder, and several inches taller than him. As a pantry-boy his responsibilities were very clear to him — taking the food from the galley to the officers' mess, serving the catering crew their food and keeping the pantry spick and span. The second steward had to look after the cabins of the Captain and Chief Officer, serve their meals and supervise the other caterers, including John.

They had hardly sailed out of London before Hutchinson called John. 'Paddy, this is your job here. You've to make my bed and clean my room.'

'No, I don't,' said John abruptly. 'You do that yourself.'

'I'm telling you. You do it.'

'Well I'm telling you I'm not. I'm not a skivvy for you or anybody else.'

'You'll do as I tell you!' he ordered, spittle flying from his lips. John still refused. Throughout the following day he picked fault with John's work. At the end of every voyage each seaman was issued with a discharge in his book with a comment on his behaviour: VG — very good; DR — declined to report, VNC — voyage not completed. A DR meant that when one produced the discharge book to register for the next trip such a report was a black mark and made it extremely difficult to find work. John was anxious to avoid such a comment.

After John had cleared away all the lunch dishes and scrubbed out the pantry Hutchinson deliberately arrived late with the Captain's dishes. John ignored the plates intending to see to them at tea-time and went to his cabin. Later the Chief Steward brought him before the Captain who fined him two days' pay for disobeying an order. He was being forced to capitulate. Characteristically, he took on the extra work with an enthusiasm which was mistaken for submissiveness but he said to Hutchinson: 'That's it. I'll see you when this is all over.'

'Huh! I've heard all you Paddies talk like this before,' the big man boasted. One day when they had set sail from the Iranian port of Abadan he went up on deck to get some sun. A cool breeze disguised the fierceness of the heat. On the sea the waves sat like cotton stitching, flecks of white on a rich blue fabric where splume was bubbling through. He lay down and fell into a deep sleep and wasn't discovered for about four hours by which time his back and shoulders had erupted in blisters. He was removed to an American oil company's hospital onshore where he spent two days. There he met an Irish nurse from Belfast who wasn't long out and she told him about the trouble back home.

In April, following protests from Paisley, the government mobilised the Ulster Special Constabulary, a totally Unionist paramilitary reserve force, also known as the B Specials or B men, which had a long record of anti-Catholic sectarianism. The government also banned all trains travelling from the south of Ireland which were carrying Republicans to commemorations of the fiftieth anniversary of the 1916 Rising. In March, April and May there were petrol bomb attacks on Catholic shops, homes and schools in Belfast.

When John was returned to the ship he was fined eight days pay for being absent from work whilst his 'self-inflicted injuries' were being attended to.

As they approached Cape Town alarm bells began ringing. Black smoke was belching from the skylights above the engine room which had gone on fire when a sudden swell overturned one of the oil spillage trays sending fuel into hot pipes. There was pandemonium on board and it took fireboats five hours to put out the flames. The following day they off loaded the fuel at the terminal but the damage the vessel suffered forced it to return to England six weeks early.

Most of the seamen had a cynical view of their union leaders. When they joined the union they had to sign a form which authorised the shipping company to deduct their dues from their wages and pay the union direct. When a ship returned to its home port the union man, carrying his brown briefcase, came on board. The first people he went to see were the Captain and the Chief Steward to hear their version of any problems during the voyage: only later would he ask the crew their side of the story. So cynical were the seamen that they reckoned that the briefcase was especially made for the two bottles of whiskey and the two cartons of cigarettes, care of the Captain, which fitted so neatly into it!

When the boat docked at Teesside John sought out the union representative. He smiled when he saw the briefcase but wasn't that dismayed. However, when he tried to complain about Hutchinson, the Captain, the excessive discipline, his fines, the union man procrastinated. He said he would need to write off to headquarters in London: he would need a full statement from him which he would get the next day or perhaps the day after because he had to see to three ships. But John had already signed off the boat which meant he had no legal entitlement to remain on board. Most of the crew were breaking up and had gone home. To stay and make a statement he would have to go to the Seaman's Mission or book into a hotel which would be expensive. He said, 'Forget it!' and the union man seemed quite pleased: he had sorted out another labour dispute.

At the railway station he placed his luggage on board the train, which wasn't due to leave for another half-hour, and went into the bar to have a few drinks with those crewmen still left. Hutchinson sat in the company and was loud-mouthed, boasting of some of his sexual exploits in Durban. When he got up to go to the toilet John followed him. They stood at the communal latrine. The Londoner said: 'Paddy, it was great knowing you. We didn't start great but we became the best of friends. Put it there . . .' He outstretched his hand. John smiled at him, gathered his fingers and thumb into a clenched right fist and hit Hutchinson so hard that he fell into the spray of water, blood spurting from either nostril. He looked up, his anger and ability to rouse himself checked by the shock of the punch.

'You'll think twice about messin' another Paddy about,' John said and left to board his train.

\* \* \*

The man melted into a little boy once she caressed him and rested his head against her breasts. It was one of those moments when silence was music. Still some sweat lay in their thighs.

'I could eat you!' he said.

'I know,' she replied, with a trailing, tender emphasis on the word 'know'.

At that they closed their eyes and gently swam into a shallow pool of sleep.

\* \* \*

'Do you ever take a break?'

'What do you mean?'

'For God's sake! You go on and on and on. You couldn't enjoy America. When you wrote to me it was all about what they had done to the "poor" Indians. Everywhere you go there's something wrong. I don't even know why you bother going away . . . or coming back . . .'

'What does that mean?' he said angrily.

'It doesn't mean anything. Look, I'm sorry, I'm just uptight.'

'I've been away too long . . .'

'No, it's not that. Ach, I'll get over it . . .' she said and kissed him on the forehead.

Doubts opened up like deep holes appearing in the path before him. He felt depressed when she went home. Something was wrong.

\* \* \*

John Scullion's funeral was relatively small given the circumstances of his death. The RUC reported that he had died two weeks after a mysterious stabbing in Clonard Street, off the Falls Road. On 26 June three Nationalists were shot as they left the Malvern Arms public house in North Belfast. The Falls was shocked when it was learnt that the youngest of the group, seventeen-year-old Peter Ward, was dead. He came from Beechmount and his funeral drew large crowds to the west of the city. Demands were made for John Scullion's body to be exhumed. A fresh post mortem showed that he also had been shot. The UVF, a Loyalist paramilitary group, had carried out both killings.

\* \* \*

John had looked forward to this day and he had planned it carefully. What had been irritating Angela, he concluded, was the instability of their relationship, or rather the fact that he was away so much that it led to an uncertainty about where she stood. He was also grateful for her honesty in telling him that she had been out to dances. How could he have been so naive as to expect her to sit in seven nights a week while he was seeing the world! But now everything would be okay. It was a beautiful, sunny August Sunday and he had borrowed a car to take her for a drive up to the Glens of Antrim. It was his intention to propose that they get engaged on her next birthday and that he leave the sea and try to get a job, any job in Belfast.

The journey from Cargan village over the mountains, down passed Glengariff forest and down the steep, twisting road was pleasant and could not have been more propitious. Although quiet at the outset Angela became more lively as they drove, and sang to the pop music on the car radio.

But then things went wrong. He caught nuances in some of her conversation, a coolness. Then she aggressively attacked some innocent remark he made about the pleasantness of a couple holding hands who passed by. His plans were disintegrating and he never found an opening where he could put his proposal.

They sat at the harbour facing the small County Antrim seaside village of Waterfoot. They sat in the car trying to resolve their differences, trying to lower the tension. She had her mind made up, there was no changing her from the decision which, she made clear, hadn't just come over her as they had eaten their lunch in the Cushendall hotel when she first told him it was over.

'Listen John, there were times when it was good, really, really good. And there were times when it was not so good. Please, let it go. Let it be.'

'But I don't understand. We were getting on really, really well. Is there somebody else? Tell me, is there?'

'You know there's not! But I need the break, I need to look at things more objectively, have some time off to consider things, which I can only do if I'm free . . .'

The last word pierced him. Free. As if he would ever imprison her! Or curtail her! All he wanted to do was put the world at her feet. He thought about what she was saying, its validity. He went over every word they had spoken during the meal. In their silence he retraced every inch of the journey before they reached here. Then he recalled their conversation and her moods the day before, the week before, what she had written in her letters. He remembered the expensive watch she had bought him for his birthday and the romantic card she sent. Try as he might he was at a total loss to explain her behaviour. It was inexplicable, it baffled him. When they had made love he *knew* from her total commitment and involvement that it was love she was making. If her unhappiness was so ingrained and outstanding — as she claimed — she certainly gave him no indication, gave him no warning, no opportunity for him to mend his ways if he was to blame.

He must have done something wrong or hadn't pleased her and he was about to promise to do this or that but his pride got the better of him. She saw the anguish in his face, and felt a bitch, but knew no easier way of breaking things off. The truth would have wounded him even more. She was even selfish enough to have entertained the thought that if she had been honest he may have thrown her out of the car, right there, and that would have been a real inconvenience. She cried a few tears at his desperation and he misinterpreted them as a further sign that he was troubling her and he comforted her with a 'there, there, now,' and put his arm around her shoulder.

The windows were rolled down and the brine from the sea below hung in their nostrils. John stared at the u-shaped glen. The hills on either side appeared to merge two or three miles up the valley. He imagined the scalping of the mountain sides, the top soil being unpeeled and the almost silent screeching of the rocks as the unrelenting, grinding glacier made its melting retreat to the depths over a thousand years. All of that powerful but inanimate violence was of nothing compared to the stabbing pain concentrated within his heart.

'Can we go now?' she said, dabbing her tears.

He pressed her to reconsider, to think things over. He maintained the appeal until she felt as if she had to make him that promise just to get out of there.

When she closed her front door behind her she breathed a huge sigh of relief. She was delivered of him and took a few minutes before she looked out the window to be certain that the car had left, that he had gone from her door. I'm free!!! she squealed into herself. 'I'm free!' she squealed aloud as she ran upstairs to lie on the bed and take deep breaths of relief.

* * *

For a full week John was obsessed with Angela. He couldn't stop thinking about her. The thought of her holding hands, walking with, kissing someone else hurt him like a ton weight strapped to his heart. But the ache wasn't physical. He felt he could have coped, could have dragged such a heavy burden around so long as he was assured that at the end of the dark tunnel she and he would emerge as their old selves, in love, content. He could take that, he could wait, provided there was a sign.

He remembered the ways he had relentlessly pursued her in the past, the stratagems he had employed to 'accidentally' bump into her. For weeks, perhaps months, from the time she had made an impression on him he had been planning how he in his gaucherie would approach the ideal girlfriend. I wonder had she seen me before I saw her or were the same invisible forces of love working to bring us together? But as soon as I saw her, I knew, I just knew, I had to meet her, be with her. A blackness came over him and he suddenly experienced an inexplicable ache within. He had had arguments with Angela before, minor rows, some harsh words, but he couldn't contemplate her responsible for this rolling and tumbling, these waves of depression, these drowning feelings of hopelessness and despair.

Clearly, there had been some mistake. He took a deep, deep breath and thought to himself, how best can I win her back? What can I do to swing her to me, to demonstrate that I love her and can give her the type of affection and attention which few others will ever receive in a relationship. He stared out the window overlooking his yard. A declaration, inside a heart, had been etched on the entry wall below: 'SP loves JJ, 1.8.53'. Whoever they are, where are they now? he mused. A crowd of children came running up the entry, banging doors and generally making a racket. They were shouting, 'Any oul wood for the bonfire? Any oul wood for the bonfire?' He recognised Jimmy and Sheila carrying off between them and three others one of those obsolete stuffed armchairs with threadbare armrests and seat. They are completely oblivious to responsibility, to passion, to the rapport between lovers, he thought. They have all this before them.

He had the idea of writing Angela a love letter which he would pass to her in the dance that night. It was daring and it was this feature which appealed to him. He momentarily considered the risk of a rebuff but this was overwhelmingly outweighed by his depression and by his faith in her sense of propriety and appreciation. He mustered all his emotional energy and powers of imagination and sat down to convert the blank page into an exposition of his feelings which would be so persuasive as to literally sweep her off her feet. He read it and was very pleased with himself. He read it again and became depressed, deciding it was over-the-top, unmasculine even. Shit, it's how I feel. He read it again. Damn it, I'll give it to her.

*Angela, my dearest Love. Let me know through a shooting star, or the draw of the plucked petals, or the buttercup yellowing my throat, or through that crack in the pavement which my foot may cross, if you are for me!*

*My eyes lay blind, sightless, until you came into my life and showed me the sparkling stars, the glowing lights of love, the brightness of our passion, the splashing colours of our joint existence.*

*Now you have gone and night has befallen my every day since. I am haunted and terrified by the darkness of your absence. Perhaps now you blaze another's trail, the thought of which pales me into a former shadow of myself.*

*I'll be here tomorrow, waiting, your obedient pet, waiting for you to return to the arms of the one who loves you. But tonight just give me a sign, please look at me, give me the wink and tomorrow, a new, bright day, I shall come running, running out of this dark hell and into your warm, heavenly sunshine.*

> *Your faithful lover,*
> *John O'Neill*

The hall was packed, the lights dim and the band music loud when John and his two friends, Gerard and Felix, came in late. They were instantly greeted by the thrill which the atmosphere generated. Most girls were dancing with other girls, some with boys. The banquettes around the walls were tightly filled to their capacity. Clouds of smoke rose from those seated and seams of heavy smoke swirled in the light each time the gent's door swung open.

Big Al, the MC, was on stage cracking jokes.

'Knock! Knock!' he shouted.

'Who's there?' the audience roared back.

'Siobhan!'

'Siobhan who?'

'Shove on your knickers your da's coming!'

There were loud cheers from some of the boys and girls giggled into their hands.

John had braced himself for the opportunity to pass the letter over to Angela and his heart sank when, despite touring the hall and repeatedly scouring the dance floor, he failed to locate her. She had been there though. She and her friends had drunk several Carlsberg Specials in a city centre bar before they loudly tumbled into the hall joking with the bouncers on duty at the front door. John had passed her twice and failed to notice her. He was expecting to see her sitting in her usual company, expecting to find her still perhaps demure and reflective after the trauma of their break-up.

She had her hair cut and curled and was sitting on her new boyfriend's knee, her lips buried in his, her arms locked around his neck, as she rolled back and forth in his lap. Only when she got up to visit the cloakroom did Patricia stop and warn her that John was searching about the place.

'Shit!' she said. 'Why can't he leave me alone?' She looked around but couldn't see him. She crossed the slack end of the floor and saw him in the distance, standing transfixed, holding something white in his folded hands the way one would hold rosary beads. His eyes lit up when he recognised her and he beamed an innocent, desperate smile in her direction. There was something of an underdog about his simpering pose which she despised. She moved the sides of her lips into a barely defined smile, but it was booby-trapped with meanness and high contempt.

That smile was hope, part of his mind argued.

In the cloakroom Angela found it difficult to restrain herself. She thought her hostility to him had plumbed its depth but she now found herself drawing upon new reserves of untapped hatred and she was disgusted at herself for ever having seen anything in him. He was boring, serious, unattractive . . . an oaf.

She came out from behind the ticket woman and John was standing in front of her.

'Hi!' she said giddily as the alcohol raced around her mind.

'I've something for you,' he sheepishly muttered, and handed her the letter. Before she could respond he disappeared into the sultry heat of the dance hall.

She appeared to be gone for a long time. Felix wanted to know what was wrong, why didn't he unwind, get a girl up to dance. Gerard asked him was he feeling all right, he was very quiet. He told them to leave him be.

He had never been so nervous before, not even when facing a fist fight against a superior adversary whom he knew would annihilate him. He was in a cold sweat and said that he would be back in a minute.

Angela returned, looked around, paused and shot a genial smile over to where John had been standing in the half light with his friends. She had read the letter not once but three times.

In the toilet John patted his face with cold water, then gulped down several mouthfuls. By now she has read it, he thought. She has read my words of love, the expression of my feelings for her. His fear was gone. His composure, his confidence was restored.

The letter, that magic letter, he sang enthusiastically as he drummed his fingers on the edge of the sink and joined the throng of people to share the humour of the MC. The band was relaxing during the last interval. The dimmed lights had been fed more power so that people and groups were distinguishable and no longer anonymous.

There was loud laughter as John made out the MC's words as he read ' . . . I'll be here tomorrow, waiting, your obedient pet . . .' Somebody barked like a dog and there were more howls of unrestrained giggling. John knew that his heart died on the spot. The humiliation burned the love inside him to a shrivelled cinder. His eyes found hers as she swung around on the arm of someone with whom he realised she was too intimate for him to have been a recent pick-up. He stood there, as his signature was read out, taking the last insult she would ever hurl at him. For a second he wanted to wilt and cry like a child. Not everyone there knew him or knew that he was the author but one person more than she to whom it was addressed was one person too many. Fifteen or twenty people stared at him, some laughing, others with mixed feelings, some empathising. Through her alcoholic swill she saw his stare, saw him stand his ground, and in defence of the action she chuckled hollowly to drown out the faint voice of remorse struggling somewhere within.

Felix took John by the arm and said, 'Let's get out of this fuckin' place and leave these animals . . .'

John hesitated briefly, looked down at the floor and glanced at her again with eyes that said, You did this to me. You did this. Then he walked out.

John's decision to suddenly leave Belfast took his family by surprise. Over recent years he had shared few of his secrets or feelings with his father, even when they went out for a drink. Catherine guessed that his departure was perhaps something to do with Angela but even that suspicion was dispelled when she called into the house two weeks later to get an address for John. She was relaxed and amiable and gave no clue that there had been a fall-out or that her boyfriend was away on anything but a routine trip. Angela had stopped visiting regularly anyway and so when the weeks passed and she didn't call back and they received lengthy letters from John which made no reference to her Catherine supposed they had just gone their separate ways

\* \* \*

'There daddy. That's for your pipe. I made you that in crafts.'

Peter looked at the glazed clay ash-tray. It was unusual in that the dimples for cigarette rests were missing and instead it was designed in the shape of a small armchair surmounted on a circular bowl.

'I came first in the class. The teacher said he had never seen a design like it when I started but he let me finsh it.'

'Catherine! Have a look at this!' She came in and genuinely admired the ash-tray which had a rest for the pipe and a bowl for discarded tobacco and match sticks. Whatever way he had painted it it looked rich and rare.

Jimmy was now eleven and had started secondary school. He showed no academic flair and indeed was below the standards of the middle stream into which he had barely scraped. But his real qualities were his humour, his generosity and his general demeanour which just about made him loved by everyone. Each time John went to sea Jimmy became depressed and hated to see his big brother leave home. If Peter and Catherine argued he would mediate with a, 'Now, now you two. Behave yourselves . . .' which usually brought them around.

*　*　*

Catherine arose early but hadn't time to light a fire before getting Peter his breakfast. When he left she knelt before the hearth and opened the grate. Fine white and grey particles rolled down the slope of a little mountain of ash below the dead cinders. She stoked the cinders again before discarding the useless bits of flake but retrieved the odd honeycombed half burnt coals which were good for rekindling the fire. She opened the back door, made a quick dash to the bin which was full of refuse and had no choice but to leave the lid-full of ashes sitting upright. The heavy rain pulverised the dust and after a few minutes left it with the complexion of heavy, wet cement.

Jimmy heard her call but rolled over onto his side. He had a terrible sore head even though he had slept soundly. Catherine brooked no compromise. Though often she would relent, he had been off sick the previous week and she saw nothing in his condition to justify another lost day. She remained firm, assured him that when he got to school he would feel better and then would be glad because afterwards he could go out and play. She sent him off and then was over-run with that guilt feeling which even the certainty of having made the correct decision could not assuage.

At tea-time they sat watching the news on television. Nearly every pupil at the Pantglos Junior School was dead. At 7 am that morning Tip 7 had sunk by ten feet. At 9 am it slipped another ten feet. Then at 9.10 am the fine tailings from the coal washing plant began to move: slow at first, until it gathered speed and raced like an express train on its 2,000-feet run. The wave of black mud ripped its way through two farms, crossed the canal and railway and crashed with full force into the primary school where the children, 109 in all, were gathered together for morning assembly. In total 144 people from the tiny Welsh mining village of Aberfan died.

Jimmy set his fork into his unfinished mashed potatoes. His lower lip began to tremble as the sombre news report revealed the extent of the tragedy. He felt nauseous, burst into tears and ran upstairs, crying, leaving everyone in the living room bewildered and embarrassed. Peter said,'What's all that about?' and Catherine told him not to go up, to leave Jimmy on his own. The others were ordered not to say anything to their brother either by way of sympathy or jest. When his mother was making tea she shouted up to him: 'Jimmy? Jimmy! Do you want a cup of tea?'

'Please,' he said, and she could detect from his tone that he had regained his composure and was ready to come down.

Some weeks later it was Halloween. From after tea-time onwards children, dressed up in old frocks and clothes as witches, devils and monsters, their faces painted in make-up, knocked on doors singing, 'Please put a penny in the old man's hat!' The first half a dozen callers were genuinely welcomed and the coppers kept aside for the occasion were soon exhausted. But as more and more called at doors which had been already answered ten or a dozen times adults' patience wore thin and soon the children realised that the begging was over for another year. Then they went on a tour of the streets and found that they were suddenly in love with those squawking babies who were terrified by the cartwheels, jumpin' jacks, roman candles and exploding rockets which their young parents continued to set off despite the hysterical squawking. So the gangs were full of 'ach isn't she lovely', and other ingratiating remarks which perpetuated the fireworks display until the last sparkler fizzed out.

Jimmy was out early collecting with friends from his own street in his own and neighbouring streets. Later they counted their separate earnings and boasted of what they would buy. He said he was going to get a book on wild birds but, unknown to anyone, he bought a stamp and envelope and sent the money he had collected, 3/7½d, to the Aberfan appeal fund.

# Chapter 6

# London I

When school resumed following the summer holidays Angela studied first year 'A' Levels English and French with little and often no enthusiasm. Because she had had to repeat her 'O' Levels she was a year behind Patricia and other classmates and she felt frustrated and slightly lonesome amongst pupils a year her junior. Her inattentiveness soon brought her into conflict with her teachers. Her copybook was well blotted from previous incidents and despite warnings and a letter to her parents in late September she increasingly adopted a couldn't-care-less attitude.

Her parents, Mary and Frank, had attempted to instil some discipline in their wayward daughter. They had tried keeping her in at nights, deprived her of pocket money and Frank so lost his temper one day that he physically scolded her and then felt ashamed. On Saturdays she worked as a packer in Lipton's city centre supermarket, giving half of her earnings to her mother. Even so, on one occasion as punishment, her parents refused her the ticket money to a concert by Donovan. She sulked and cried in her bedroom and locked the door against Mary Ann who had been playing there. She lay on the bed and remembered how this difficulty hadn't arisen in May when Bob Dylan played in the Ritz. She had casually mentioned the concert in a letter to John, with no hidden intention, yet he had picked up her words and sent her the money, telling her to enjoy herself. She thought about him and realised that she missed him and would have liked to be receiving his love letters once again but clearly she had squandered that. He had never replied to the two letters she had sent him and which contained a half-hearted apology since she couldn't be certain of her true emotions which fluctuated so much. If only he hadn't been so serious and old fashioned, she consoled herself.

By November she was expelled from school. It was at a time when Mary had plenty of worries over debts, but, more particularly, over the failing health of her younger sister Maureen who had fallen repeatedly ill.

The incident which broke the patience of the nuns, Mary later admitted, wasn't that outrageous but it had followed a history of

Angela being continually upbraided over her truancy and bad behaviour. With several friends she had gone down town one lunch-hour and took a change of clothes in her briefcase which she changed into in the toilets of a cafe, before going dancing in the Plaza ballroom. She was an hour late returning to school, was caught climbing through the science classroom window and was brought before the Mother of Discipline and then expelled. The injustice, she protested to her mother, was that those girls who hadn't bothered coming back in the afternoon weren't detected at all as having gone missing. She could hardly complain about that, her exasperated mother commented.

Angela then took a notion that her vocation was to be a secretary. Her parents somehow found the fees to send her to Orange's Academy where, they had to admit, she at last showed promise, conscientiously bringing home with her at night note-books full of Pitman's Shorthand. They bought her an old Olympia typewriter on which she battered away in the evenings. It proved, they said and Angela agreed, that once she set her mind to something she could accomplish it. In January 1967 she got a different Saturday job working in a record shop. Even though the wages were less than before she couldn't believe her luck — getting paid for listening to pop music and meeting interesting fellahs.

Angela loved Saturdays when she worked with two other girls her own age and when Patricia would call in for a chat even though they saw each other throughout the week. She got to know regular customers, among them groups of long haired youths in their late teens. Some of them would ask for 'certain sounds' and the two girls would giggle as three particular fellahs would close their eyes and shake their heads to the rhythms and beats as the booth filled up with the grey smoke from a shared reefer. When pressure of custom eventually forced the youths to give way to other people they still loitered about the premises chatting up girls.

'Listen man. London's the place to be. Everything's happening there . . . the music scene . . . fashion, ' said Eddie who had his long hair in a pony tail. They spoke about the 'pads' they had stayed in, the 'joints' they smoked, the 'swell' parties which lasted days on end. Angela was fascinated by all the talk but Patricia would express scepticism.

'No man. You're wrong!' Eddie insisted. 'I've been, you ain't, ' he would argue in a feigned mid-Atlantic accent.

'Well, I'm going . . . ' put in Patricia, surprising even Angela who had noted in the last year her friend's increasing self-assuredness. 'But it'll be nowhere near you wee boys.'

'Whadda you mean?' Eddie said, getting ruffled.

'Here, go in and listen to this,' ordered Angela placing a new LP on the turntable. She wanted to hear from Patricia what was going on.

'Me and a couple of others are going to London to work for the summer, at Kings Lynn, in the canning factories, or wherever we can get a job.'

'Gee! You're so lucky! When did this all happen?'

'Rose's older sister, Bernie, who's at Queens University answered an ad from students in London who were looking for some people to rent out their flat while they're away picking grapes or something in France. We're all heading over at the end of next month if things go according to plan.'

'Oh Patricia! You're so lucky. I'm dead jealous!'

'I knew you'd be. But listen there's still a chance that one of the others will pull out. I can see no reason why, if you were chipping in your fair share of rent, you couldn't come with us . . .'

Her eighteen-year-old heart was pounding at the thought but it was impossible. Her mother would never let her go. Besides what would she work at. In Belfast there were contacts for jobs and one could always fall back on family. But the idea of such freedom made her dizzy: strolling through the leafy suburbs of London, lying on the grass in Hyde Park, boating on the Thames with some nice boy, frequenting boutiques, bistros, dances, bars, drinking without having to worry about your father smelling your breath, falling in love . . . !

\*   \*   \*

'I know you from somewhere?' asked John of the new galley-boy, who looked eighteen but was actually only fifteen.

'Yeh, I used to knock about with your wee brother, Jimmy, but I'm not from around your way. I live just around the corner from O'Neill's. They're cousins of yours aren't they? And near the McCann's. You used to go out with Angela, didn't you?'

'Yes, I used to . . . I remember you now! You used to knock us up out of bed in the summer holidays to see if our Jimmy was going out,' John laughed. 'What's your name?'

'Stevie Donnelly.'

'Is this your first ship?'

'Yeh.'

'Well, I'll look after you. You'll have no problems though I'd say you could look after yourself . . .'

'Yeh,' said Stevie, smiling.

\*  \*  \*

'Who the hell is that at the door!'

Angela was upstairs but still heard her mother's voice raised in disbelief. Frank looked out the window also. 'He looks like P.J. Proby,' he laughed. 'Give him a few coppers.'

Mary Ann opened the door.

'Hello little girl. Is your big sister in?'

'What do you want?'

'Angela. Tell Angela that Eddie's at the door.'

'Mary Ann! Come in!' Mary pulled her daughter in. Behind her, Seán stared at the amazing figure in the colourful clothes and with hair longer than any girl's in the street.

'Who are you looking for, son?' Mary asked.

'Is Angela there? I've to see her.'

Angela came running down the stairs, panting. 'It's okay mummy, go on in. It's Eddie, a friend of mine.'

Her mother glared at her. 'Come here till I see you a second.' Eddie was left at the door, seemingly oblivious to the shock he had caused. 'Is he on drugs! What the hell are you going out with the likes of that for! Well? A bloody screwball . . .'

'That's it, ' interjected Frank. 'You're not going out. I've had enough of you. Tell him you can't see him . . .'

Angela felt the tears well up inside her, at her mortification, at their narrow-mindedness. . . 'No, I won't!' she shouted, and ran out the door, grabbing her coat but leaving her handbag behind. Her father made a dash for her but stopped short at the door so as not to cause a public scene.

'Listen babe,' Eddie comforted her. 'They're all old bags. Mine were the same. Didn't respect me till I got a pad of my own. Here, have a smoke. Wanna stay the night with me?'

'No, let's walk,' she said and poured her heart out to him.

\*  \*  \*

'What are you doing out of bed?'

'I'm okay,' replied Maureen, who had lost considerable weight over the past number of months. Doctors had discovered a lump below her right breast and she had to have a mastectomy performed. Although she was still being treated she personally felt that she had conquered the disease.

'Angela's up in our house in case you're worried.' Desmond closed the door behind him.

'I'll kill her, Maureen. I'll kill her!'

'Now, now. Calm down. She knows I'm down here. She's looking after Gary.'

'You've no idea. You wanna see the tramp called here tonight for her . . . I'm just sick, sore and tired of her. I give up, I honestly do,' said Mary.

'She's talking about going away and getting a job. It mightn't be a bad idea . . .'

'She's going nowhere with that thing!'

'She wants to go to London. I think you should let her.'

'Jesus Christ, Maureen.' Mary stood up. 'Do you need your head examined. London! In with a lot of drug addicts.'

'Listen. Listen,' Maureen pleaded. 'Not with your man. With student friends, just for the summer holidays. The experience would do her good. Going away helped me.'

Mary shook her head and sat in silence. She was caught between her parental responsibility, her maternalism, and the tiniest of suspicions that perhaps they needed a break from each other.

*    *    *

The long train journey from Heysham in the north to London in the south gave them the impression that England was a vast place. The three of them — Angela, Patricia and Rose — had been warned not to talk to strangers but it was Patricia not Angela who broke that rule with the first man to engage them in conversation. Rose's older sister, Bernie, had flown over on Friday because the English students would be leaving that day for France.

The girls fought for the windows as the train pulled into Euston Station.

'Gee 'Tricia! Where are we?' The platforms were full of black people and other races who appeared to outnumber the whites.

They had never seen such a busy place: it was more hectic than Donegall Street in Belfast during Christmas shopping, said Rose. They decided to walk to Holloway Road in North London and spent an hour trying to find the Thames in the belief that once they established their bearings the rest would be easy.

But when frustration built up they had to concede that London was so big that they'd have to resort to transport. By buses and experimenting with tube routes and asking directions they eventually, proudly, made it into Archway, around tea-time on Saturday evening.

'Where were you?' asked Bernie, a little worried.

'Sightseeing!'

'It was fantastic!'

'We're starving!'

'Well there's been a little mix-up and the people here aren't leaving until Sunday afternoon,' said Bernie. 'There's a shortage of beds but we'll manage. Go straight up the stairs . . . Here, give me some of your bags.'

After they had something to eat they were introduced to the English students, all of whom were from the provinces, daughters of vets and teachers, although the father of the odd one out, Jane, was a Durham miner.  But even Jane struck Angela as being eloquent and socially adept as well as showing the most hospitality. In the large communal living room they sat on comfortable sofas or pouffes on parquet flooring. A Persian-style rug hung from the wall: traffic hazard lamps had been converted into red lighting on one side of the room — candles burned from wine bottles on the mantelpiece. There was a dining-table and chairs in a small ante-room: and records of the Righteous Brothers and Otis Redding dropped in turn from the rest-arm on to the turntable. It was all so chic and atmospheric. Angela was very impressed.

They spoke about British politics and Vietnam and completely lost the Belfast girls: only Bernie joined in but with what appeared to be a limited knowledge of the subjects.

'Do you have television in Ireland?'

'Pardon?' said Angela in disbelief. Her tone of incredulity at such a stupid a question forced a retreat.

'I mean, do you have a television back in Ireland?'

'Yes. A colour one. And there's newspapers and records.'

'Uhm.'

When the English girls departed the following day leaving them in control of the two  upper  floors of the four storey house they all felt more relaxed.

*    *    *

In the cut at Waterloo Angela got a job as a telephone clerk in a bookmakers which took on summer workers during the racing season. Every morning as she walked close to her workplace she was moved by the sight of the alcoholics who had been turned out of the nearby Salvation Army Hostel. It was the same sight at Charing Cross, vagrants and old people living on the pavement, sleeping on the streets as if no one cared. She would throw them whatever change she had. She discovered a similar attitude from people to domestic disputes. One night a wife was hanging out of a window shouting, 'He's gonna kill me, gonna kill me!' but no one intervened. Her immediate reaction was that the priest should be called but a neighbour laughed at her and offered instead to phone the police. The police said that the couple fought all the time and refused to come out.

Angela was also disgusted with the Irish people who regularly emerged from a nearby ballroom  drunk and fighting. She wouldn't have minded them drinking and enjoying themselves, she pointed out to Bernie, but the arguing and physical rowing was so juvenile and primitive that they let the side down. Bernie had been increasingly losing her patience with her guest for some weeks.  It began when Angela started bringing  Eddie back to the house. He was living in a flat — a squat, Bernie called it — over in Kensington. 'He can smoke whatever he likes over there,' Rose's big sister would insist, 'but he's not smoking dope in this place. Right?'

'Don't be so old-fashioned!' Angela would retort before storming out and staying out that evening.

As the summer passed she became more restless. Eventually she wrote home  and said that although Patricia and the girls were preparing to return to Belfast she had decided to stay on a while longer and had found somewhere else to live. There was no money with the letter, she explained, because she had to make some basic household purchases.

*    *    *

From the Trucial States they sailed to Durban then to Cape Town. John and two of the galley-boys, Stevie, and Dave from Southampton, left the ship after 7 pm when the day's work was done. They had a few hours' leave and the docks were a considerable distance from the city centre. Unable to afford a taxi they hopped on a passing single decker bus. All the passengers were black people. They stared at the three whites and some moved up the seats. Before they left the ship seamen were warned to stay away from blacks and not to interfere in anything they saw. The Chief Steward told the crew of an incident four or five years previously concerning an Irishman from Carrick-fergus, whom he himself had briefed. Then, a few hours later, with complete disregard to the advice given, he was caught with a black girl, was arrested and received twelve lashes of the birch.

'Where are we going?' asked John.

'To a night club!' said Dave excitedly.

They found the bar was packed with sailors of different nationalities, drinking, smoking, playing cards and singing. Prostitutes, all coloured girls, with patently false smiles on their faces, hung around the shoulders of the sailors. Instinctively John didn't like the place.

'Ach, come on and stay a while. Just for me,' pleaded Dave who ordered three brandy squares, a local drink. The only way John could tolerate the place was by guzzling the spirits into his stomach. He had taken five or six but the misery of the place acted like an antidote to the alcohol. He thought of what his mother would think of him if she could see him here. His conscience snapped and he got up to leave.

'Where's Dave?'

'Gone off to see a friend,' replied Stevie, who was amazed at the place. 'You know I've never been in a brothel before,' he added.

'For God's sake, keep your voice down. Don't let anybody hear you call it that.'

Dave returned a few minutes later, smiling, tripped on the leg of a chair and fell into John's arms.

Outside, the evening was still fiercely bright and the light hurt their eyes. A black beggar stood in the shadows against a wall. He emerged and put out both hands. Stevie threw him his change.

'What do you think you doing! Eh!' screamed a white policeman, gun holstered to his hip, to Stevie. 'Fook off out of here I tell you. Git now!'

A black policeman carrying a sjambok rhino whip thrashed the black beggar who turned to run but ran so quickly that he stumbled and dropped the coins. Dave quickly sobered up and grabbed Stevie by the shirt, restraining him. 'Don't be a fool, man! This isn't Ireland! Come on, let's go!'

'Come on, Stevie. There's nothing we can do,' urged John, who had similar experiences before. The white policeman hit Stevie across the back of the head with his palm as a schoolmaster would do to a truant boy and ordered him away. Stevie turned around. The limp beggar, despite being painfully whipped by the black policeman, picked up all the money before fleeing.

*  *  *

'Where's Mandy Anjie?' asked Eddie's friend Pete.

'What?' answered the girl with long, plaited hair, turning her head to understand the question above the thumping hippy music which resonated from the loudspeakers day and night.

'Where's Mandy Anjie?' the tall figure in grimy jeans asked again. Tiny bells sewn on the ends of the frayed legs jingled around his sneakers.

'Out.'

'Out where, honey? In space,' he laughed.

Through a mirror the girl painted flowers like a garland across her forehead. Outside, the London traffic passed by but there was no sensation of street life in the Kensington flat above, only songs about flowers, love and San Francisco.

'She's gone to market to sell a suit.'

It was late September. Angela wandered through Kensington Market, strolling through the clothes and knick-knack stalls. She had enjoyed marijuana joints all summer but had begun experimenting with tablets and various other concoctions combined with alcohol. Some of the trips she experienced whilst hallucinating had been so heavenly and sensuous that they expunged all worries and abolished any modesty she ever had. She had convinced herself that she and the guys — as everyone in 'the pad' was referred to — were in the real world and that everyone else, outside, was in a rat race. She became quickly addicted to mandrax barbiturate tablets — thus her nickname Mandy.

She found the stall she was looking for and didn't haggle about the exchange. She simply handed over the suit, which her

mother was still paying off in a catalogue club, thanked the girl
and clutched dearly the mandrax tablets which were in a small
capsule. She sung into herself with happiness and made her way
back to the flat and decided against dinner, which was invariably
ginger nut biscuits or corn flakes.

*    *    *

Angela was now so dependant on drugs that she schemed and
lied and stole in order to feed her habit. There was a hollowness
about her life which she intuitively recognised.

By mid-November she hadn't written to her parents for almost
six weeks. In the 'pad' everyone wrote poetry, and recitations were
awarded with fulsome praise.

'One moor, one moor,
'A tree did fall
'Upon
'One moor, one moor!'

They were all spellbound at the tribute to evolution and time.
They sat on mattresses scattered around the floor, holding hands,
couples kissing. There was a constant incense from burning joss
sticks and through the mist hung the threads of smoked hashish.
Posters adorned the walls: one was of a head peering through a
big toilet seat which Angela thought was particularly hip. A new
'guy' had joined them, even though he was actually passing
through and making one of his regular calls. Cool Jonathan
traded in drugs and he was there to help them 'get it together.'

'Hey! That was a bad scene out there, yeh?'

'Yeh.'

Earlier they had gone to the pub and had ordered
some drink but one of the fellahs had been refused
service because he wore just a suede waistcoat on top which
revealed his armpits. He was barred for showing 'pubic' hair and
they all left in solidarity.

Jonathan tried to interest them in his samples.

'What are they?' asked Angela, expressing curiosity.

'Tabs of acid, Mandy. Acid tabs, for special-paying-friends.
And other samples.'

The music was pumping through the room. Angela took a long
drag from the reefer and popped some tablets into her mouth. The
guitar twanging and drum-beats became gentle and symphonious

and a cool breeze blew. Leaves daubed softly with a greenness suddenly burst into pinnate formation and fanned her naked body, then tickled her and made her laugh a refreshing happiness as the blue sun glowed in a spongy sky.

In the early hours no one saw her lie back and search Jonathan's coat.

'Hey you guys,' Jonathan was agitated. It was near noon.

'Some one's ripping me off. We'll have none of that. Come on!' He sounded angry.

'No, man, you're wrong. You'll find it, you'll find it.'

They all awoke and began searching the unfurnished room. Angela was shaking and her eyes were bulging.

'You bastard, you bastard!' Jonathan viciously hit her across the face but she fell over without making a sound, though her left hip made a large thud as it hit the fireplace. 'That bitch'll pay for this. She'll fuckin' pay!' He kicked her again and the others were too terrified to intervene. Eddie appealed to him.

'Hey, take it easy, It'll be all right, you'll see, you'll see. How do we help her, Jonathan. What do we do?'

'Cook her in the oven and then get out of here. Your time is up,' he shouted and stormed out of the room. Eddie tried to bring Angela around but nothing worked.

'When did she take them?' he asked but nobody knew.

'Make her sick,' suggested one of the girls.

'Get me the sugar and a cup of water.' He diluted three quarters of a cup of sugar with some water. They prised open her mouth and poured the syrup down her throat. There was no reaction. She didn't even cough.

'Give her some more and it'll work!'

More was prepared and again they poured the solution down her throat. Her face was chalk-coloured but she was still breathing. Eddie looked around and the others were leaving. She couldn't hear their words. Her body was in a state of immobilised panic, her mind was in a state of shock.

'We're splitting the pad. This is a real bad scene,' he was told. He was worried himself about Jonathan's threats. Angela vomited and then coughed and began shivering. Eddie wrapped a sleeping bag around her.

'That's good. That's good. You're okay now. Listen. I have to go and so should you. Rest a little and then get out of here. I don't like leaving you like this but you understand . . .'

'What time is it?' Her voice was feeble.

'It's two o' clock.'

'It's very bright for two o' clock.'

'It's two o' clock in the afternoon. Why, did you think it was night?' She didn't answer but rolled over and slept. Eddie packed his small items into a plastic carrier bag. The others had removed the record player and records and all other possessions.

She lay shivering on the mattress until the next day. Each time she dozed she had horrific nightmares. By the second night she was able to get some proper sleep and when she awoke her throat was parched. Her mouth and lips were covered in ulcers. Every hour or so she would remove a piece of paper preserved in an envelope in the back of her jeans. The single page was folded in quarters. She would carefully open it, read its words and have a quiet cry.

One minute she felt clammy and the next the sweat reduced her to a shiver. When she woke up on the third morning her nose was blocked and her chest was heavy and wheezing. As soon as she yawned a tickle forced her to cough and the rattle unpopped a thick plug of phlegm which set the small, air passages in her lungs seething. This forced an involuntary cough which brought up more phlegm. She painfully rose — there was an agonising throbbing in her hip — and went to the cupboard. There were two crackers and an inch of curdled milk at the bottom of a bottle. She ate the biscuits and sucked cold water from the tap. She then hobbled out of the flat empty-handed since she had sold all her clothing bar that which she stood in. On each bus she fumbled for her fare and then declared that she must have forgotten it. Only one conductor ordered her off.

The girl at Archway opened the door.

'Who are you?'

'Do you remember me? I'm Angela. I stayed here during the summer . .?' Jane also came to the door. 'What's happened to you, Angela? You look awful! She can come in. She can stay in my room,' she said to the other young woman who scowled.

Jane gave Angela clean clothes and though debilitated by her trauma and by months of neglect she started working as an office cleaner the following Monday. By Christmas week she was looking forward to going home and to putting 1967 behind her.

# Chapter 7

# The Pogroms

John and Peter stood together looking across the greenish-blue carpet of sea, sparkling in the late afternoon sun. Behind them on a well-spread check blanket sat Catherine and around her, munching sandwiches, picking out grains of sand, and thirstily drinking tea from two flasks, were the rest of the family. They were holidaying in County Donegal and had rented a cottage a few miles outside the seaside village of Downings. They had borrowed an old banger of a car and most of the scenic places had been brought within visiting distance.

On one splendid sunny day they drove to Gweedore and Burtonport. On another day John took Raymond and Jimmy to Mount Errigal, the highest summit in Donegal, and they climbed to the peak before their big brother would allow them to drink the bottle of lemonade and eat the sweets and chocolate he had carried. On some of the evenings Peter, Catherine and John would walk to the Singing Pub, a thatched house which was tucked up a lane behind a few trees, and by closing time — a time often determined by the last customer — Peter and John would be crooning to the stars as the only sober one guided the three back to base. There was no television or radio in the cottage and Catherine had to cook in the living-room on an old range into which Jimmy fed amorphous lumps of brown turf. He would then sit on an armchair, put his hands up to his nose and take deep addictive sniffs from the earthy stains on his fingers. The others washed the dishes in turn and gave Catherine a break.

The air was so clear and clean, the sky so luxuriously blue, the lanes and fields so quiet and peaceful that Catherine experienced a deep pride in her husband and children — which is how she still saw even John who was twenty-one. The thirteen days had shot by so quickly: they were leaving early because trouble was expected in Derry, the following day, Monday, 12 August, 1969.

John skimmed a stone across the water, his longish hair flicking with each throw. Each time he had come home he sought all the details from his father of political developments and was usually disappointed at Peter's lack of precision and poor recollection.

A Civil Rights Movement, demanding justice and reforms, had been launched ten months previously. The Unionist government and its supporters attacked the Movement and in a number of confrontations three Nationalists had died at the hands of the RUC. But the repression had only brought more international scrutiny of the abuse of power by the Unionist party which had been in government for 50 years. Now, the British government — which established and guaranteed the existence of the Northern Ireland state — was also becoming involved.

'And what have you been doing with yourself?' Peter asked.

'How did you get on at that school you went to?'

John told him about his course at Ruskin College in England where trade union and maritime law, board of trade regulations and how to conduct meetings, take and log complaints, were explained in great detail to him and several others who were interested in labour law. As a result of an official strike in 1966 seamen had won shipboard representation. Corrupt trade union officials had been pushed aside — the militancy had paid off and realised for the seamen many of their rights. Ruskin College produced a cadre of representatives for many trade unions and gave workers the opportunity for some further education.

'Tea up!' Catherine shouted at the two.

'This holiday was a great idea, son. I really enjoyed it.'

'So did I, da. It was a good break and I think my mammy had a nice time too.'

*   *   *

When Angela returned home twenty months earlier she was greeted with warmth and affection by her whole family. Mary commented on how much thinner she had become but all queries about the details of the life she had led became unfocused and then lost in the bright, new atmosphere of their relationship. They became friendlier and Mary had to admit to her sister Maureen that she had been correct in arguing that Angela be let go. Neither of them knew the truth about the autumn of 1967 and Angela saw no need to acquaint them with the distressing facts of her past.

She went steady with one boy, then another who used to call for her and about whom her mother would joke that he would make an ideal husband such were his manners. At first Angela worked in a tie factory, typing invoices and taking calls but she was made redundant when the factory closed down and the contract went to Crumlin Road Jail in Belfast. She then moved to an accountant's firm in the city centre where she was an audio typist.

Her mother and father were happy that she had settled down at long last.

*    *    *

The decision to allow the Loyalist Apprentice Boys to triumphantly march along Derry's walls which overlook the Nationalist Bogside did lead to trouble.

Rioting broke out on the periphery of the march. The RUC baton-charged Nationalist youths and fired CS gas. The youths erected barricades and used petrol bombs to keep the police out of the Bogside. Rallies and protests were called for other towns to demonstrate solidarity with them.

The Dublin government called for the introduction of a United Nation's peacekeeping force and called upon Britain to recognise 'that the re-unification of the national territory can provide the only permanent solution to the problem.' After three days of continuous fighting in Derry the RUC were exhausted and demoralised and it was widely feared by Nationalists that reinforcements would be drafted in to the maiden city. On Tuesday night B men opened fire on an unarmed Catholic crowd, wounding three people. More protests were organised to stretch and tie down state forces.

John and Felix joined in a march of about 200 people to Springfield Road barracks which was in the process of being modernised and rebuilt. There was a rising mood of militancy inspired by the battles in Derry where the Nationalists had taken control of their areas. The feeling of protracted defiance was new and thrilling, compared to the Divis Street disturbances five years previously, but was nevertheless accompanied by an apprehension about the outcome.

They sang Republican songs whilst a deputation went up to the door of the new barracks to hand in a petition protesting against police brutality in Derry but an RUC sergeant hiding behind the hoarding refused to accept it. The crowd then returned down the Falls but not before smashing four windows on the first floor. They heard that RUC personnel carriers had been spotted on the fringes of the district where young people had begun stoning them.

When the crowds arrived at Hastings Street barracks they saw three agitated RUC men posted at the front door. The weather was mild but they shuffled from one foot to the other as if from cold.

'There's the bastard that arrested me!' someone shouted; a shout which was followed by a confident fusillade of bottles and bricks. The policemen ran into the barracks and radioed to nearby mobile patrols which had been anticipating just this sort of development. Commer personnel carriers turned from Millfield into Hastings Street and drove at the crowds, scattering them. John and Felix ran into side streets.

Shortly after 11 pm trouble broke out in North Belfast on the Crumlin Road where Nationalists from Hooker Street and Loyalists from the Shankill Road fought with stones and bottles. Around the same time youths on the Falls broke into the car showrooms of Isaac Agnew, dragged five cars out across the road and set them on fire. At other points tyres were laid across the road but still the RUC stayed away.

'What do you think?' Felix asked.

'Looks like they're just gonna leave us alone, most of them must have already left for Derry and that's why they're not taking us on,' replied John.

'Don't say that!' added Gerard, whose older brother Dominic was in the IRA. He was married and lived in Divis Flats. 'Our Dominic says if Derry falls we're finished.'

Although most of the traffic had stopped moving, especially cross-town traffic which bisected the Falls at Northumberland Street, through the Shankill, a few cars had still travelled some of those routes.

'We got a report there,' said Felix, 'that Loyalists are gathering on the Shankill. An ambulance driver said that there's hundreds of them at the top of North Street, in Third Street and in Cupar Street.'

'I heard they were out at the top of Dover Street and Percy Street.'

'We'll have to keep our eye on them,' added John, aware of how vulnerable the Falls, and indeed other Nationalist working class areas, had been in the past.

'We're gonna attack Springfield Road barracks,' declared a fellah who was pointed out to John as an IRA Volunteer.

'Get milk bottles and start siphoning petrol.'

It was now approaching 12.45 am when the crowd crept up the right-hand side of Colligan Street. Then, suddenly, they rushed on to the main road. There were crashes of glass and large flames momentarily licked the front of the building and ignited the footpath where petrol from the majority of the molotovs had splashed. From the first floor windows revolver shots rang out and two people were hit — but they were not critically wounded. Commer personnel carriers then raced up the road, frightening people back around the corners.

The crowd ran back into Colligan Street and turned into McQuillan Street where an informal conference was hurriedly held.

'Jesus! Did you hear that!'

'Were they real bullets or blanks?'

'The bastards!'

'I'm going back out!'

'So am I!'

'Let's go and get more petrol bombs . . .'

When they were organised they returned to the scene and ineffectually attacked the barracks. The one and only time that a petrol bomb exploded behind a broken window and sustained some flames an RUC man on the roof of the barracks opened fire with a Sterling sub-machine gun, apparently over their heads. As they scattered, satisfied with the night's activity, about three-quarters of a mile away Loyalists looted a public house owned by a Catholic at Argyle Street on the edge of the Shankill area and Ian Paisley met with the prime minister, Major Chichester Clark, and offered to organise 'a Protestant force to assist the government.'

John rose at about 10 am the following morning. He was due to go back to sea on Sunday night but the situation was so volatile, so full of expectancy, that his plans were in doubt. Again that day's news was dominated by events in Derry where the RUC were suffering serious defeats and, thought John, could only occupy the Bogside if they used fresh forces or used fire power.

\*　　\*　　\*

A soft blue mist seemed to hang over the Falls Road. Thursday, 14 August, was a warm and bright but tension-filled evening. Between 5 and 7 the First Battalion of the Prince of Wales Own Regiment moved into Waterloo Place in Derry and began setting up wire barriers, taking over police lines at Castle and Butcher Gates and in Bishop Street. The RUC sheepishly withdrew but news of this major development and its implications came too late to stop the demonstrations now beginning . . .

John, Felix and Gerard had been in Divis Street from around seven, at first in Dominic's flat eating tea and sandwiches and listening to RUC broadcasts which reported large gatherings of Loyalists along the Shankill Road. They then went out to the forecourt of Divis Tower where youths and men were congregating, some armed with hurleys. Many families who lived in those streets between the Falls and the Shankill had moved out for the night and boarded up their windows. Gerard confided in his two friends that Dominic had been very apprehensive about the turn of events. It was the first time that John had learnt of the disagreements which had been smouldering within the IRA over the lack of preparedness for a crisis. The revelation struck the young men as being so fantastic as to be beyond consideration.

A crowd marched on Hastings Street barracks and those at the front threw stones and bottles at the building. Two men came running from the side street beside the barracks and joined the throng. One shouted, 'They've brought three Shorlands and a Humber around the back . . . They've got machine-guns mounted on the Shorlands . . . Something's up!'

Shortly after ten, two separate groups of Loyalists ran down Dover and Percy Streets smashing windows. The men of the houses, joined by the others, engaged the Loyalists in hand-to-hand fighting until a rough border was established behind which each side retreated, exchanging stones and bottles. Two shot-gun blasts were fired from the Loyalist ranks and then a line of uniformed B Specials appeared with batons and charged at the Nationalists who turned and ran a short distance until growing numbers forced the B Specials to retreat.

News of the attempted incursion spread quickly up and down the road and increased the people's fears.

About half a mile further up the road the same thing was happening: the RUC, behind whose lines were hundreds of Loyalists, would charge from the direction of the Shankill down Cupar Street and Conway Street. The Loyalists tore down hoardings placed over windows, smashed the glass and then proceeded to throw petrol bombs into the houses. Families who had been naive enough to stay or who believed that the RUC would protect them were fleeing towards the Falls, some in just their pyjamas and nightdresses. A group of Nationalists who attempted to turn back the petrol bombers were fired on by the Shorland armoured cars. The rattle from the Browning guns could be heard for miles around. After midnight more gunfire was heard. Two people were shot in Conway Street, two others in Balaclava Street, and one person was wounded in Raglan Street, all by RUC and Loyalist gunfire. Each time Nationalists petrol bombed the Shorland cars the response was a heavy burst of gunfire which sent tracers through the night sky.

John helped some men build a defensive barricade close to Ardmoulin Avenue, a street which ran between Dover and Percy Streets. Before it was finished the RUC baton charged them. However, stones and bricks drove the RUC back to the Loyalist side where they were given binlids to act as shields. Again just before the barricade was completed an RUC armoured Humber and three Shorland cars came down from the Shankill and broke through. Behind them came several hundred Loyalists armed with sticks and hatchets and carrying petrol bombs.

Suddenly the Loyalists burst into Divis Street. They were triumphant and were singing and waving Union Jacks. The first crackles from burning homes lit up the sky which was engulfed in dark, expanding clouds of curling smoke. There was screaming from women in the flats.

'They're coming into the flats! They're gonna come into the flats!'

John looked down towards the town centre. Shorlands, Humbers and Commers were lined up almost across Divis Street. Behind them were riot police. If they were able to join up with the Loyalist forces at Dover Street corner, the flats themselves could be attacked and burned with catastrophic consequences.

'Where the hell is the IRA?' shouted a man in the middle of the crowd, articulating the frustration, helplessness and vulnerability felt by everyone. A human chain was formed from the ground right up to the roof of the Whitehall block of flats. Stones, bricks, petrol bombs, pieces of gratings and scaffolding tubes were transported up to the fighters who battered the advancing group of RUC men, hurling missiles and petrol bombs down into the street below. After two minutes the RUC gave up and pulled back to Hastings Street barracks.

Amid all the roars and cheers shots rang out from the corner of Gilford Street across into the mouth of Dover Street where the Loyalists were singing and dancing, having looted and set on fire the Arkle Inn. A Loyalist fell dead in the road and three RUC men were grazed. Two RUC men fired wildly in John's direction, forcing people to dive to the ground. Some minutes later, a little after 1 am, a Shorland car sped up Divis Street, slowed to a steady cruise, trained its heavy machine gun on the flats and let loose with a burst of automatic fire. John couldn't believe his eyes.

'Jesus Christ! They're mad!'

'They're gonna kill us! They're gonna kill us all!'

From within the open walks around the maisonettes there came several distinct screams. The men on the street continued to put up a good fight with stones and petrol bombs but the Loyalist crowds and the B men had set dozens of homes and shops well alight. The newspaper shop at the corner of Percy Street was burning fiercely. Uniformed RUC men led a mob against St Comgall's primary school trying to set it on fire. An ambulance arrived at the back of the flats and nine-year-old Patrick Rooney from St Brendan's Path was taken out in a stretcher. He had been shot and seriously wounded as he lay in his bed. Six other people suffered gunshot wounds.

A few minutes later there was more gunfire. RUC snipers on the roof of Hastings Street barracks opened fire with rifles at the Whitehall block, seriously wounding two men. When John arrived Hugh McCabe, who was a member of the British army home on leave, had been brought down from the roof to one of the flats below where he was given the Last Rites by a priest and was then declared dead.

In the Ardoyne area of North Belfast it was the same story: the RUC baton-charged Nationalists, and led raids into their areas. Then petrol-bombing Loyalists followed and set homes on fire. In Herbert Street the police fired through the window of Mr Samuel McLarnon, killing him as he sat in his sitting-room. Three other houses were shot up. In Butler Street the RUC opened fire and killed Michael Lynch who was defending his area. Twelve other people were wounded.

Back in the Falls the Shorland armoured cars fired down Derby Street on four or five occasions at people who had erected a barricade to protect St Peter's Chapel from being burned down.

From the side of St Comgall's school John and about eight others threw petrol bombs at the RUC men on the opposite side of the road. Felix called him to the side of the building: 'Here's the IRA!' he said. 'They've got guns!'

'It's about fuckin' time. Do they want to go into the school? Come on, we can break in through the back.'

John broke a window, unfastened the latch and let the IRA man and several others into the corridor. He had a Thomson sub-machine gun the sight of which mesmerised the young men.

'Right. Youse can leave now. Get out!' he ordered to all but the two who were with him. John felt extremely disappointed. Outside the screams were reaching a crescendo as petrol bombs continued to crash against the solid walls of the school. From the roof of the building the IRA man opened fire towards Percy Street, wounding eight Loyalists. The loud roar of return fire from a Browning cut chunks of masonry out of the front walls and brought them back to reality. The IRA man reappeared a minute later and said, 'Right, that'll do.' Then he disappeared. He moved to another part of the district and opened fire to give the impression not just to the Loyalists and the RUC that the Nationalists were well armed but also to the Nationalists.

'Did you hear the news?'

'No, what did it say?' asked John of the newcomer to their team — the group of twelve or thirteen men who had informally joined together in the absence of any directives and any organisation, even though each probably only knew two or three of the gang.

'The B Specials have shot dead a civil rights demonstrator in Armagh City. There's rioting all over the North . . .'

'Worse than that . . .' added another man. 'There's word from the hospital that that wee lad, Patrick Rooney, has died . . .'

'Fuck me. That's desperate.'

The Nationalists were convinced that Loyalist snipers had been operating from the roof of Andrews Mill and the New Northern Mill since some had seen what was assumed to be muzzle flashes.

'Things are getting bad up at Conway Street. We'll have to head up there.'

'Yeh, let's go.'

They ran up Ross Street, which was parallel to the Falls Road, as far as Millikin Street which took them onto the Falls. Everyone in the district was out at their doors, nursing the injured in rudimentary 'field' hospitals, or making petrol bombs, or feeding the menfolk who returned every now and again for a short rest or a drink of water.

It was traditional on the eve of 15 August for Nationalists to light bonfires to celebrate the Feast of Our Lady, the mother of Jesus Christ. This year, in view of the gathering political storm, the tradition was abandoned but there in place of the bonfires were burning houses, twenty-five in all in Conway Street as John and his friends got within sight of the area. The Loyalists had just looted a public house and many were dancing in the street, drunk, with bottles swinging by their sides.

It was now 3.30 am and the last gunfire of the night was heard from Divis Street where an armoured car again opened fire on St Comgall's school though the armed IRA man had left there long ago.

'What a night,' yawned John. 'Thank God it's over.'

'May we never see another like it again.'

The rival crowds, apparently drained of all energy, kept their distance. Up towards the Shankill the RUC and the B Specials sat on the kerb among the Loyalists. They were being given tea and cigarettes. Perhaps, thought John, in the sober light of day it has now dawned on them exactly what they have done.

Families who had fled Conway Street the evening before slowly began to return to the corner. Those who had lost everything stood dumbfounded or else sobbed out loud which had a profound emotional effect on all who watched. There were women who insisted that they would never live in the street again but that they wanted their furniture, the children's clothes, family albums, retrieved from their homes before the Loyalist mobs returned, though the lull seemingly had a secure quality to it. John sat down and took a cigarette which was offered to him, despite the fact that he hadn't smoked in six years. It had been a long, exhausting night but strangely enough he still didn't feel like sleeping.

'There's the gypsies with lorries! Come, let's evacuate the rest of these houses!' shouted a short, stocky man. 'Don't worry they've realised what they've done. They'll have been given orders to do no more shooting. They're bloody well ashamed of themselves.'

It was an eerie peace. People walking to work from their homes further up the road stopped and were appalled at the devastation. Most of those from estates had heard gunfire but didn't realise that the Falls ghetto had been under such sustained, violent attack. Some Nationalists walked up to inspect their homes whose windows had been broken. They were within hostage-taking or striking distance if the Loyalists so wished. Amongst the opposing faction were even neighbours whom they had grown up with. However, it was only when other Nationalists came up the street to lend a hand to the evacuation that the Orange mob got very restless. There was a sudden clash as if some force pulled each side into conflict and for several minutes there was hand-to-hand fighting in the street before RUC men on foot fired over the heads of the Nationalists. As the RUC advanced a few yards at a time, people turned and ran. Behind the police the Loyalists advanced bit by bit setting fire to two or three more houses until over two-thirds of the dwellings were ablaze.

As one area quietened down, another seemed to flare up. Not far from Conway Street was the district of Clonard. On Thursday Clonard Monastery had received a threatening telephone call stating that it was going to be burned out. Fr McLaughlin, the acting Superior, allowed two local IRA Volunteers into the building. They were armed with a shot-gun and a .22 rifle and the unit to which they belonged was one which had been at loggerheads with its IRA superiors. Some men felt that other comrades had been unfairly drummed out for objecting to the IRA's demilitarisation strategy.

Though Clonard escaped the shooting and burnings which the Falls and Divis experienced, families began leaving on Friday for relatives' houses, complaining that they were being intimidated out of their homes in Cupar Street and in the other side streets off the Shankill.

In the afternoon some small barricades were being erected and stones exchanged.

Fr McLaughlin telephoned the RUC at Springfield Road barracks on a number of occasions and was told, 'Rest assured; if an attack comes from Cupar Street, they'll never get through.'

Soon, the Loyalist invasion of Clonard had begun. Petrol bombs set alight a house in Bombay Street, the family escaping through the front door. They ran to the monastery for help and a priest again phoned the RUC for assistance.

By now more petrol bombs had set other homes alight. It was all young people who were fighting on the Nationalist side against a large crowd of Loyalists, some of whom were carrying arms. Rifle shots rang out close by and hit Gerald McAuley, a fifteen-year-old Nationalist youth. He fell on to the footpath and writhed in agony. Within minutes he was dead. The people of the area were now in panic, fleeing their homes as teenagers, some as young as thirteen and fourteen, overturned a big Scammell lorry. The Loyalists were also attempting to invade the area from another street. Someone ran into the bell-tower of the monastery and rang the bell to summon help. The two IRA men arrived and one opened fire with a shot-gun, hitting a Loyalist and forcing the crowd out into Cupar Street. Young Republicans began breaking into some of the homes of families who were on holiday, for legally-held shot-guns. They were lucky at one house and three youths with one shot-gun and about 100 cartridges between them took up a position on the second floor of St Galls school in Waterville Street beside the Monastery.

Much of Bombay Street was now in flames and people feared that the whole district was going to be overrun. Fr McLaughlin again telephoned Springfield Road barracks.

'Why are you not coming up to help us? Is it because your own side are doing the attacking?'

'What do you mean?' the RUC man answered back.

'You know very well! The people of Cupar Street . . .' He slammed down the telephone out of frustration. Older residents of the Monastery were moved out to safety and the Eucharist was removed from the church.

* * *

Earlier that day Loyalist crowds had again assembled in Percy Street and Dover Street. They watched as the Nationalists pushed a bus across Percy Street and began evacuating their homes, loading pieces of furniture on to lorries, handcarts, prams, or simply carrying chairs, tables and cardboard boxes of clothes by hand. In all the side streets along the left hand side of the Falls Road travelling countrywards people had been busy for hours building fortified barricades made from flag stones which they ripped up from the pavements, from scaffolding and concrete set in trenches. Thousands of petrol bombs were being prepared.

All over the south of Ireland the IRA were collecting shot-guns and any other old weapons they could lay their hands on to be smuggled into the beleaguered Nationalists.

\* \* \*

In the early hours of 15 August the most senior officers of the RUC in Belfast admitted that the situation was beyond their control. The Unionist government then made a formal request to the Home Office in London for military aid in Belfast.

At 3.10 pm the British government gave approval for the deployment of troops in Belfast. The Unionist government was jubilant: it was getting the British army with no strings attached. London was not going to interfere in Stormont's affairs and the constitutional relationship between the two islands was not to be called into question.

At tea-time British soldiers arrived in the Shankill Road and slowly advanced southwards towards the Falls where people were relieved to see them. For fifty years the Nationalist people had lived under the boots of the RUC, but now here were the 'impartial' English.

'Good for youse, son!' an old woman shouted to the young soldiers who had bewildered looks on their faces as they took up positions on the Falls Road, though it was made clear by the men that they weren't getting behind the barricades. For behind the barricades a new IRA was being built to ensure that Nationalists were never left defenceless again.

It was 8.30 pm when a small party of British soldiers, 26 men, led by Colonel Napier, made their way to Clonard Monastery. Fr Egan brought Napier into the residence and took him into a room overlooking a stretch of Cupar Street. A man with a shot-gun was at a window and moved aside to allow the uncomfortable Colonel to survey the Loyalists milling about in the distance.

When soldiers were sent out to establish where the dividing line actually was Loyalists at Argyle Street threw petrol bombs at them before being dispersed. The soldiers then received orders to return to the Falls and when they did so the Loyalists resumed their attacks on Bombay Street, overcoming the brave resistance of the people, and setting ablaze the remainder of the houses.

At 9.30 pm the British army returned to patrol the area. Some people called them 'cowardly bastards' but it was generally felt that their presence was more needed than not. As the patrol was crossing Kashmir Road a Loyalist opened fire with a shot-gun wounding a private. As he lay on the ground there was a second discharge which grazed his ear. A soldier fired a covering shot whilst a colleague rescued the wounded man. The British army appeared confused and unable to handle the situation.

It was 2 am on Saturday before the British army consolidated its positions and before the Loyalists withdrew.

# Chapter 8

# The Honeymoon Period

'You're wrong!' said Dominic to a more mature man who had been interned towards the end of the IRA's 1950s border campaign. 'You're definitely wrong!'

'Look Dominic and listen. You saw for yourself. The people are giving the British tea and sandwiches. I had to stop my own bloody wife from cooking for them. The wee girls of the area are even going to dances and discos in the mill. Generally, the British are welcomed and we have to take that on board. Without them on the 15 and 16 August the rest of the Falls would have been burned out . . .'

'That's nonsense. We would have been okay from then onwards. Bits of gear were starting to arrive. The Brits didn't come on to the Falls to protect the people but to protect the government. You're forgetting what you told us down the years about British imperialism being ultimately responsible. Besides, by the Fifteenth we had started a rumour that we were gonna invade the Shankill because of what they'd done the night before. The Loyalists were terrified by then . . .'

'Will you let me finish? Okay?'

'Okay. Go ahead. I've heard it all before.'

John entered the room.

'Sorry. Am I interrupting?'

'Come on in. It'll do you no harm to hear this,' said Dominic. John had joined the IRA in an auxiliary capacity and had got the house they were in for the others to meet. There were a lot of discussions and arguments and talk of a split.

'We are in a very strong position. The B Specials are going to be phased out and the talk is that the RUC is to be disarmed. With the spotlight on this place we can get all the reforms we want pushed through . . .'

Dominic interrupted him again: 'That's fuckin' nonsense. Stormont hasn't been suspended, the Loyalists are still in control. There's no chance of the RUC being disarmed because if they were unarmed there wouldn't be a Loyalist in the North prepared to join such a Boy Scouts organisation. We are in a prime position but for different reasons. For 50 years the British have been able to ignore this place, they've internalised it and it's been forgotten about. Now we've got British soldiers back on the streets . . . British soldiers! Think about it. You always told us about British imperialism and here it is confronting us, even though it's in a peace-keeping guise. We should get organised and get stuck into them.'

'Same old dreaming. Same old dreaming that's cost us dearly down the years. First, the soldiers are highly popular. Second, we still haven't enough arms even to properly defend the areas. Third, there's plenty of people supporting us whilst we defend our own areas but would soon throw us out if we turned on the soldiers. Fourth, we haven't the right kind of equipment. Fifth, we've no money. Sixth, the British army is very professional and would steam-roller over us in about a week. Seventh, we'd lose sympathy, I mean international sympathy. Eight, do you think the Loyalists would take it all lying down? Nine . . . for Christ's sake the reasons are endless and you want to get stuck into the British army! All objective conditions, the circumstances, are against what you say. Besides, the leadership is opposed and that's that,' he said, attempting to conclude the discussion.

'Dominic's right.' The next speaker was an old Republican who had been interned in the 1940s for a time, and again in the 1950s. 'We've got the British by the balls. Nobody can persuade me that they're here to protect me and my family or the Catholic community. I've prayed for this day all my life. If we miss this opportunity we may forget about everything.'

John was fascinated by this discussion and others which were raging but rarely did he vouchsafe his opinion which was still crystallising. He could see truths on both sides but could in no way visualise the attitude of goodwill which the Nationalists had for the British army being overturned. That would take a mental revolution in attitude, he thought. When he considered the Vietnam War, the anti-war movement, the student's protests, he had had a romantic notion of guerrilla warfare and revolution, and these Belfast streets just did not fit the bill.

The words of the speaker opposed to Dominic rang through his head: 'This isn't 1916 and the British army of today is not the Black and Tans.' That was true.

Stevie had been at sea, on his way home, when he heard about the Belfast pogroms on the world service of BBC radio. When his ship anchored at Las Palmas in the Canaries he borrowed £80 off a Scottish crew member who doubled as a money-lender. Having made some discreet inquiries he met with a shady character in a bar who sold him two .22 pistols and 500 rounds of ammunition. He then smuggled them ashore in England. At Heathrow airport before boarding the plane, and while in the queue at the ticket desk, he got to know the name of another Belfast-bound passenger. He tagged the small bag which contained the guns in that person's name and sent it through. When he landed at Aldergrove airport he simply reclaimed the baggage as his own.

Back in the Falls Road he showed John the weapons which both of them turned over and over, loaded and re-loaded and endlessly admired. It was these two weapons which had helped cut through red tape and 'bought' them their IRA membership.

Behind the barricades both young men had received weapons training in mostly old guns. Ironically, the majority of the training was given by men who because of high unemployment had in their youth left the Falls and joined the British army. Now they were bringing their skills to bear for the Nationalist cause.

Four weeks after they had been erected the barricades were taken down. Manning had been a major, exhausting and exacting affair. Republicans encouraged people to maintain their guard but lost the argument to the persuasive reassurances from Catholic clerics that the British army would protect the Nationalists. With the barricades down a sort of normality returned even though a clandestine army was still beginning to take shape.

Such was the genuine hospitality experienced by British soldiers — officers and privates alike — in West Belfast that they came to take goodwill for granted, came to take the people who could bestow kindness on strangers for fools, and then couldn't come to distinguish between hospitality and patronisation. Each night a patrol would call into Stanley's bar in Stanley Street, close to the bottom of the Grosvenor Road and on the edge of the Pound Loney, the oldest part of the Falls. It was in this bar that a soldier gave John and Stevie, and, in their turn, about a dozen other Volunteers, a detailed description of the Stirling sub-machine gun and the SLR.

'Have another beer, go on!' John encouraged one of the uniformed and armed soldiers who was a regular nightly caller, after he completed patrolling the district from the mill.

'Okay, Paddy. Just one more.'

'And what do you call that part?' asked Stevie, innocence blooming in his cheeks.

'Ah, that's the safety catch. I showed you already how it worked. Are you stupid? Watch again, right?'

'Yeh, he's stupid okay,' laughed John. 'Aren't you?'

'Yes, I'm Paddy Irishman,' replied Stevie at the soldier who took out a coin and showed them how to begin stripping the weapon.

After some weeks the two men were frustrated by the lack of action and the divisiveness within the IRA. The uprising, the revolution — terms too grandiloquent to aptly describe the Nationalist community's partial realisation of itself — appeared to die through the want of a crisis or intolerable repression.

John asked Stevie what he thought of the situation.

'What do I think of the situation?' Stevie replied, after long thought. 'Well, it's a bit slow for me. I can't see anything happening in the near future and I'm thinking of going back to sea next week. What about you?'

'I think you're right. We'll not be missing anything . . . And if we do, we can always come back.'

There was such a large turnover of recruits in the IRA in the autumn of 1969 that their departure was of no significance and no one objected. The IRA was just glad to have their guns and the Officer Commanding their unit, their O/C, told them that if there was ever a possibility of them coming across other weapons they should go for them and contact him.

\* \* \*

As the dust settled on the situation there still appeared to be no sign of an end to 'the honeymoon period' when Nationalist disenchantment with the British army would set in. In early September there was an incident when Nationalists who rushed out of their homes fearing an invasion by Paisleyites up Broadway towards the Falls suddenly found that the soldiers turned on them with fixed bayonets. There was a number of other clashes close to the peaceline at which baton-wielding soldiers, organised as 'snatch squads,' ran at rioters to allegedly remove the ring leaders. It was usually onlookers or passersby who took the brunt of their gusto.

Shortly after the two men went back to sea the situation at home did slowly change. In late September more Catholics were burnt out of their homes just yards from Hastings Street barracks, and opinion was that the British army had made little effort to defend them. In October a British government Committee of Inquiry into the RUC and B Specials recommended that the RUC be an unarmed force and that the B Specials be disbanded and replaced by a new part-time force, the Ulster Defence Regiment. Loyalists rioted against the proposals and on the Shankill Road used firearms on the British army and RUC on the night of 10 October, shooting dead Constable William Arbuckle, the first RUC man to die during the crisis.

*   *   *

In November John and Stevie joined a shipping line and set sail for the east coast of America to pick up passengers for the Caribbean winter cruises. A deck-hand, Andy McLean from Clydeside, was the seamen's convenor and he congratulated John for being nominated the catering representative, which was the biggest single section of the crew. There were trade union representatives also for the deck-hands and engineers.

The cruise was to begin on the Hudson River in New York but two hours before they were due to sail one of the engines developed a fault and the passengers had to disembark. The crew were just as disappointed as the passengers — they relied on tips to survive, tips which usually amounted to more than their wages. It appeared that the crew was to be ship-bound in New York over Christmas. The Irish ones had no great difficulty going to relatives but it would be a difficult and lonely enough time for the rest, most of whom were English fellahs.

John went off for a couple of days to spend Christmas with cousins of his father. When he returned to the ship he discovered that there had been uproar. As their money ran out the sailors had gone to the Chief Purser to get subs to tide them over, which was standard practice. Under orders from Captain Robin Kellner the money was refused on the grounds that it hadn't been earned yet. John thought this nonsense: there was a North Atlantic bonus available for non-USA nationals working out of east coast ports on cruises. It was about £14 a month and was to help compensate seamen for the cost of living. John went and saw Andy McLean and suggested that they pursue this line but he wasn't enthusiastic.

'Look,' said John. 'We're gonna have to do something. These men are going crackers. We're gonna be held up here for another two weeks. As the men's reps we have a duty to examine every option and drawing on the North Atlantic bonus is the answer and will keep everybody happy.'

'Okay, okay!' replied Andy. 'I suppose we'll have to go and see the Captain.'

Twice they were palmed off with the excuse that Captain Kellner was busy. John was getting angrier and Andy told him to keep his cool. When they eventually met, John had tactically regained his composure.

'Look Captain. There's a lot of bad feeling among the men. They've been here three or four days over Christmas with no money . . .'

'What! What has that got to do with me. If they were more frugal they would have savings. I can't be held responsible because they fritter away their money on beer and women.'

'Well,' said John, remaining patient. 'What we were thinking was that the men could have a sub on their North Atlantic bonus. That would maybe help them out and get us over this hump?'

'No, no, no! There's no such thing, no such thing! There's no North Atlantic bonus, South Atlantic bonus or South Pacific bonus . . . ' he said with an imperious smile. For all the use that Andy was, John felt he was on his own.

'That,' said Kellner, 'only applies when you are leaving an American port. Since we haven't left, it, therefore, does not apply. Thank you gentlemen.' He stood up from the table and Andy rose but John sat on, feeling the psychological disadvantage of being towered over.

'No,' insisted John, who had read up on the laws, customs and practices of his job. He was confident of his position. 'It applies when you arrive.'

'It doesn't apply until you are leaving and that's final . . . I'm not listening to you people, anyway. Get out! Get out!'

'Hold on a minute, Captain. We are elected representatives of the men. We've been appointed by the Shipping Federation and by the seamen. You can't adopt that attitude. You'll have to at least listen to us.'

'I do not have to listen to you or recognise anybody. I'm the Captain on this ship . . .'

'So let's get this right,' interjected John, his dander rising. 'You're not recognising the National Union of Seamen?'

'No!'

'Ach, hold on man,' said Andy trying to cool the situation. 'Take it easy.'

The Captain had re-taken his seat and began to fill an impressive looking meerschaum pipe. 'You know my position. I have made it clear.' His words were as clear and smooth as they were contemptuous.

Andy wanted to stay on but John was setting the pace. 'No, let's get out of here. This man's a complete blockhead.'

A general meeting was summoned and the situation explained to the men. When they were told that the Captain refused to recognise the union there was much bawling and yelling: they were in an angry mood.

'We were supposed to have shipboard representation,' said John, referring to the gains of a previous strike which were still very slowly being realised, 'and the first time an issue arises that Captain just totally refuses to recognise us . . .'

'Then we'll refuse to recognise him!' someone shouted from the back and received loud cheers of support. The union representatives were mandated to fight the Captain, an endorsement which made Andy feel uneasy. He had been around much longer than John, he later argued, and knew the power of the ship-owners. The 1960 strike had started on passenger boats out of Liverpool which were on the Canadian/Pacific line, and it spread to the Union Castle boats and Cunard. After a few months it was successfully broken by the companies. John told him not to be so despondent. He was their overall convenor, their leader, and shouldn't have a defeatist attitude: it could rub off on the men and the whole protest would then crumble.

After two days John went to the Chief Purser.

'There's gonna be serious trouble here if there's not something done about this.'

'The Captain has made his position clear and that's his position.'

The NUS in London was telegrammed and made aware of the situation. When the men received no reply they telephoned and were told by a union official that the company was being lobbied and that we re trying to do something to ease the situation.'

'Ease the situation!' bellowed John down the phone. 'We want it fuckin' resolved in our favour!' He slammed down the receiver.

As the days passed and there was no progress the Captain became confident that soon the men's representatives would be knocking on his door. It was true that the men were getting a little uneasy. Repairs to the engine were almost completed, the ship would be ready in two days' time and the returning passengers were shortly due to arrive. At Ruskin College John remembered being told about the value of always keeping the men informed of what was going on. Even if nothing was happening it was important to call meetings and gauge the degree of commitment to the positions which they had adopted and to know, before the employers, if a strike was going to collapse. He urged Andy to call a meeting and was pleased with the response. It was, as Stevie had told him, unanimous. The men were not sailing under Captain Kellner and that was that. Nor were they leaving the ship to allow on board another crew, that is if scabs could be found.

The occupation was now making news in New York and the company was getting nervous and anxious that passengers might switch to other cruises or that the strike would spread. John was interviewed on a number of radio stations and by several newspapers. The Captain also publicly tied his colours to the mast and a deadline was looming.

Throughout, John had a number of friends and advisors in whom he confided. The two most important ones were an elderly seaman, Peter Osborne, a communist from Liverpool, and, surprisingly because of his youth, Stevie Donnelly, who John joked, had a serious disease called stubbornness. 'Let's hope you catch it!' Stevie jested.

He met both in his cabin.

'Did you get the meetings set up?' John asked.

'We've to see the tugmen at 9,' answered Peter.

'I've seen the rep from the . . . the . . .' Stevie smiled. 'The Stevedores . . .' He smiled again at the name. 'We've a meeting in a bar on the wharf at 10.'

That evening they went ashore. The tugmen were enthusiastic: 'We're behind you all the way. Stick at it!' One of the two Stevedores' representatives was called Murphy whose grand-parents had emigrated from County Mayo. 'Listen you guys there's no problem. None of our men will handle the baggage, of that you can be definite. Sure wasn't the word boycott invented in my own part of Ireland. Take no crap from the bastards. We're with you! Just keep things quiet and we'll spring it on them at the last minute when the passengers arrive. That'll ensure success and keep our people, who could be afraid of it spreading, off our backs. Good luck!'

John now knew they were in a very strong position. The men were ecstatic when they heard the news but he told them not to breathe a word of it. Early the next morning Stevie received a message and left the ship. He returned gloomily and sought out his friend. 'Our brothers in the Stevedores are being put under big pressure by their national leadership. They're annoyed that the element of surprise has been lost, or given away to be more accurate. They said Kellner had wind of what was discussed at our meeting fifteen minutes after it broke up.'

'Some bastard is squealing. But who is it? When have you to see them again?'

'Murphy will be talking to his men about now. He thinks he can carry them.'

'Let's hope so.'

By the afternoon things began to move. The Stevedores stood firm. An NUS official from London flew out. When John saw him with a black brief case he asked him where was the brown one but the well-dressed Londoner gave him an inscrutable look and asked for a complete blow by blow account of the dispute. A senior management representative, Mr Van Eyck, flew in from the company's headquarters to join the New York manager. A meeting between all sides was called for at 8 pm in the restaurant. Before the meeting John went and clarified the demands and received a fresh mandate not just from catering staff but from deck-hands and engineers. He had emerged as the natural leader, a reputation which the actual convenor Andy McLean resented but was powerless to prevent.

Very quickly John established that the company — despite the protestations of the Captain — would bend on the issue of the bonus and they also proposed, unsolicited, that the men be given £25 each for the disruption they had experienced over the Christmas period. But that was no longer the real issue, he insisted, despite Andy tugging at his sleeve and muttering something about compromise.

'This Captain refused to recognise the truly elected representatives of the National Union of Seamen. The men themselves have decided that they are not going to sail under him! Take it or leave it but the ship stays until he goes.'

The Captain stormed out.

'But this has never been done before. This is unheard of,' said the New York shipping manager, clearly having difficulty getting his words out.

'This is mutiny!' exclaimed the representative.

'Call it what you want,' said John, stretching casually back in his seat.

'I'm afraid we can go no further. The £25 disruption offer is withdrawn.' He pushed back his chair to rise, momentarily delayed by clearing the edge of the table with his beefy paunch, but his bluff was punctured by John who rose first and was quickly out the door.

'Well?' asked Stevie, excitedly. 'Have we a new Captain or not?'

'Not yet,' smiled John confidently. 'But we will have by the time passengers arrive in the morning.'

At 12.20 the trade union representatives were sent for again. The Captain was absent.

'We've thought things over,' said Mr Van Eyck. 'In the interests of common sense, in the interests of the seamen, who have suffered enough hardship, and of our passengers who would be extremely disappointed for a second time if the ship failed to sail, we have come up with a proposal which we sincerely believe will resolve the deadlock.'

'Fire away,' said John smugly. 'We're listening.' They proposed that the Captain, John and Andy would stay off the ship, let it sail as normal. They would all be flown to the company's headquarters for further talks, would be booked into a first class hotel and would be generously compensated for their loss of earnings. John ruled it out immediately.

'I'm not going off the ship . . . I came here to earn my living and that's what I'm gonna do. There are no negotiations about it. Andy and I are not leaving the men.'

'Listen John. You go ahead. I'll stay behind and keep things right. We need a good man talking for us if this is to be resolved.' The London NUS official agreed with the Scot.

'No, I'm not leaving the ship but I'm leaving this table right now.'

At 5.30 am they were all called to a further meeting.

'Okay,' said Mr Van Eyck. 'The Captain goes, but we want a joint statement. Will you go along with that?'

'You can say what you like. You can say he won the pools or ran off with another woman. As long as he gets off this ship! We're not worried about saving face so you can say what you like.'

'We are saying that Captain Kellner has been promoted to take over one of the company's biggest supertankers . . .'

John started laughing. 'Very good, very good. I like your style.'

'You handled that well, like an expert,' Andy afterwards congratulated him. The new Captain — who had flown in from London two days previously in the event of a company climbdown — was introduced. 'We'll meet everyday,' he promised. 'There'll be no communications problems, I can assure you.'

Up on deck John bid Van Eyck goodbye. Mr Van Eyck turned to him. 'I never thought I'd see the day when this would happen. You are a very pig-headed man.'

'I'm not pig-headed,' rebutted John. 'There's the pig-headed man going down the gangway now. He created the situation. He's a Captain Bligh. He could not live with the changes that are happening today. He couldn't stomach it.'

When the ship sailed the seamen were in a euphoric mood and there were no other incidents during the cruising season apart from one. Andy McLean suddenly disappeared off the boat after the first trip and later John learnt that he had been a company plant all along.

In April the ship returned to England to resume the regular Liverpool-to-Montreal-to-Liverpool run. Stevie signed off and went home. On the second run John got a very sore throat, he presumed from inhaling paint fumes after the living accommodation had been redecorated but hadn't dried thoroughly before he moved in. He didn't want to go to the doctor in case he was paid off sick. In a few days time they would be docking in Liverpool and he could take off a week due to him, and recuperate in Belfast. However, when his throat got worse — it was almost closed over and he could barely swallow even liquids — he was forced to get the ship's doctor who was about to recommend that he get paid off sick but relented when John explained that he was going home on leave.

*   *   *

The most changed feature about life in West Belfast, noticed John, was the high level of troop activity and the coldness of the people towards them. They were no longer the British army but were now called the 'Brits'. Confrontations were regular occurrences and John couldn't believe the turn-around in attitudes. People were now complaining that they were seeing the British soldiers ten times more often than they had ever seen the RUC. They had merely swapped oppressors: nothing had altered.

At the Republican Easter parades in 1970 there had been many clashes between marchers and the British army and some tension in Beechmount Avenue between the two rival Republican groups which had now formally split. In Derry a woman who struck a soldier on the chest with her hand was sentenced to a month's imprisonment. On the Springfield Road British soldiers who protected an Orange parade through a largely Nationalist area were stoned and petrol bombed. The rioting lasted three nights and in the Ballymurphy ghetto of Springhill the soldiers saturated the area with CS gas, baton-charged the Nationalists and were followed into the area by Loyalists who smashed windows and seized a tricolour.

The British army announced that petrol bombers could be shot dead if they persisted. The IRA issued a statement which said that in the event of this happening, 'retaliatory action will be taken by our units in occupied Ireland.' There were also confrontations in Ardoyne and the New Lodge Road where, in mid-May, the British army carried out house-to-house searches for arms. Since arms had only been used in defensive actions these particular types of raids incensed Nationalists

When John reported back to his IRA contacts, as had Stevie some weeks before him, they discovered that the organisation had split, as newspaper reports had indicated. A temporary provisional Army Council — later to be dubbed the Provisional IRA or the Provisionals — re-organised the IRA and attracted those disappointed with the degree of 'Official' IRA preparedness for August 1969.

John grabbed Stevie by the lapel at their third meeting and said, 'My good man, you and I are going back to sea.' His friend thought he was joking him: after all, Stevie was into the swing of things and even had a girlfriend! But John was persistent and explained the purpose and after some thought Stevie agreed.

\* \* \*

'You have to see the doctor. You got paid off sick.'

'I didn't get paid off sick. I went home on leave,' John insisted.

'Nothing to do with me, chuck,' said the Liverpool woman behind the glass. 'There's a medical report here says you got paid off sick. You have to see the doctor.'

'Okay. Okay.'

'What's up?' asked Stevie.

'I have to see the doctor. Some mix-up.'

He went to the ship's hospital where there was a stranger, a middle-aged man, sitting in a three piece, pin-striped suit, waiting to examine him.

'You're not the ship's doctor!' said John rhetorically.

'No. No. I've been sent from the shore.'

'I never heard of that before.'

'Oh? It's happened quite often enough before.'

'How many people are you seeing today?'

'Just yourself.'

John knew something was not right. Out of every crew it was usual for about ten or twelve men to have been signed off sick. When they returned they had to report to the doctor to be given the all-clear before signing on. The examination was usually cursory — 'open your mouth, stick out your tongue. Drop your trousers, cough. Okay. All clear.' His suspicions that something was unusual were confirmed when the doctor began a lengthy probe of his medical history, asking about parents and grandparents, then took blood and urine samples, did eye and hearing tests, checked his scalp, even measured him. It took three-quarters of an hour. He's going to find something wrong with me and pay me off this ship for all the trouble I've been causing, thought John, who was conscientious about his fitness and physique.

'Doctor. See before you fill in your report and comment whether I'm fit or unfit I'm gonna tell you something. You've been brought here to do a specific job and that's to find me medically unfit. That's not because they are concerned about my health. There was a trade union dispute on this ship as I'm sure you heard on the news or through the grapevine.

'The company wants me off and if you are going to do their dirty work for them I'm going to insist that the same medical examination, the same standards that you apply to me, be applied to everybody on this ship and before she sails. I mean Captain, officers and crew. That'll take you and several other doctors — on overtime — about eight days.'

They looked at each other's eyes.

The doctor snapped close the file.

'Perfectly fit! I've never seen a fitter seaman in all my life,' he smiled, indicating that he would have no part in the company's game. The Captain and the officers were aghast when they saw John head for the cabins.

'How long have you got to live?' Stevie shouted, laughing, so that they could hear.

\*   \*   \*

The ship sailed up the St Lawrence River and docked in Montreal. Some weeks earlier John had noticed guns for sale in a large sports store in the centre of the city. On the ground floor were fishing tackle, nets, heavy clothing and camping equipment. Upstairs were row upon row of weapons. John had investigated the conditions of purchase which were lax — a name and address within the state which was easily gleaned from the telephone directory.

'Have you seen anything you like?' asked the floor manager, a fat man with a Zapata moustache.

'Could I have two M1 Carbines please and a 1,000 rounds of ammunition.'

'Certainly. Have you decided which of these you'd prefer?'

'Yes, that one and that one there, sir,' said John.

Stevie was amazed.

'Huh,' said John, 'Two water pistols from Las Palmas!'

'That'll be $120 please,' said the manager, handing him the wrapped package.

'Pleasure doing business.'

'Call again, thank you.'

'Where'd you get $120?' inquired Stevie.

'You know that wee post office on the Donegall Road? Well . . .'

They had no problems getting on to the boat and hiding the weapons in air vents to escape the customs men back in England who would often bring on rummaging-squads looking for contraband. The weapons were easily smuggled by other Republicans into Ireland since there were yet no permanent checks or widespread searching of vehicles. By the third trip they were so well organised that they were buying and smuggling ten rifles and several thousand rounds of ammunition, telescopic sights and cleaning equipment. Their boat tied up in Liverpool just across from the sheds near which the Belfast/Liverpool ferry was berthed so the weapons didn't have to be shifted out of the docks.

In late June, by which time John had decided to devote his entire energies to the IRA in Belfast, the British government announced that it was sending 3,000 more troops to Ireland to reinforce the 7,500 already there. On the last weekend of the month serious rioting erupted in different parts of the city. Three people were shot dead on the Crumlin Road. In East Belfast Loyalist gunmen attacked the Nationalist Short Strand area and petrol bombers attempted to set fire to St Matthew's chapel. Two more people were killed in these clashes, one of them Henry McIlhone, an auxiliary member of the IRA who died defending his area.

The following Friday, 3 July, six British army trucks and an RUC car drove into Balkan Street in the Falls and sealed off both ends of the street. A raid commenced and in one house guns belonging to the 'Officials', or Stickies which they had since been nicknamed, were seized. A few stones were thrown by youths at the troops as they withdrew and this was met with fusillades of CS gas and the quick surrounding of the Falls by troop reinforcements. It was clear that the British army brass had anticipated that they would be given the pretext for a much broader confrontation: they had 3,000 troops on standby for this operation.

In Omar Street a Saracen armoured car ran over and killed 36-year-old Charlie O'Neill, an invalided ex-serviceman. The people were outraged. Gangs of youths began hijacking buses and commercial vehicles which were turned into burning barricades. The soldiers then indiscriminately fired CS gas into the streets and over rooftops. Many old people and young children were evacuated from the area, which was quickly being sealed off.

John was summoned to a meeting in Servia Street of 'D' Company, his IRA unit. There were eleven Volunteers in the house. His O/C, Charlie, was a man in his mid-twenties. On the ground in the corner lay a number of weapons and a bag of blast and nail bombs.

'The Brits have just shot and killed Billy Burns on the Falls Road,' Charlie said. 'General Freeland has declared a curfew but we're gonna defy it. We've got enough gear to hurt a few soldiers . . .'

'What's the Stickies gonna do? Does anybody know? They've still got gear in a house in McDonnell Street. Do you know which house I'm talking about, Charlie?' said Dominic, who had wanted to steal the weapons but had been refused permission for fear of causing a feud. Earlier that year, in January, the Stickies had beaten up those Republicans who had rejected their authority and for a time most of the men of 'D' Company were forced out of their homes in the area and had had to stay elswhere.

'They've quite a few dumps,' Charlie answered. 'I expect they'll fight. We'll see.'

They discussed their strategy and then the weapons were distributed. Brendan, an ex-marine commando, ran out first, across to the bottom of Bosnia Street. He was armed with a .303 Lee Enfield rifle. British soldiers were at the other end of Servia Street and Albert Street. Brendan gave cover fire while the others dashed out of the house in formation, close to the brick walls. They headed towards Cyprus Street, carrying several Lee Enfields, a Thompson and Sten sub-machine guns, three short-arms and with blast bombs and matches in their jacket pockets. In Cyprus Street the soldiers poured concentrated fire at them, pinning them down in open doorways. They returned fire and John, who was armed with a Luger pistol, lit and threw a blastbomb up towards a parked Saracen. The bang shook the whole area and was followed by a sudden peace as everyone gathered their wits about them. The IRA unit then pulled back into Servia Street. A woman peeping from behind an upstairs window shouted down to her husband who shouted out to Charlie that the soldiers were in Varna Gap. One of the Volunteers fired blindly into the gable wall at a sharp angle.

'What the hell are you doing?' shouted his O/C.

'Richochets. We might hit them with richochets.'

'For God's sake catch yourself on and pull back!'

At the lower end of the Falls not everyone had heard the British army helicopter or the troops with loud-hailers towards the top end of the district announce that the area was under curfew. In Marchioness Street 62-year-old Patrick Elliman, an elderly, asthmatic man, went to his front door for some air, believing that the night's troubles were over. In his shirt sleeves and bedroom slippers he walked to the corner. It was shortly after 11 pm. The British soldier who spotted him, took aim and shot him in the head, fatally wounding him. A nephew from the same street dashed to his aid and risked gunfire to summon a Knights of Malta ambulance from its base in Sultan Street. Soldiers delayed it going to the man who was still breathing.

Later that night the soldiers broke into Elliman's home and quartered themselves there during the curfew, sleeping in the beds and cooking themselves meals.

\* \* \*

Saracens began to trundle into the area and 'D' company retreated, exhausting most of their ammunition and improvised grenades after an hour. The shooting, however, continued: soldiers firing at imaginary targets or in response to the gunfire of their colleagues in another part of the Falls.

John got separated from his comrades as the encirclement got smaller and smaller. The place was saturated in a mist of gas causing most people to retch and vomit. He ran into a supporter's house, his eyes streaming from the stinging effects of the CS gas. He cleaned his Luger, wrapped it up in a tea towel and hid it and a spare nailbomb in the rafters of the toilet shed outside in the yard. He then sat there, nervously talking to the old man who lived alone and who was even more nervous than John. They waited and waited on the door being broken in. The soldiers took their time coming, clearing and searching one street at a time, seizing weapons mostly belonging to the Stickies, only a few of which had been used in brief exchanges.

\* \* \*

Zbigniew Vglik, a young Londoner of Polish extraction, with an interest in amateur photography, was over in Belfast as a freelance journalist. He stayed in the Albert Street area until about 1 am and then decided to return to the Wellington Park Hotel where he was resident. Rather than risk going through the curfew zone he left the area through the back of the house in Albert Street. British soldiers who had commandeered a house shot him dead.

\* \* \*

In every street there were arrests and beatings. Several hundred people were taken into custody. At 7 am on Saturday morning the sacristan was refused permission by the British army to open St Peter's Church. A girl from Bosnia Street was prevented from going to her wedding. Two people who attempted to reach St Peter's — which was outside the proclaimed area — were arrested.

Later that morning two Unionist government ministers, John Brook and William Long, drove through the Falls standing in an open back military lorry, imperiously inspecting the military operation.

\* \* \*

When news of the curfew, and news of the resistance began to reach the outside world, the international media came flocking in. By Saturday afternoon rumours of the house-wrecking and beatings inside the cordoned off area began to slip out. Nationalist politicians and Catholic clerics condemned the actions of the British army. The British announced that shops inside the sealed zone could open for two hours but that there was to be no movement of people or supplies inside or outside the curfewed area. Pressure was now building on the British government to call a halt to the house-to-house searches. British army officers, under pressure of time, now began selecting at random a quota of houses in each street or, in some cases, on just one particular side of the street.

John sat agitated as he watched the soldiers enter the homes just opposite him. When no one answered the knocks the door was sledge-hammered. Inside, the house was found either to be deserted or terrified members of a family would be huddled together in some corner, awaiting the worst. In different parts of the area a number of men were caught with weapons. John was now awaiting his turn when suddenly the soldiers moved off out of the street — leaving behind patrols based in sandbagged emplacements at each corner — to begin to search the next street.

'Isn't it ironic?' said the old man

'What do you mean?' replied John.

'These streets where we live. Balkan Street, Bosnia, Raglan, Sultan, Omar . . . They were all named by the government of the time after the British battles, where the British fought during the Crimean War . . .'

'That isn't ironic. It was deliberate. That's the way the Brits work. They invade your mind, take over everything. I mean everything, ár teanga [our language], our streets. Our very souls they take over with the importance of their ways and customs and ideas. Fuck them!'

By Sunday people were again running out of food since most of the main shops were outside the area and access to them had been denied. At 7.45 am a British army helicopter announced that people could go to Mass. However, the first families to make their way out-doors were ordered inside again at gunpoint. For some time there was confusion but people outside the area were now organising their own offensive. Several hundred women gathered at St Paul's church on the Falls Road and marched into Leeson Street distributing food which was quickly snapped up.

Several hours passed.

John heard a noise in the distance of chanting, of singing, of screaming but not in a frightened sense. It got louder and louder and brought people to their windows, then, to their front doors. Thousands of women from Andersonstown, Turf Lodge, Bally-murphy, St James and Rodney and from areas on up the Falls, hearing about the first break of the blockade, marched down to the British army cordons and pulled the barbed wire barricades aside. They were carrying bread, milk, vegetables, meat parcels, biscuits. Some pushed prams, some were old people outraged by the curfew and who had never felt strong enough or motivated enough to act so defiantly before.

'Come out! Come out!' they screamed. 'The curfew is broken! The curfew is broken!'

John turned around. He was excited. He turned to thank the old man standing behind him but the old man was crying and sobbing from relief, from pride, from a renewed faith in his community at a time when he felt so isolated and devastated.

At every corner the soldiers were swept out of the way and booed. The women marched through the streets, their numbers growing as the imprisioned families rushed out to greet them. John joined the triumphant throng and made his way to another street where he met up with some other Volunteers.

'We're shifting the weapons!' he was told. Several Volunteers of Cumann na mBan, the women's branch of the Republican Movement which helped the IRA and took part in operations, were among the crowd, pushing prams whose springs were almost collapsing. When the British army pulled back to their billets and the area was eventually clear 'D' Company did an inventory. They went into the curfew with eleven weapons. Now they had eighteen: those extra had been recovered from manholes and roofspaces where they had been discarded by Stickies. They were well-armed and supplies were also coming into the country at a fair rate. They were now ready to take on British forces.

\* \* \*

Stevie said to the guns' salesman: 'How come when I first came in here a while back the carbines were only $40 a piece and now they've doubled in price?'

'Ah,' said the man, smoothing down the thick bristles of his black moustache. 'These weapons are now in great demand. Everybody is after them. We've even had the Black Panthers in, the Weathermen, and then there's your crowd — the IRA . . .'

Stevie gulped and looked around. He paid for the weapons and walked out. He wouldn't be back in that shop or, for that matter, in Canada. He had missed the curfew and the first shots fired at the British army and he was kicking himself. For security reasons alone someone else would have to resume purchasing for the Second Battalion of the Belfast IRA.

\* \* \*

Angela sat sipping her tea in the packed canteen of Bostock House, which was connected to the Royal Victoria Hospital complex. Her friend had left to return to the office. She was now working as a clerical officer having left her previous job. 'A year in an accountant's is long enough. I simply got browned off with it,' she explained to her peeved mother.

She opened her handbag and took out the postcard from Patricia who was holidaying in the south of France. She sighed. Not only was the deteriorating situation in Belfast depressing but romance had recently gone out of her life. Four weeks previously she and her steady boy broke up, their relationship dying of boredom. Since then she had placed all notion of the opposite sex out of her mind and had been pleasantly surprised at how more relaxed and reflective she felt. But now, in the middle of a hot summer, and against a background of friends coming into work each day, talking about boys and dances and holidays she began to feel left out. In recent days her friends' attentions had been drawn to a group of young doctors, some from Manchester, who were surrounded by a clean-cut antiseptic aura of sophistication. Their crusading, humanitarian qualities were almost palpable and the legendary stories about their dissolute private lives created something of a tantalising, moral paradox, to be explored should the rare opportunity arise. In the office, speculating about their lifestyle and pairing off such-and-such a doctor with such-and-such a pretty staff nurse were innocent enough pastimes which most of them indulged in.

'Excuse me, may I join you?'

Angela looked up at the young man before her. He was tall and casually dressed. He held a tray and obviously had trouble finding a space in the busy canteen.

'Yes. Sorry. Go ahead. I didn't see you.'

He carefully buttered a piece of wheaten bread and cut a piece of cheese to fit. He looked from side to side, mildly curious. As he did so, Angela snatched quick glances of him. He was not stunningly handsome but was attractive all the same and this became apparent the more she studied him. She felt that he caught her staring but as if he didn't notice he merely commented, 'Busy, isn't it?' She caught the inflections of an English accent.

'Yes. Always is at this time. Have you not been here before?'

'No. It's my first time, though I'm based in the complex.'

She acknowledged his comment, smiled and then noticed the time. 'Are you late?' he asked.

'Just a few minutes.'

'Maybe I'll see you again then,' he remarked and stood up, gentlemanly, as she left.

A few days passed and she saw no further sign of the young man. As their meeting was of no consequence she felt no need to mention it to her workmates. The following Monday she was again finishing lunch when he showed up and asked could he sit down beside her and her two friends. When they saw that the two knew each other the girls cleared off, ignoring Angela's assurances that they weren't interrupting anything.

His name was Roger and he was not a trainee doctor or a laboratory technician, as she first thought, but worked in communications. However, he wanted to know more about her and although he did mention his upbringing in Yorkshire and his tastes in music he was more receptive to her views on life than anyone she had met for a long time. And so she heard her own voice, at his alluring encouragement, indiscreetly range unbridled over such matters as love and marriage. Then, the following day she sat talking to him again. Roger was fascinated and asked would she go out with him but Angela, now embarrassed at the looseness of her tongue, declined the invitation. He said he was going back to England for a week and she agreed to possibly seeing him when he returned.

When, after a fortnight, she did see him again she couldn't believe her eyes, though on immediate reflection some of the things he had said suddenly made sense. It was late Friday afternoon and by sheer accident she and some of her freinds had called into the canteen for a snack. Roger walked over to her table and her friends left immediately. As he sat down Angela at first laughed at the British army uniform and at the thought of how silly she had been not to make the connection. Roger produced a diamond engagement ring from its box and suddenly the situation slid completely out of her control.

'This is for you, Angela. Please take it . . .'

She was taken aback at the present and his generosity but it was all so ridiculous. 'Look Roger, this is all a mistake. I can't. We barely know each other . . .'

She was the focus of many stares. Although soldiers occasionally frequented the canteen Nationalists had, since the curfew, begun to stay well clear of them. Catholic girls who went to British army discos were attacked by Republican supporters for being 'soldier lovers' and some had even been publicly tarred and feathered or had their heads shaven.

Angela said, 'Roger, I'm sorry. It's all been a big mistake.' She rose from the table but he just felt that it was early days and that the surprise had slightly disorientated her. 'Hey, it's okay. I understand,' he laughed. 'I'll see you on Monday or Tuesday. You'll feel better then.' He bent over and kissed her and then left.

Angela started to worry about the repercussions and her mood fluctuated between how obvious was the mixup to anybody who chose to look at the situation in all its innocence, to one of sheer panic. Her face began twitching and she broke out in a cold sweat. She opened a packet of cigarettes but discovered that she had no matches left. She crossed the floor and asked a couple of men, whom she knew by sight, if they had a light. She found it unusual that they claimed to be out of matches also. Catch yourself on, she told herself. You're falling to pieces.

Back in the office she felt that those who hadn't gone home yet, were whispering about her. The snack rumbled sourly in her stomach and she had to go to the bathroom until she was sick. Eventually she calmed down and composed herself. Having conquered her fears she then realised how foolish she had been: that of course any half-wit who saw or heard about what happened could appreciate how surprised she was to find out in the one breath that not only was she almost engaged, but she didn't even know! She laughed at the thought of just how ridiculous it was. The girls from the Road to whom she urgently wanted to explain the whole matter were not among those still on duty.

'He did what!' shouted her mother when she told her what happened. 'Angela, I'm going to ask you one more time. Are you sure you're telling me the truth because to be honest it just sounds like something you would do, leading a fellah on . . .'

'Mammy!'

'Well what do you expect me to believe. You have brought more trouble on this house down the years than five daughters . . .'

Walking through Tullymore estate later that evening Angela felt that all eyes were on her. She was extremely uncomfortable and fearful on her way up to see her Aunty Maureen who would contact someone in the IRA, and sort it all out. She recalled how before moving up to Andersonstown some years earlier she had despised the close-knit streets of the Falls, the narrow entries, the dogs and cats, the lack of open space and greenery. Parochialism, narrow-mindedness, choked her. Despite her bad experiences in London she relished the sense of freedom and anonymity offered by the British capital and she wished she had never come back.

'How could you have been so stupid!' pronounced Maureen.

'You saw that he had short hair. Did you not realise he was a radio man in the British army? And all that time you didn't know he was a soldier? Are you sure you weren't seeing him somewhere else?'

'I swear to God, Maureen. The whole thing is so incredible.' Maureen said she believed her, that she would see someone and that Angela could more or less set her mind at rest.

\* \* \*

'Two girls were asking for you at the club last night but I told them you hadn't been there for weeks? What's up? You've gone all white . . .?'

Angela told her friend everything.

'Jesus, you don't think they were gonna shave your head, do you? You know, don't you, that there's a rumour you're pregnant?'

\*   \*   \*

'The whole talk is that you're getting married to a soldier.'

'Who told you that friggin' rubbish?' She was angry but more frightened.

'Everybody's saying it. There's talk that it's gonna be a military wedding. Angela, I think you're in big trouble.'

'I know. I know,' she said, biting off her once carefully manicured finger nails.

\*   \*   \*

'Mammy, I can't settle and I want to go.'

'But what would you work at in England. You've nobody to go to.'

'Bloody IRA!' said Frank. 'Who do they think they are. Just let them come near this door. So much for your sister being able to sort it all out!'

\*   \*   \*

'It's okay. Everything's been cleared up.' Her mother's voice across the phone was reassuring. 'You can come home.'

'But mammy I've only arrived and I've another interview tomorrow for a job.'

'Angela.' It was her father's voice. 'The right people have been seen. Only one side of the IRA was told. The other group had it explained to them and everything's okay. I'm sure you're glad?'

'Yes, daddy. But I'm shattered by the whole thing. And if you and mammy don't mind I think I'll stay here for a while. To tell you the truth I was getting fed up with Belfast anyway.'

# CHAPTER 9

## 9 August, 1971

As the double-decker hijacked bus, minus its passengers, approached the British army billet it slowed down. From upstairs Stevie opened fire with a machine gun into the breeze-block nest, cutting chips of brick out of the observation post. The soldier inside dived for cover and when he felt sure that it was all over — even though he still expected the roar of an explosion — he peered out to see a number of armed men alight from the abandoned vehicle and disappear into the Kashmir Road.

'Well did you get him!' John shouted to Stevie as they and another Volunteer ran up the street.

'I dunno! I dunno!'

Two youths with nailbombs were in the side streets to deter any patrols which may have been in hot pursuit of the unit, but no soldiers came into the area immediately. Before they sealed off Clonard district the British army would wait until they had considerable reinforcements.

'You should have gone slower,' Stevie complained to John in the debriefing session they held in the call-house — the home of a sympathiser supplied to the IRA as a meeting-place.

'I wasn't used to the thing and I was afraid of it stalling,' said John who was the O/C of this battalion Active Service Unit — an ASU. He knew from his comrade's statement that they had inflicted no casualties. Other Volunteers returned from operations and swore until they were blue in the face that they had shot dead not one soldier but two or three along with him. A whole myth had arisen that the British army couldn't admit to high fatalities, but were secretly burying their dead and writing them off as killed in car accidents in West Germany. John was totally sceptical and never accepted a Volunteer's claim — distorted by the heat of battle — about dead soldiers. 'Did anybody see blood on the pavement?' he would sardonically ask. Stevie always erred on the side of caution so when the late morning news announced that no soldiers had been injured John agreed with the BBC.

Since the curfew IRA activity had been steadily increasing. There was no clear-cut strategy. Indeed, many operations were carried out unofficially as the IRA leadership — based in the south of Ireland — was more cautious about intensifying activity than were the people on the ground in the North. There had been no real debate among Republicans about how to proceed. Rural units of the IRA, besides attacking barracks, were blowing up key installations — electricity pylons, sub-stations, telephone exchanges — or customs posts. Activity was largely a probing exercise: discovering how the government and its forces would respond to this blatant challenge to, and undermining of, its authority. The Belfast Brigade during the 1970 curfew had set off bombs outside banks in Andersonstown in an attempt to overstretch the British army and RUC and lure them away from the Falls. It had also planted incendiary devices in city centre shops to create a similar diversion. As units proliferated a very low level campaign of bombing commercial and business premises in the centre of Belfast was begun. It took the war out of the Nationalist ghettoes and forced the extra deployment of soldiers in city centre checkpoints who would otherwise be engaged against the IRA in its bases.

In February 1971 the first British soldier to be killed on duty in Ireland since the Black and Tan War, before partition, was shot dead by the IRA in North Belfast.

Every day the IRA was in the news, mainly through speculation that it was responsible for the military attacks since its claims of admission came slow and irregularly as it had yet to develop a propaganda machine capable of politically exploiting successful operations and defending the organisation when an operation went wrong. But it was forcing government ministers to respond and in March the gathering political crisis had forced the resignation of the prime minister, Major Chichester Clark. His successor, Brian Faulkner, at first boasted that the IRA was 'on the run' and 'would soon be crushed'. In the British parliament on the 28 July Home Secretary Reginald Maudling said that he considered that 'a state of open war now exists between the IRA and British army.'

John was kept busy. He had been attached to 'D' Company — the Dogs, as they were nicknamed — for several months before he was noticed and promoted into a more flexible and prestigious Battalion Active Service Unit which had access to more resources than each Company. When he wasn't planning an operation or carrying one out he was attending his Irish language classes and was now fluent.

In March relations with the Stickies reached an all-time low and a feud erupted which lasted several days. During this feud one man lost his life — John's former O/C, twenty-seven-year old Charlie Hughes who was ambushed by the Stickies. He was the first Republican to be killed in such circumstances since the Civil War, sixty years previously.

John's ASU had been involved in a whole series of bomb and gun attacks. It had bombed RUC/British Army barracks at Queen Street, Roden Street, Springfield Road and Henry Taggart. It had killed two British soldiers and seriously injured several others. The Volunteers were confident of closing down Roden Street barracks which was indefensible. Two Volunteers had been wounded and both were brought across the border for hospital treatment. In a two month period, over forty youths had applied to join the Battalion's companies — units based in, and drawing their membership from, specific districts.

John and Stevie interviewed some of these recruits.

'Why do you want to join the IRA?'

'Gabh mo leithscéal. Abair sin arís, le do thoil.' [Pardon me, Could you repeat what you said please.]

'Oh, a gaeilgeoir! Certainly, I'll repeat it.' John was pleasantly surprised.

'Speak in English. I don't understand.' Stevie insisted, sounding irritated.

'I've always believed that Ireland was a nation long before England. I believe that we're entitled to our own heritage and to freedom. I'm a great admirer of Pádraig Mac Piarias and have read all his poems . . .'

His starched white shirt annoyed Stevie.

'Could you throw a nail bomb? If I told you to shoot somebody could you do it?'

'Well, if I was trained properly I could throw a nail bomb but I wouldn't shoot anyone unless I was absolutely convinced that it was the right thing to do . . .'

'Could you take being hated?'

'What do you mean?'

'If an operation goes wrong your ma or girlfriend could be calling the IRA 'bastards' and it might have been you who was responsible. You'll hear it from the priests during Mass. You'll read it in the papers that we're wrong. When you're arrested the Brits and cops will hate you with a venom you've never seen before. The screws in the jail will detest you. So could you take being hated?'

'Umm, I'll have to think about that.'

Stevie gave him more cold treatment. But not all of potential recruits were so naive.

'Why do you want to join the IRA?'

'The Brits won't leave us alone when we're standing at the corner. They're always fuckin' us about.'

'Why do you want a united Ireland?'

'I'm not that fussed. Haven't thought about it much.' He shrugged his shoulders to show that he had no burning enthusiasm for political rearrangements.

'Everytime you stand at the corner they come along and tell you to move off. I'm fed up with it and just want to have a blarge at them.'

'What do you think?' John later said to his comrade.

'You know me. I'm not into the language thing, the culture. We'll make a fighter out of the last one, and his politics can come later, but I wouldn't be for the first one.'

'I totally agree,' said John.

Given the rising level of IRA activity something had to break. Everyone was told to stay out of their houses. An old word came back into circulation — 'billet', a safe house for sleeping in: 'Get yourself a good billet and you'll be all right.' And the golden rule: leave the women of the house alone. There was talk of internment without trial being introduced. The government would attempt to arrest all IRA Volunteers in their beds. It had been successfully used by the northern state in the past. But on those occasions the IRA was terribly weak and had no significant base in the towns and cities, where the Nationalist population was largely apolitical and cowed.

On 23 July there were dawn raids in Belfast and nine other towns, followed by widespread arrests on four other mornings before the end of the month. People had only been detained for short periods. Internment was talked about so much that it was expected after every operation. When it didn't happen it became a boring topic and a certain lethargy crept in.

John was at home only at weekends, usually if he was out drinking with his father. He had had a bad row with his mother back in February when he had been out with hand grenades fighting British soldiers. They had not told his father about the argument and it was smoothed over. In the July raids his home wasn't searched. He was a bit surprised they hadn't raided for him and he concluded — from other reports he had received — that their intelligence files were not that good given that many of those arrested in the swoops were not active militarily, and that some others were active only in the Civil Rights' or Students' movements.

At their meeting after the gun attack from the bus they discussed the next operation. That night a bomb was to be prepared for Springfield Road barracks and a van was to be got for the next morning, Saturday, when it was intended kidnapping two RUC men from the City centre, bringing them up to the Falls Road and tarring and feathering them outside St John's Chapel.

The bomb was to be made up of ten pounds of gelignite with a 12-second delay fuse.

John was dropped off in Crocus Street. He lifted out the hold-all bomb. A scout went to the corner: there were no soldiers in the street. He broke the phial of acid which lit the fuse, turned the corner and hurled the bomb over the barbed wire fence towards the makeshift look-post that had been erected following a similar bomb attack which killed a paratrooper in May. As he ran away the soldiers suddenly opened fire and he tripped on the ground, lying there for a few seconds. There was an almighty explosion and the buildings appeared to momentarily shimmer. Two women, apparently not too traumatised by the blast, thought he had been shot and when he got up they shouted: 'Run son! Run!'

He ran into Colligan Street but at the bottom corner soldiers were dismounting from their vehicles, unaware of what exactly was happening, but cutting off his escape route. Peter was among the crowd to emerge from Maguire's bar where the explosion had shaken the walls and cracked the windows. He saw John run down the street and was almost sick with dread thinking he was going to be killed or captured. Dozens of soldiers, none of whom had been injured, streamed out of the barracks and began forcing people — women and men — up against walls, ordering them not to move. Peter started a hullabaloo and encouraged others to engage in punch-ups. Somebody got bottles from the bar and threw them at the soldiers, and a small riot began.

John burst into the first open door he found and ran upstairs.

His ankle was twisted and sore. The old man of the house, realising what his unwelcome guest had been up to, was terrified and John calmed him down.

'Can I get out the back? Can I get out the back?' he shouted and attempted to open the bedroom window but it was sealed with coats of paint. There was a loud knock on the front door and John was convinced he was a goner.

'Don't open it! Don't open it!'

'I have to, son. I have to . . . Who is it?'

'Open the door. It's okay,' said a woman's voice.

The old man opened the door and she stepped into the hall. She shouted up to John: 'Are you one of Liam Hannaway's men?' referring to a senior IRA man.

'Yes,' he said, still agitated.

'Quickly. Come with me.' She took him out, across the street, which was still in uproar, and into another house. He was helped over a yard wall, into a house in the next street and then out the front door and into a car. Stevie, chewing gum and blowing bubbles, was behind the wheel.

'Bet you thought you were gone there,' he smiled as they drove off.

Peter walked home. He was shaking from tensions he swore to God he was never placed on the earth to experience. He felt as if two blood streams were gushing through his veins in opposition to each other. One had determined the instant justification of his action and it was also spiced with excitement. The other more powerful flood, was of his own nature and his revulsion at the use of violence. His eyes filled with tears which he was too embarrassed to show and which he felt run down the *inside* of his cheeks. He had nobody to talk to, to help him sort out the moral dilemmas of the situation. Catherine just couldn't cope with being acquainted with the details of their son's activities even though deep down she knew. He just wished that it was all over and that there was peace. And yet strangely he felt closer to John than for as long as he could remember.

\*   \*   \*

'A man's been shot dead outside Springfield Road barracks!'

'What happened?' said John to the young Volunteer who had brought the bad news.

'He was in a van, driving past. It backfired and the soldiers opened up.'

'Anybody seen Stevie? Is he back with that van yet? Jesus, I hope it's not him.'

The kitchen door opened and Stevie walked in. 'I know. I heard. The Brits told the locals they were fired on but they weren't. There's crowds gathering. We'd need to cancel that op on the two cops, there'll be bigger trouble now.'

Rioting broke out on the Falls, Ardoyne and Ballymurphy and on Saturday night a crowd of 300 attacked Springfield Road barracks. On Sunday a soldier was shot dead in Ardoyne and six others wounded.

'The Sticks have five .303s out in Raglan Street,' Stevie reported.

'How many have our people out?'

'We've two armalites, a Thompson and a .45. Whoever's in charge of the Brits hasn't a clue. Snatch squads carrying only batons are chasing the rioters into the area. The Dogs are out at Lower Clonard Street and Spinner Street waiting to cut the dung out of them.'

The trouble lasted well into the night and since most of the shooting was of an opportune nature John's unit was not needed after 10 pm. Some of the men stayed around just to be in the middle of things but John left and phoned up Geraldine to see if she fancied a drink. He had been introduced to her at a *scoraíocht* — a fund-raising party — three weeks previously. She gave him companionship and support and was more in love with him than he realised or could reciprocate. He met her as arranged and they called into a club which his father patronised. They joined Peter, who sat with a pint of Guinness in front of him, and Catherine who sipped at her tomato juice. For years she stayed at home and rarely ventured out to socialise but since the children had grown up she occasionally went out with her husband and found that she had enjoyed the sing song and light-hearted banter though she would certainly not allow alcohol to cross her lips.

Peter immediately made the two welcome and gave his order to a passing waiter.

'Big round of applause for Tony now,' said Macksie the guitarist, 'and a bit of order because he's not wearin' his teeth. Come on now, a bit of respect, Tony's one of the nicest fellahs you'd ever meet . . .'

The singer, a small elderly man in a faded suit was a well-known favourite of the audience. Clutching a cigarette, which acted like an informal baton, he incoherently mumbled the words of an old song but was drowned out by the chorus from the floor who then went on to give him a rousing ovation. 'More! More!' they shouted. 'Sing again, Tony. Go on, sing again!' He got back up and as bold as brass proceeded to sing the same song to much applause.

A woman in her late twenties lifted her handbag from a table near the top to visit the ladies. She had had too much to drink but thought she was sober. She knocked over a glass, which fortunately was empty. As quick as a shot Macksie responded facetiously: 'Watch you don't knock that glass over, love,' but she continued on her way oblivious.

John was enjoying himself, relaxing after the feverish activity of the last few days.

'I saw you last night,' Peter whispered to him when the group resumed the stage for the final half hour.

'What are you talking about?'

'On the Springfield. You know my views but I was really worried for you. I hope you young people know what youse are doing. Be very careful . . .' and he winked at John who winked back. It had taken so long for them to arrive at this understanding, he thought. So long

'Will you have a whiskey, daddy?'

Peter looked at Catherine and saw that she intuitively read that the two of them were in really good form.

'Aye! Why not! What about you Geraldine, will you have a wee vodka?'

'Yes, thank you, Mr O'Neill,' she replied, even though it was John who was buying.

John sat next to his girlfriend with his arm around her chair, whispering to her in between sipping at his pint of beer and glass of whiskey. A ginger-haired youth entered the club with the doorman who pointed John out. He came over and gave him a message which irritated him.

'I'm sorry folks, but I have to go. Something's cropped up.' His father despite being philosophical just seconds earlier, now felt as if he had been showered with splinters of ice, felt the Republican Movement once again reach into their lives. Catherine grabbed John's hand.

'No. It's nothing like that. It's just that I've got a message and I have to find various people before the morning. Geraldine, are you coming?'

'Look, why don't you let Geraldine stay if you are rushing off,' said Peter. 'I'll walk her home. She's still got drink in front of her.'

This appeared to suit everyone.

John had received word that ten new recruits were to go to a training camp, leaving early the next morning. The Brigade training officer, a personal friend of John's had gone to a billet and only John could trace him so he set out to deliver the news. It was after 2 am before he got back into the Falls. He was staying in the street next to his own but noticed his living room light on. He called into the house and discovered that his mother was vomiting: apparently she had earlier complained that one of the tomato juices tasted odd. Peter made her a cup of tea and then helped her to bed. When he came down the stairs he said, 'Shouldn't you be somewhere else?'

'Ah they're probably well tucked in now. I'll stay the night if that's all right with you?'

'You know you're more than welcome.'

*   *   *

Before John had time to assimilate the crashing sounds, the noise of boots on the stairs and Sheila's and Monica's screaming, the paratroopers came in on top of him. They had sledge-hammered his front and back doors and had not brought in their rumbling Armoured Personnel Carriers — APCs — until the raids commenced so as not to give their victims any warning. As Raymond was away in England and Jimmy was staying in his granny's house there was no disputing who — Peter or John — was the 23-year-old.

'What's going on? What's going on?' Peter demanded.

'Never you mind old man. John O'Neill I'm arresting you under the Special Powers Act. Tie him up!'

Catherine was shaking and sobbing as were Monica and Sheila. 'Leave him alone! Leave him alone!' his youngest sister protested but she was pushed aside and his hands were tied behind his back and a rope put around his neck. This was the price that had to be paid, John kept thinking but cursed himself for being at home having chided the others who had fallen back into the habit of creature comforts. If only the house *had* been raided in July then I wouldn't be here now, he thought. Peter ran out into the street and stuffed a packet of cigarettes into John's trousers pocket. But the escort wouldn't accept John's shoes and socks. Though it was still dark, people had gathered and were shouting abuse at the soldiers. There was a sudden, hushed silence when the noose around John's neck was tightened and he began choking.

'Get your bin lids out and start rattling!' shouted a neighbour, Peggy Carson. Another, Mrs Clarke, comforted Catherine and went to make her tea. John was made to lie on the floor of the armoured car, soldiers' boots on top of him. 'What about Donnelly?' he heard someone ask.

'We missed the bastard.'

They arrived at Mulhouse Street barracks. He was taken inside and roughed up. Radios were crackling, and APCs were arriving and departing in a frantic commotion of shouting, cursing, and horns being blasted. For those arrested, ripples of fear came with every sigh. He was brought into what appeared to be an assembly hall where there were many other prisoners similarly bound. A soldier was appointed to each prisoner.

There was a loud explosion close by: probably a nail bomb, thought John, as they had discussed what to do if internment came. As soon as the crowds came on to the streets the units would begin moving weapons out of dumps: one, to have a go at the soldiers and demonstrate that the IRA was still intact and, two, to move the armed struggle into a higher gear.

The sun came up to reveal in the sky palls of black smoke rising from Nationalist areas as the rioting spread. John was bundled out of the hall and placed on plank seating with others in the back of a canvas-covered lorry. Of the eight prisoners only John was an IRA Volunteer, while a few were supporters and the rest had a small local profile in street politics. The lorry drove out of the base and turned down the Grosvenor Road. Shooting from the Leeson Street area could now be heard. The soldiers fell quickly to the floor but jabbed the muzzles of their rifles into the prisoners forcing them to sit upright.

'Boys, this is Pocky Logan, Pocky Logan! Don't be shooting! Hold your fire!' shouted the Republican sympathiser sitting closest to the back flaps. John felt disgusted at the spinelessness and noted that the soldiers who had slapped them for asking questions or speaking earlier didn't interfere or interrupt Logan's screams.

At Girdwood Barracks John was bodily thrown out of the lorry. There was a queue of silent prisoners waiting to go into a gymnasium. Many were badly injured, blood pouring from head-wounds. One complained that his fingers were broken and was struck with a baton across the shoulder blades. There was an old man, stiff in his movements, who had just received a black eye from a military policeman for refusing to comply with an order. A soldier protested at him being hit: 'This is feckin' desperate, corporal. Look at 'im — he's only an old man . . .'

'Mind your own business and carry out your orders,' said the MP who was his senior.

In the gymnasium several hundred prisoners were sitting on the floor, some in pyjamas, with their hands on their heads. The MPs were in control. Fractious detainees were hit with batons and ordered to do press-ups. Names were called out and then those persons were marched out to interrogation rooms.

John's wrists were still behind his back. He was photographed and taken to a room for questioning. As he approached the room he heard a loud groan. Two RUC men in plain clothes, whom he took to be Special Branch officers, were interrogating a prisoner who was handcuffed and hanging from a round iron bar cemented into the wall. On the other wall was a framed colour picture of Queen Elizabeth and the Duke of Edinburgh, smiling.

'No more, no more, please! I'll talk. Let me down, please!'

The fear in the room was palpable but John was suspicious of the quasi-crucifixion. Activity in the room had only begun when he was a few yards off and there was too much blood on the prisoner's face. He had heard from old Republicans about being put in the same cell as someone who would claim to be from another IRA Brigade area but who was actually a plant, trying to get information. He decided that this was a set-up.

One of the RUC men flicked through a thick file: 'Ah, so you're John O'Neill. Take him away!' He was surprised that that was all that was said. On the way down the corridor he had to pass MPs who were standing about.

'Here's the bastard that shoots our mates in the back!' one shouted. They began punching and kicking him. He ran as fast as he could but two of the MPs had their arms through his and considerably slowed him down. He was put back on the floor. The beating had helped restore his faith in his convictions. The bruises were sore but he was not bleeding and he stared ahead of him, curiously enjoying the thought of a cigarette, inhaling the stream of blue smoke like it was an intoxicating draught. He was also more anxious about his family being worried than about himself because at least he knew what to expect.

The cord around his wrists was cut off and he was ordered up off his feet and taken to the toilets. 'Here, clean them!' he was instructed. He let the scrubbing brush fall to the ground.

'Clean them!' the voice roared — bad breath — inches from his face. John refused, was punched in the stomach and grabbed by the scruff of the neck. He was flung to the floor and caught some of the kicks before they did him harm. He was brought back to his position. Hours passed. The prisoners were called up to a table for tea. There were only about twelve cups for the entire hall and the fact that they were being re-used without being washed put John off. Since his days at sea he had a fastidious attitude towards delph and cutlery based on hygiene but he was so thirsty that he drank the awful concoction. Out of the side of his eye he caught sight of other prisoners washing windows, brushing the floor and two carrying mops and buckets out of the toilets.

'O'Neill! Out here!'

'Kah! Out here!' When prisoner Kerr realised he'd been called he wasn't long responding. Another four were ordered out. John was escorted out the door into the daylight and fresh air.

'Hands out front!' He was tied with plastic cuffs.

The engines of a Wessex helicopter were started up and they were ordered to climb in. John was last. Behind them the doors locked like a vacuum seal. They took off and the flight lasted about fifteen minutes. An MP grinned at John and shouted: 'Can you swim? I said, can you swim?' John nodded.

'Well then, can you fly?' The prisoners got very worried. 'Did you ever see the Viet Cong getting thrown out of the choppers? Eh? That's what's gonna happen to you fuckers . . .'

The door roared open and air shot in. John was kicked out and his heart gave one last hard pump, but he fell only a few feet into a dog compound where whorls of canine faeces sat like deposits of giant lugworms on a beach. The other prisoners landed beside him and the helicopter quickly rose into the sky. Snarling alsations came running at them and the prisoners formed a group with their backs against each other, kicking at the animals who were on leashes staked beside their kennels, but long enough to present a danger. A gate opened and handlers rushed in, grabbed the men by the hair and trailed them through the barking animals. Other soldiers standing about as observers, shouted their approval of what was happening.

The men were taken back into the gymnasium where the number of prisoners had significantly fallen. They were then individually called for stew which turned out to be cold. It was covered in a white layer of grease and was unappetising. Anyone who refused to eat was beaten, so John was again pummelled.

His name was called. An MP grabbed him and frog-marched him out of the hall. He was taken into a large hole, which apparently had been blown in the wall dividing Girdwood Barracks from Crumlin Road jail, and was led through. In the basement of D wing his hands were untied. The RUC found the cigarettes and confiscated them. John's watch and ring had already been stolen. 'These will be placed in this bag outside your cell and you can collect them when you're going,' an RUC man said whilst a prison warder locked him up in a cell. John was jubilant and was singing to himself, 'I've survived! I've survived!' The prisoner in his cell stared at him, 'My God, what have they done to you?'

The young man, whom John didn't know, tore some linen from the bed, wetted it with water and washed the wounds. He rinsed out the makeshift flannel in the bowl which instantly turned bright red. John thanked him. He then realised the extent of his injuries. His lips were split open and the air was like acid eating at them. Both eyes were black, one was almost closed over. Blood had coagulated on his scalp and had dried over the skin creases. The door was unlocked and an RUC officer appeared.

'You, get out! You shouldn't be in there with him.'

He was left on his own and pondered over what sort of arrangement was it that had RUC men and MPs in charge of prison warders, telling them where to put prisoners and when to open and close cell doors. The door creaked open again. He recognised a senior officer in the Special Branch. They had nicknamed him the Bouncer. The Bouncer introduced himself.

'You must know where there's a few guns knocking about, John, my old friend. I'm not after names, just guns and bombs, you know the sort of things. I want you to think about it son. You look like a nice fellah. I know everything about you but I'm a reasonable man. There's £20,' he said, extricating two £10 notes from a thick wad. 'Now, just you think about it. There's plenty more where that came from, as you can see. I'll call back later after you've rested.'

John placed his ear to the door and listened carefully until the Bouncer had finished his rounds. Then he banged on the cell door until a warder opened it.

'Any chance of a smoke?' he asked. 'I've fags just sitting outside in a brown bag.' The warder gave the bag a glance. 'Piss off.' He proceeded to close the door. 'Wait, wait, wait! Just a minute . . .' John dug his hands deep into his pocket and pulled out the £20. 'This is no use to me in here. Here take them, go ahead, but give me a smoke.'

'Let's see,' said the jailer. 'Okay, what's the harm.' He gave him the packet, lit him up one of the cigarettes and pocketed the money in his breast pocket, fastening the silver button. The barefoot prisoner lay back on his bed, one leg over the other, smiling at the high, yellow ceiling.

When the Bouncer returned John had enough smokes for a week.

'Well, have you thought about it?'

'I've thought about it and I'm not interested.'

'You'll be sorry. I have something special in mind for you. Now, give me my money, I mean, our money back.'

'I haven't got it.'

'Where is it then?' His face discoloured quickly.

'He has it,' said John pointing. 'That screw has it in his top pocket. I gave it to him to mind for you but he must have forgotten.'

The warder stuttered and then conceded without arguing. 'Oh yes, here you are, here you are.'

'Why wouldn't you take the money?' the burly interrogator asked.

'Money wouldn't buy my pride.'

'Well, you'll have plenty of time to think about your pride.'

All that night the lights were kept on and the cell doors were banged. It was only possible to lightly doze.

On Tuesday morning MPs took John out of the jail and forced him to run an obstacle course made of barbed wire and broken glass. He was once again confused and afraid because he had thought it was all over once he was in jail. His moods swung between spiritual highs and demoralised lows — what if they're right and I'm wrong? Could we really have expected to take on the British government without retribution? Were we upstarts, dreamers, doomed from the outset? Then he would draw upon his convictions which were buried under the weight of the brutality, and he felt an inner peace. I am right, I am right! he silently screamed. And when they saw the trace of that defiant smile which this declaration produced they beat him all the more.

Late on Tuesday night, shaken and hungry, he was brought outside into the darkness. There were three other prisoners whom he recognised but did not acknowledge. Their hands were tied behind their backs with plastic cord. The MPs stood in front of them, silently. Slowly and deliberately they produced eight hoods — hessian-type bags — and put one hood inside the other. Then they walked behind each prisoner and pulled the hoods over their heads. The man on John's right began to scream and he heard the dull thuds of fists pile-driving into a stomach. The terrified prisoner quietened down after that.

Someone twisted the bag at the back until it tightened and John felt as if he was choking. A helicopter landed and they were pushed and kicked on board. Within seconds it took off. It flew for over three-quarters of an hour. When it came to ground they were again kicked and forced to run over rough terrain. The length of the journey made John think he was in England or Scotland.

He was brought into a brick building. The floor was cold and bare. From the sound of his escort's boots he felt that they were going down a corridor. His hands were untied. He was brought to be medically examined. The doctor sat in a swivel chair. The small room was spartan, clinical and white-walled.

The doctor sounded fat and English: 'Any ailments?'

'I've a bad heart,' John lied through the sweaty hood.

'Take his clothes off.' He cursorily examined him: 'He's all right for interrogation.'

The hood was wrenched tight and he was forced out of the room. He was bundled into a boiler suit, two sizes too big.

'Up against that wall!'

He didn't understand the order because of a loud hissing noise and was forcibly spread-eagled by two or three people with English and Scottish accents. He tried to reduce the angle by a few inches, and thus ease the pressure on his limbs, but his feet were kicked even further apart.

'Now, maintain your posture or else . . .'

Hours dripped by and a snow-plough went through his brain, scattering cells, splattering red flakes into the ditch, returning and churning up more furrows, shaving his brain smooth, opening the road to allow the interrogators' traffic through.

'What time is it?' he asked.

'It's August and don't you leave that wall!'

He fell and was beaten, then he was helped into the spread-eagle position and told: 'Resume the posture!'

More hours passed by.

'Come with us.' He was taken into a room. The hood was removed and a number of men sat behind arc lights which were trained on him where he stood.

'You asked to see us.'

'I didn't ask to see you,' he whispered.

'What did he say?'

'He said he didn't ask to see us.'

He was hit across the head and fell on the concrete floor, but got on to all fours. His interrogators wore track suits and plimsolls and their faces were hidden. He was frog-marched back to the wall.

'Resume the posture!'

Hours passed. More beatings each time he fell. The noise drove holes of excruciating pain through his head.

'Can I go to the toilet?' he mumbled, pitying himself.

'You are shit, so shit where you are!'

He had no bowel movements and had been given no water. He dreamed he was urinating against an entry wall and urine dribbled down his leg, hot and stinging as when he was a child and a few drops always came out even when he thought he was finished, leaving his thigh chafed.

'Out!' Corridor. Room. Lights.

'You asked to see us?'

'I didn't ask . . .'

Another beating. Back to the wall, back to the Devil's screech.

'Out!' Corridor. Room? No room. Air. Lorry. Drive. Helicopter. Sky. Earth. Jeep.

'Get him through the hole in the wall.' Crumlin Road jail?

The hood was removed. Three RUC officers sat in front of him. 'Are you John O'Neill?'

'Yes.'

'Here is a removal order empowering the RUC via the Civil Authority to remove you to any place where your presence is required and question you for any length of time. As you can see it has been signed by the Minister of Home Affairs, Mr Brian Faulkner. Okay? Here you are.'

It was stuffed into the top pocket of the boiler suit.

He was taken back out through the hole in the wall, hooded, placed in a jeep, driven to the helicopter and was soon back up against the wall in the spread-eagle position.

Hours. Hood removed.

'You asked to see us?'

— Silence.

'I told you he asked to see us, didn't I!'

'Yes, you did. Do you think is he ready?'

'I don't know. Let's ask. You did ask to see us.'

His convictions were hanging on to the edge of a cliff with one finger nail. You were a tout before, O'Neill. Are you going to be a tout again? What about Paul McShane? Paul McShane . . . Paul McShane, McShane, the shame; the shame of squealing on McShane. School days, so long ago, so innocent, before all this. He hauled his whole mind up from where it perilously dangled, used the pause, the silence, as breathing space and muttered: 'I didn't ask to see you . . .'

'Fuck ya, O'Neill!' The lamp was knocked over and one of the provoked figures kicked him in the groin. The whole world went dark.


'And what do you think you'll be doing in five or ten years time?' Angela asked. It was late July 1965 and she was lying with her head in his lap, staring up into his eyes. The thumb and forefinger of his right hand made an inverted C at the base of her right breast.

'Oh, who knows? Living in Paris, London, Berlin . . . who knows? Why do you ask? Would you come with me? Would you live in a spacious garret with me, and in the winter mornings I would go out and buy hot croissants. When I came back you'd have the coffee made. We'd spread butter and strawberry jam over the hot rolls, eat and drink, and then we'd climb under the continental quilt and make love as the snow fell outside our window?'

'Where's the guns?'

'Where's Stevie Donnelly?'

'You blew up the jeep in Brougher Mountain!'
'You killed the three Scottish soldiers!'
'Two of them were brothers, you bastard.'
'Yeh, and seventeen years of age.'
'You blew up Roden Street barracks!'
'You blew up Sergeant Wallace in Springfield Road!'
'You planted incendiaries in Anderson and McAuley's!'
'Where's the guns?'
'Where's Stevie Donnelly?'

Some of the questions and statements meant nothing. He wasn't talking but most of the time there would have been no time anyhow to have answered before the next question or statement came.

'Do you want to go back to the music room, John?'

The music room, that's what they called the room where the high-pitched hissing sound, the 'white noise', went on and on and on.

Days passed, days of blood and bruising . . .

John turned the minute hand of the chubby alarm clock back, to give the workers an extra half-hour to get out. Stevie covered the doors. As John ran to get out Stevie dropped his gun and grabbed him in a bear hug, like a madman.

'For fuck's sake Stevie let me go. Let me go! This place is gonna go up! I've planted bombs. It's gonna go up, up, up! . . . '

'What's gonna go up? What's gonna go up?'

He awoke, handcuffed to a radiator — the rest room.

'Okay, back to the wall. Resume the posture! You'll talk. You'll talk!'

The doctor saw him twice more: 'Fit for interrogation!'

'Where's the guns? Where's the guns? Where's the guns?'

'Where's Donnelly? Where's Stevie Donnelly? Where is he?'

John sat at the top right hand corner of the ceiling, out of sight, impish, giggling, as they punched him in the ribs down below. Next, he was being rolled about on the ground. They were rubbing his neck, massaging his muscles, restoring his circulation. They lifted the hood up and he sipped some water through his parched lips. They gave him a piece of broken bread which almost choked him.

'Right. Resume the posture!'

Spread-eagled again. Legs kicked out. He tried to cheat by using his head to take the weight off his arms but they fired rounds of ammunition which forced him back on his fingers. He thought of his mother and she appeared before him and he felt happy. He did not feel like a person: he was either a mind or an aching, sore body: never the two together at the one time.

He felt like crying: he had just shit himself. It had been a painfully slow bowel movement and the little warm balls stuck between the cheeks of his buttocks. They gave off, he imagined, a thirty yard diameter of stink and reduced him to a baby. He was helpless.

'John? John?' It was a friendly, soothing voice. 'John, it's okay. The hooded treatment is over.'

His eyeballs returned to his head. His head, arms and legs returned to his torso from the distance to which they had been kicked. He listened hard. His eyes shot from side to side within the blackness of the hood.

'It's over, John. I'll take the hood off in a minute and tidy you up but I'll have to put it back on when you move back to Crumlin Road jail. These people don't want you to know where you are or to see their faces. Okay? Now, take it easy . . . '

It was a Belfast accent. He was worried that his mind was playing a trick on him. The RUC man's assurances made him even more afraid. The hood did come off and John stood trembling. He couldn't move his arms. His legs were locked cramped in the standing position.

'Come on. I'll help you. It's over. You have my word. I'll be travelling with you.'

John burst out crying as he shuffled barefoot down the corridor and into the toilets. His ankles were swollen and he had fluid in his knees. His friend shaved him, cleaned and wiped his backside. He rubbed and softly chopped at his arm and leg muscles. 'John you have to be photographed. Come with me. It won't take long.'

He was photographed in the nude and the cameraman appeared to be hundreds of yards away in the distance. He was taken back to the corridor. He couldn't talk but hung on to the one-who-had-shown-mercy. He held onto him when he thought he was leaving him.

'Look. It's okay. It's time to go. Trust me. Help me put on the hood. We'll do it together. That's it. Now, I have to handcuff you.

Then we'll get on board the helicopter. When it lands I'll remove the handcuffs and the hood but don't look back. You're going away from here, back to your mates. When you go to jail there'll be a tribunal. You're not a bad fellah, you know. After 30 days you'll be able to go to this tribunal and sign a form and you'll be out. If I ever meet you in the street would you buy me a drink?'

John spoke to him for the first time: 'I'll buy you all the drink you want . . .'

'We're going now.'

When the helicopter landed he said: 'Don't be looking back. Good luck,' and he pulled the hood off and pushed him out. The doors whooshed closed and other RUC men put him into the back of a landrover and then drove him to the jail.

He was brought into the basement of D Wing. The prison doctor weighed him. He had lost 16 lbs.

'What day is it, doctor?'

'It's Tuesday.'

'It couldn't be. I was here on Tuesday. It must be Thursday or Friday.

'No. It's Tuesday, Tuesday the 17th August.'

John shook his head in disbelief. He just shook his head.

# CHAPTER 10

# LONDON 11

When Angela left Belfast in August 1970 she went back to London in search of a new life. Her morale had struck rock bottom but she was fortunate to find work almost immediately and able enough to throw herself into it with absolute commitment and no distractions.

Even the other typists in the law firm of the partners Stevenson, Scott and Bevins had to admit to her conscientiousness. An agency had arranged the interview and Mr Bevins' supervisor took to Angela right away. The different jobs she had held down could have been interpreted as flightiness, but her references were impeccable and Miss Richards, despite a stern exterior, chose to see instead that the 21-year-old had a wealth of experience behind her. Her shorthand was excellent and she could speed type at 60 words per minute. But she did tactfully warn Angela that despite being with Mr Bevins for over twenty years she still found him cantankerous at times. 'Often', was the word she could have used, as Angela soon found out. When he and his wife had had an argument he would be in a foul mood. He would lock the door of his office and dictate swears and all onto the recording machine. Then he would simply slide back the glass window, hand out two hours of tapes without comment and later slide back the window expecting the letters to be typed up. If they were not finished by five he didn't scream or shout but coughed aloud and then simply sat on, loudly drumming his fingers on his desk whilst the girls typed away, doing overtime without pay.

Angela had been promised that her wages would be reviewed, depending on her efficiency, after three months. Time passed and when she had been there six months she spoke to Miss Richards. Miss Richards told her that Mr Bevins had personally to clear all increases in salaries for his girls with the exceptions of those in the typing pool who worked directly for Misters Stevenson or Scott.

'When shall I ask for a rise?' Angela had said to a colleague after three months.

'You'll not have to. He knows you're a good worker.'

It was now time to knock on his door.

'Mr Bevins, as you know I've been here for six months now and pay-wise I am still below some of the other girls who have less experience. The new girl who started last month, Maggie, is getting exactly the same as me. So I was just wondering . . . '

'Don't worry, Miss McCann,  I'll discuss it with colleagues and let you know.'

One week and then two weeks passed.

'Excuse me, Mr Bevins, but have you had any chance to discuss the matter of my pay with . . .'

'No, I haven't. But I'll organise it.'

A month passed and there was still no rise. She then heard that he had booked a fortnight's holiday for himself and his family at the end of the month. Angela grew increasingly irritated. One morning around this time she had difficulty rising due to the ache in her hip which still caused her pain four years after Jonathan struck her. She decided to go see a doctor for a further opinion. She was given the all-clear and arrived in work, still with the dull pain, at just after 11.

At the end of the following week when she examined her pay slip she noticed a shortfall. She thought it was a mistake and checked with the bookkeeper who told her she had been docked for being off.

'But I've never been off. Not once in six months!'

'Nothing to do with me. See Mr Bevins.'

'I will.'

'What are you coming in here for? Can't you see I'm trying to get away?' He threw his briefcase into a corner.

'Mr Bevins you have docked me for going to the doctor and you have been promising for weeks now to give me a pay rise. What about the extra hours I have worked? I even worked on a Saturday so as you could get your legal aid money. If that's all you think of me then you can keep your cheque . . .' She threw the cheque on the table and stormed out.

The whole office, including Mr Scott, heard the commotion. Angela began clearing her desk and packing her handbag. About a minute later Mr Bevins, slightly embarrassed, emerged from his office.

'Here. Take this cheque. It belongs to you.'

'I won't take it until you rectify it. Maybe you want me to hand in my notice. Is that it?' asked Angela, feeling sorry for herself.

'Don't be silly, girl. I'll sort out your increase when I return. Meanwhile, take your cheque.'

She stood stubbornly before him and he stared at her until his patience ran out.

'As from now we'll take it, Miss McCann, that you are on a month's notice! Now, if you'll excuse me!' He thumped the cheque on her desk and walked out.

'I'll not be seeing you again!' she shouted after him and whispered, 'you baldy bastard.'

Mike Scott came over to her.

'You'll be cutting your own throat if you leave. Come over to my office for a talk.'

He ordered two coffees and Angela explained what happened. Outside, the leaves on the trees were turning green to catch the bright, warm April sunlight.

'I know he's hard to work for. But don't commit yourself to leaving. I could do with someone extra. June is leaving to get married and is intending to become a proper housewife, which she will regret but that's her decision. Come and work for me . . .'

'Oh my God!'

'What? What is it?'

'He's written a new cheque. It must be for all the overtime. I'm skundered. What am I gonna do?'

'What did you say you were?'

'Skundered. It's a Belfast word for being embarrassed.'

'You certainly are skundered, especially since most of the office heard you referring to him as having no hair!'

They both laughed.

'Think about it,' he said. 'Think about coming to work for me.'

\*   \*   \*

'How long have you been married?'

'Ten years. But it's been stormy as I said to you before. Having no kids hasn't helped either.'

This was the third occasion in just as many weeks that overtime had detained them in the office together and that they had subsequently stopped for a drink, she having accepted his offer of a lift to her flat. She had only been working for him two months when he promoted her to his personal secretary. She had suddenly then found that she was in a position to buy clothes *and* save at the same time. Angela sipped at her drink, a dressed Pimms, and Mike ordered another brandy for himself. Their conversations had been slowly becoming more personal.

'What about you? Any steady boyfriends?'

'No. Not this long time. I'm working an evil past out of my system!' she laughed.

'I don't believe it,' he said.

'Well, I'm not joking.'

'Tell me please. I'm really interested.'

She scrutinised his face and saw a genuine expression of concern. 'Well, before I do,' she said, pinning him with a comically raised eyebrow to denote that if he should betray her he would suffer indescribable retribution. 'Before I do, promise me you're not a British soldier!'

'What!' he gasped, completely baffled but smiling and realising his privilege in hearing the cathartic confession of this strange woman.

She told him about school life under nuns, her wild teenage years in West Belfast. About her first lover, John. About living it rough in London, in the squat, on drugs. About the eruption of fighting in Belfast, her terror at being mistaken for a 'soldier-lover', her return to London. About taking a fancy to him shortly after starting in the firm. Whilst she included some of the details of her past flirting, she omitted to tell him of how she had publicly humiliated her first lover. At times his mouth fell open in a gape but at all times he sat attentive and fixed to his seat, fascinated. When she finished she said. 'Now what do you think of all that?'

'You've lived three times and you're only what is it? Twenty-three? Twenty-four?'

'Twenty-one! It wasn't that rough a life.'

'I'm sorry,' he said, anxious to assuage any offence he caused.

'It's all right!' she laughed, turning her empty glass around and looking at him.

'Waiter!' he called. 'Waiter!'

*   *   *

Angela came back home for a holiday in late July. Nothing was said by anyone she met why she had fled Belfast the previous August. For some days she had been trying to gently break the news to her mother and father that she was living with a married man. She confided in her sister Mary Ann but she just listened without commenting as if there was nothing that Angela could do that would surprise or appal her.

Frank's sister and her husband were visiting and he was boasting about the success of his daughter in England.

'Yes. She's doing very well for herself.' Angela smiled and passed the sandwiches. 'She's a private secretary and has moved into her own house and even has her own cheque book!'

Mary was very proud of her and Angela couldn't muster the courage to shatter the illusions her parents held after so many years of disappointments. But she had determined that her days of deceit were over and just as Mike and she had traumatically faced Vera, his wife, with the announcement of their love — even before they began an affair — she intended breaking the news to them by the time she was set to leave. The day approached and she decided to wait until the last possible moment so as to minimise the time available for tears and rancour.

'Mammy, I've something to tell you. Where's daddy, I want him to be present.'

'He'll be back in a second.' Her mother sat down slowly, perched on the edge of the sofa. She bit her lower lip, not liking the tone of seriousness injected into Angela's speech. 'I think you better tell me before you tell your father,' she said. She thought of the worst thing possible: 'Are you pregnant? Is that it, Angela?'

'No, mammy, I'm not expectin.'

'Thank God for that. What is it then? What's wrong?'

'Well actually I don't think anything's wrong. Not in my eyes . . .' Despite this being a sling-shot at prevailing moral prudery, as well as a hint of what she was getting at, she saw the cloud lift from her mother's face and a ray of relief beginning to show. Immediately she added: 'I'm sharing the house with someone.'

'So?'

'We're buying it together.'

'It's a man, isn't it. You're living with a man. My God, what's your father gonna say!'

'He's married . . .'

'Jesus, Mary and St Joseph that's all I need. That's all I need. How could you? We'll be the talk of Andersonstown.' Mary started to cry. Her son Paul wandered into the room, saw the tears, and quickly backed out. 'I am ashamed of you. You're nothing but a brazen hussey. You've brought me nothing but shame and trouble . . . Shame and trouble . . . What'll your granny think . . . ?'

'But mammy he loves me and I love him . . .'

'And what about his poor wife. Think of her or are you so full of yourself.'

Frank came into the room. 'What's all this then, eh?'

'Go on, tell your daddy what you told me. Go on, tell him.'

'I'm living with a fellah, daddy.'

'Well, you would be, wouldn't you, you selfish bitch.'

'That's not all Frank. Go on, tell him.'

'He's married daddy but he's getting divorced.'

'Fuck, I've heard it all. I've heard it all.' It was the first time he had ever used an expletive in front of his daughter, or inside the four walls of his house.

'Get.'

'What? What do you mean?'

'Get! Get going and don't come back.'

Angela was too stubborn to cry and went upstairs to pack. There, she made no attempt to rally Paul, Sean or Mary Ann to her side. She wasn't asking anybody to support her, nor was she going to be a cause of division. But what annoyed her was that whilst communications had now broken down between her and her parents for the foreseeable future they would lie on each occasion when someone asked after her and her circumstances. That fact of narrow-minded life hurt her.

The taxi pulled up at the door and sounded its horn. 'I'm going now,' she shouted into the sitting room. Paul grabbed her case from her and took it out to the car. 'Thanks,' she said. Mary Ann and Sean stood about the hall at sixes and sevens but still bid her goodbye. She kissed them both.

Paul opened the door of the vehicle. 'I'll see you big sister. Take care of yourself.'

'You too. Tell mammy and daddy I love them.'

'I'll do that okay. Time will sort it out, you'll see.'

* * *

The small house in south London which they shared was one of several properties owned by Mike's wealthy father: the others he had converted into flats and sold them off at handsome profits.

The firm had been handling the conveyancing when Mike had his marital crisis and as his father never got on with Vera and lost no sleep over the break up, he had no hesitation in selling him the house at a knock-down price.

Mike accepted that Angela's parents would eventually understand and come to terms with their relationship. He was concerned not just from the point of view of legitimising — though not formally, but in terms of attitudes — their arrangement. He also wanted, for Angela's sake, to at least de-criminalise it in the eyes of her parents in the same way as it was acceptable to many of his friends who frequented the house and socialised with them.

Angela enjoyed cooking for her partner and looking after him. She bought ties to match his shirts and in the office prioritised his interviews and supervised his workload. The other girls respected and liked her because she was loyal to them, arguing their interests and representing them in disputes. The only person who avoided her and kept contact to a minimum was her former employer, Mr Bevins. But Angela would ignore his taciturn attitude and would shout after him: 'Beautiful weather for September, Mr Bevins, don't you agree?!' He would huff and all the girls would laugh at his seriousness as the dumpy little man waddled down the corridor.

\*    \*    \*

Whilst Mike gently snored beside her she stared at him. He wasn't handsome, indeed was plain-faced and gangly-limbed. She thought of how redundant this choice had made all her previous criteria. How she used to take a fancy to men who had an attractive exterior and only later consider their personality. She stroked his black hair with its premature silver streaks and he awoke and smiled in the dawn light. 'Okay?'

'Yes, I'm okay,' she whispered, amazed at how content she was in this bland relationship.

\*    \*    \*

There was one girl in the office not prepared to keep the secret and that was because Angela had been especially friendly with her and had taken her out to lunch a few months before to discuss a personal problem she had. By the end of the week Angela had lent her money and told the girl to pay it back when she could afford it.

'Angela. This may hurt you but you should know. All the other girls have been talking about it and I don't think it's fair.'

'What are you talking about?'

'Mr Scott is seeing his wife again.'

'I know. He sees her occasionally. They're sorting out the divorce.'

'Angela, it's not like that at all. He was seen two or three times in the same bar and they were clearly intimate. I thought you should only know.'

\*   \*   \*

'Have you been seeing Vera again?'

'No! Who told you that?'

She gave him one of her 'let's be honest' looks and he went and poured himself a drink.

'Angela. I'm sorry. It's true I have seen her. She's been really hurt and upset since I left. I know you have given up everything for me, your home, family, you've accepted my friends and what can I say. You have been wonderful to live with, we've never argued and you're a great lover. I have been happy, really happy with you but I have never been able to overcome the guilt of leaving Vera . . .'

'Be honest with me Mike. Is it just guilt?'

'I think so,' he said. 'I feel so responsible for her. I was her first and only boyfriend and my leaving shattered her morale and prestige. I love you Angela, I really love you.'

They made love there and then on the rug, more passionately then ever before. They spent the next few days kissing and exchanging intimate glances at every opportunity but by the fourth day something inside both of them knew that the furtive activity was not a sure sign of eternal bliss but was really their relationship exploding and expending itself.

\*   \*   \*

Angela was annoyed and hurt but not shattered. It was ironical: Mike said, 'Vera and I have a lot to thank you for. In many ways you brought us back together and we have learnt many lessons.'

Even Vera had begun talking to her in friendly, sisterly terms.

'You know I can no longer work for you Mike,' said Angela, a few days before he removed his clothes and belongings.

'I've thought about that. I've sorted things out. Here,' he handed her papers.

'What are these?'

'The deeds of the house. It's yours. Stop! Don't say it. I know what you're thinking and it's not like that at all and you'll only be belittling yourself if you say it. You deserve it. You've had nothing but hardship. And anyway you have no choice. Mr Bevins handled the small print and it's yours to knock down or sell. What will you do? Will you stay here? It has its memories.'

'Oh, I don't know. Life's a bit of a challenge. I've been homesick a lot recently. My friend Patricia from Belfast will be staying with me for a few weeks. I've a lot of thinking to do. In fact, I've to sort out my life. Don't feel guilty, Mike. We had a good time. A short time mind you! But a good time.'

'I'll never forget you Angela. You're a great girl. Kind and understanding . . .'

'Shut up! Or you'll have me crying over this girl whom I've never met!'

# CHAPTER 11

# AMBUSH

Stevie arrived at the house first; he was always prompt. The others followed singly, through the back door, down the steps, through the small kitchen and tiny living room and up the stairs where they stunk out the back bedroom with the constant smoking of cigarettes which steadied their nerves.

This call-house was new: a young husband and wife with Republican sympathies had become active supporters about nine months before, converted by the violent excesses of the British after the introduction of internment. There had been many such converts, and even more following the shooting dead of thirteen civil rights' marchers in Derry the previous January on a day soon known as Bloody Sunday. With quite a number of houses at their disposal, the unit changed call-houses every day, picking up the address from a trustworthy local shopkeeper. Those Volunteers on-the-run usually moved into the call-house during the early morning rush to school. Other good times for moving were at lunch-time and between half-three and half-five in the afternoons when the streets were busy again. Now, with the onset of school holidays, street routine had changed and moving about between operations could be as nerve-racking as actual active service.

Some Companies — those which were surviving the high rate of attrition through a mixture of shrewdness, recruitment and luck — were actually using two or three call-houses together.

In one a float could be in planning. On a float Volunteers in a car with one or two weapons would drive around — or 'float about' — until they found a British army target. Youths acting as scouts could be posted at street corners but often accidentally alerted the soldiers that something was afoot. It could be more dangerous than a set snipe in which an occupied house was usually commandeered and the Volunteers patiently waited for a patrol to turn up. But at least on a float they were always active and the operation — their day's work — could be over and done with inside an hour.

169

Stevie, the Volunteers knew from loose talk, had actually gone out on floats by himself, without transport, and had once opened fire on two foot patrols using an AR 15 — an armalite with a folding butt — which he had hidden inside a Marks and Spencer's carrier bag.

In another house a bombing might be planned. In another the officer commanding the Company and his staff might be based. Co-ordination with other battalion units was vital as often three, four or five bombing units were going in and out of the city centre and criss-crossing each other. Where bombs were not planted in physical take-overs of premises but were left in car bombs or smuggled into shops, warnings had to be arranged.

Houses and local support — a base — were absolutely crucial to the continuation of the armed struggle. Some sympathisers were prepared to billet Volunteers, others would allow their homes to be used for meetings but not as a jump-off or run-back point for operations. Other supporters — the ones who commanded the greatest respect of the Volunteers — were prepared to hold weapons and explosives.

Contacts in the areas passed on the names of potential supporters who were then delicately approached and sounded out to see what use they could be put to — the demand for dumps always being the most pressing. As layer upon layer of support was built up, an extensive network came into existence; sympathetic houses, car owners, people in employment who passed on intelligence. The people became the eyes and ears of this people's army and the word 'sound' when used to describe a supporter or another Volunteer took on a meaning more significant than the usual definition of reliable. Sound people could be absolutely depended on if the IRA was stuck; could be depended upon to give an objective opinion, to be truthful; could be depended upon if a Volunteer was in a tight corner.

'Joe, open that bloody window, the smoke in here would kill you,' said Stevie as he fanned his face.

There was a knock at the door. It was opened to the woman of the house who left in a tray of buttered baps and mugs of tea. The baby's room had recently been decorated and carpeted. It had a Magic Roundabout lamp shade hanging from the ceiling and curtains patterned with scenes from a zoo. The clinical, spartan smell of fresh paint was being coated in cloying, stale nicotine fumes.

'Do you want an ash tray?' she asked, a little bit anxious.

'My apologies for these men,' Stevie replied. 'They should be put out in the yard!'

She smiled back, acknowledging the concern. Her husband and herself had a fastidious and proud attitude to their small home but she self-consciously mellowed when she thought about these lads and what they were facing. She returned shortly afterwards with ash trays.

'By the way, I'm making a fry for Eddie later if any of you would like one. He's to go to work at two, he's on a shift.'

'I'd love a fry,' Stevie said. 'I'm starvin'.' He munched at his second bap.

When she left, Patsy let his envy be known.

'How the hell could you eat a fry? I'm having trouble keeping down this tea.' He had also been to the toilet twice and would be making more visits before the operation, though once they moved out and were actually on the go his equanimity would return. He knew this from his first three operations: throwing two nail bombs at soldiers on patrols and then driving on his first float.

'Not only could I eat a fry, ma boy, but I could eat yours as well,' answered Stevie hungrily. 'Anyway, down to biz.'

'I've cleared a float with the double-O,' he said, using IRA argot for Operations Officer. 'If we don't "touch" we have to wrap up before half-three.'

He made no reference to the explanation for the time limit but Joe knew that a car-load of explosives was due in the Falls around tea-time. Other Volunteers had been detailed to empty the door panels of the nitro-benzine mix and to dump it in sealed plastic bins under man-hole covers in a particular entry. The electric detonators gave off no tell-tale smell and were easily kept hidden in a house.

'Joe, I'll be on foot and youse float behind me. I'll stay around the front of the road; we'll "touch" quicker there. Tell Geraldine to take the thirty-eight and for her and Liam to take a car at the zebra crossing. They're over in McDonough's but they need to get another house to hold the driver. Hold his licence just in case he's an Orangeman and bolts. Tell Geraldine not to be hijacking any women — they'll only scream and things'll be fucked up.'

Stevie pulled out various articles from the parcel he had asked Joe to bring.

'Whadda you think of this?'

They all burst out laughing. He had pulled on an old cardigan and put on glasses with round metal frames which gave him a silly appearance. From beneath the bed he produced a borrowed pair of hedge-clippers. Finally, he dipped his comb in the tea and within seconds stood his hair on end.

They admired the lengths to which he went. Some of the Volunteers experienced a thrill, unmasked, undisguised, running through the streets, armed. The Brits don't wear masks, so why should fucking we, pride would foolishly dictate, as they left it to fate that 'dead' soldiers would never be able to ID them.

*   *   *

*I see the patrol and I smile to myself. They haven't been shot at in two weeks and they have relaxed. They have probably believed the bloody know-all intelligence officer in the barracks who put Gerry, Peter and Sean away in Long Kesh and thinks he has cleared out the unit. The second foot-patrol — their minds split between their profession and their home — is about five hundred yards behind, too far to be of tactical use in our maze of streets.*

*'Joe, get the gear. Tell Patsy to put the car beside Murray's house, facing up the street. We'll get them from the corner against the hoardings.'*

*They stop outside the post office, the Englishmen, Scotsmen, Welshmen, the uniforms, I don't give a damn. One detains a woman shopper and rummages through her bag. I can make out her protesting, giving off, and, like a cat baring its fangs, some gland flushes a vengeance through me that tautens every muscle and sinew.*

*The radio-man stops a young lad. I can almost hear that jarring British accent ordering him to put his arms up higher and get them legs out. He's feeling his jeans, frisking the body of the frightened kid.*

*Oh, I'm in control okay. I run my finger along cold steel. I stroke the smooth wood. Here they come, their sight of me bordering between curiousity and fear until I raise both hands and, with a clip, level the last section of the hedge. Like coagulating blood the juices rush to the white wounds. And the soldiers relax. I whistle The Rifles of the IRA, so cheekily, so contemptuous of their ignorance, with so much daring, almost challenging them, that it excites me and I am pleased with the aura of deception I have carefully fostered.*

Don't say I didn't warn you.

*Here they come. They don't see me even though they are looking directly at me. I look so happy and serene and domestic, standing with my hedge-clippers now tucked under the arm of my woolly cardigan.* Greenfingers is hardly going to cut our heads off! No self-respecting English youth would be seen dead wearing that polka-dot shirt, fastened by that kite-sized tie! *And because I am a twenty-year-old gawk, and bespectacled (with clear glass), and because this is a strange land, because this is Ireland, I know they shrug me off. Innocence oozes out of me. The leader of the patrol does not mentally mark me down to be p-checked. He comes up to me, me with the clownish grin, specky four-eyes, and I use our exchange of glances to impart a duplicitous trust and friendship. I have that brotherly respect for both of us that opposing combatants share in war, but I cannot confide in him in the way that his battle fatigues mark him out for me. Fraternisation, communication, pity, restraint, humour, is always their gift, depending on their mood, depending on what side of the bed they crawled out. Favourable responses, replies, repartee, and their eyes sparkle as if they've just seen light at the end of the tunnel. But these are never sentimental exchanges across no man's land. There's no football at the Christmas front. The Brits remain implacable and we cling to our cunning.*

*As he now passes me, me whom he'll never see again, I turn into the side-street of my youth and run across a few feet of cobblestones before the tarmac takes over. From here I can almost touch the house I was born in and the entry where standing in darkness we fumbled at first making love.*

*I stop my mind and note that in these few seconds of running, a thousand reflections, experiences, mixed feelings and considerations, and a few specks of golden wisdom panned over twenty years of my life, have gushed through my muddy consciousness.*

*I move as natural as this sunny afternoon's light breeze across the Falls Road, an imperceptible shift of air that would hardly tickle a fly. I am honed for the delivery of this stroke like the finely pointed lead of a sharpened charcoal pencil between the fingers of an artist. I am immortal: I shall see tomorrow. This will be that corporal's last day.*

*I think of this man. He is somebody's son, perhaps a good man, maybe even a loving husband. We both speak the same language, could have stolen the same bars of chocolate from the corner shop, told the same juvenile jokes to our mates, and sheltered from the same storms as they fell a few hours apart on our lands. I came up on the same music and television as he did, the Beatles and Coronation Street. But the British public — his ma and da, their governments — didn't even know we existed and cared nothing. When I pieced things together for myself, when I listened and watched, I understood it all — the police batons, the house-burnings, and then my decision to fight back. Sitting with the patience of a prophecy was my Irishness, waiting to be tapped and to explode.*

He probably doesn't even want to be here.

*Already I can hear the familiar sermon echoing all the comparisons and lecturing me, the killer. I can see those comparisons myself right down to our mutual likes and dislikes in food, Granny Smith's apples, flowing butter on warm white bread, plenty of salt and vinegar on the fish and chips.*

*We may even have supported the same team for the FA Cup.*

He probably doesn't even want to be here.

*Everything can conspire to scream at you, to weaken your resolve. Everything I've been taught, from the words of my mother, to my schooling, my religious teachings, my own beliefs, were all part of a moral system whose effects are to cripple this action and deter me. Then there is the smug power of the status quo and the awesomeness of existing authority.*

*My own body's bowels could burst as a signal of cowardice, a warning of the danger, a call to self-preservation. A twinge of conscience, yesterday's bloodshed, can become a black nightmare. (I have seen that in comrades who fell away 'because of the wife', because they found an ideological difference or used personality clashes as a pretext. In others it was the ghosts who broke their health or minds, or they had a flawed commitment to begin with.)*

He probably doesn't even want to be here, but he is!

*And that's my edge over him, over all their arguments. That's why I have blood like oil lubricating my calves and thighs, my buoyant steps, which take me through these close streets and into Murray's street, ahead of the Brits.*

*He has no right to be here and if he doesn't want to be here then he shouldn't be here. He can kid himself, and may well have done so, but when all is said and done here he comes, sauntering up my road with his gun in his hand, doling out his mood to pedestrians, ever nosey and curious, ever the law, on top, dashing for his survival across open spaces because he knows we don't want him. He would just as quickly rob me of breath if ordered or if the fancy took him. But I am just too smart for the poor bugger. Governments may have us, the foot soldiers, at each other's throats but I am a soldier and a general, a politician and a* civilian. *I am my own government, but without him there is no government, no British rule.*

*I am not claiming the certainty of God's blessing for my actions. I am not that conceited. I believe in a God. I see the beauty of God's creation all around me, especially in this man with the clean face and short hair who'll never shave again, in the red roses over there bathing in the floating warm air, in this demonstration of power and fate unfolding and the tragedy of trapped people. My conscience reminded — not beset — by the occasional doubt is also a remarkable process which keeps me right. I entertain doubts precisely because they strengthen my single-mindedness, my convictions. The fact that I am doing this in spite of myself, against the grain, against my nature, and not because they ever killed anyone belonging to me but because I have rationalised this confrontation and carry it out on behalf of others, proves that it isn't personal revenge. I take up a gun for every arthritic Irish man who fucks the English up and down (and not really the English but these Brits and their system). I am here on behalf of all those too weak to retaliate or who lack the stomach for violence or lack the courage to risk their own lives.*

*I am the history maker. This is my power, this is my cause, and behind me lie centuries and  centuries and a thousand lands where similar foreign fuckers with rifles or bayonets, not ever wanting to be here or there, were around just the same, doing their missionary work, civilising us natives, maintaining their peace.*

*Oh, they have their doings well sewn-up, well wrapped in a law and a morality whose smartness only the likes of me can really smile at and appreciate, because I am an arsonist with their property and institutions and I know the thief below the bow and wrapping paper.*

*Yes, the God thing and thou shalt not kill. It's even harder for us. The Brits were suckled on superciliousness, on empire building, that others were Coons and Paddies and bloody Kaffirs.*

*The pulpits say I'm for hell! We were reared to conform, not to kick, so it doesn't come easy to copy the killers and kill and even-up history a bit. I'll even stretch my imagination and allow that a Brit can be a relatively innocent being. So I snuff out an innocent life and — bingo — he goes straight to heaven. I've done him a favour, before he committed any serious transgressions and sentenced himself to eternal damnation. On the other hand, if he's a bastard and was heading for hell anyway the most I've done is put him there prematurely. So where's the sin?*

*I'm being silly.*

*I'm not as callous as this and there's always, always, always, a psychological unease, a sense of violation and wrong, about killing this* man, or the other three soldiers I shot and blew up. *Experiences and intellect, the slide into violence, eliminate the compunctions and Time absorbs the inhumanity. If I go to hell for this, I'll go to hell. My soul will burn eternally not for something I did only for myself but for what I did for others. And God's not up to much, if he'd burn anyone forever and ever. Imagine having those screams on your conscience!*

I pass the garden shears back to one of our supporters, an old man who sits on a chair at his front door reading the Irish News.

'Good luck and be careful,' he says solemnly.

'The Gardens are clear,' Joe shouts to me. 'So is the Drive and the Road.' Wearing gloves he opens the boot of the Cortina.

'Wait a minute,' I order. He snaps it shut. I walk out to the corner for a last look. *I am on stage. The cobalt blue sky, the blazing sun focus on me, the main character, me with the magic fore-finger, fate-maker, sorter-out of British soldiers come to do you harm.*

'Quickly, they've stopped some fellahs again.' But as I turn I see two armoured cars come down the Falls Road.

'Wait!'

They whine. They trundle past, beeping their hooters to their friends who wave back. The air is pungent with the foreign smell of their exhaust fumes. *It all becomes so real, so critical, so deliberate.*

My comrade opens the boot again. I put on my gloves, place the silly spectacles in a side pocket of my corduroy trousers, pull on a cap, and lift the Garand rifle which I prepared myself earlier. Patsy, our driver, turns over the engine and I note his nervousness. Joe takes up a position with an Armalite to cover my back. The area is not too busy. Traffic is light. Two big lusty mongrels bare their teeth and slabber at each other as they canter after a blonde little poodle whose self-importance rises with each sniff and growl from the competitors.

I peep around the corner. *We used to sit here when school was over and play cards and whistle after the girls from St Louise's — the 'brown bombers' we called them. Little did we know the use of corners.*

Mr Corporal is just about one hundred yards from me, down on his hunkers, finishing the frisking of a young lad. A colleague holds his weapon. Another soldier leaning over a wall and pointing his SLR directly at me, concerns me, but I am gone from sight and I have made him doubtful I think by the time, a few seconds later, when I re-appear with my raised rifle, the butt resting comfortably into my shoulder, into my spine, down to my firm feet, like it's a part of me.

And it is now that I make my thunderous finale. The corporal's back collapses inwards under the severe punch from a bolt of lightning lead *but I too feel an unusual recoil as the top furniture of my rifle is splintered by the shots returned from the alert marksman.*

*We turn and run, Joe firing a burst into the air which keeps the Brits pinned down under fake fire. It's a good excuse for some of the yellow bastards to stay put. A woman has fainted but some kids start cheering and clapping our performance. The weapons are thrown into the boot and my two comrades, as arranged, drive off; Joe to hand over the weapons to the quartermaster; Patsy to dump the hijacked car in the Kashmir district where Volunteers from another unit are waiting to use it as a lure in an ambush. I run into side streets, air streaming across my brow, blowing through my hair, curving my body. I run up an entry where a stout woman, her grey curls loosely pinned around a falling bun, is brushing some rubbish from her back door. 'Jesus Christ, what was that son?'*

*'I don't know missus, but I think somebody opened up on the Brits.'*

*She blesses herself and rolls her eyes. I cross into another entry and push open a back door. My clothes I put into the washing-machine. I switch on the thermostat, though the water is still warm, and turn on the motor of the twin-tub. I like this house because it also has a shower.*

*As I climb into its spray I can hear the engines of armoured personnel carriers, of landrovers.*

*They don't even know where to begin.*

*Pellets of water pummel my face.*

*I hear on the news that the corporal is dead, that he was married with two children, aged four and one. I clench my teeth and swallow hard and I will often think of this man.*

*I curse the life that has brought me to this; then I focus in on the British government. I think of the corporal who might have hated his job, who might have been buying himself out of the army.*

*I'll live for him and in some sort of communion with him.*

*One thing is for sure.*

*I'll think about him more often than his commanding officer.*

*I'll maybe even be still thinking about him when his widow has stopped.*

*Who knows?*

# CHAPTER 12

## SOMEONE AT THE DOOR

A battered, blue mini-van, which Catherine did not recognise, arrived outside her house and Peter got out from the passenger side. Hair unkempt, he was furtive, odd looking, as if he was a six-year-old creeping to the biscuit tin in the middle of the night or a gun-runner. No, he definitely wasn't a gun-runner. One IRA man in the family was enough, she thought.

'Is she about?' he said.

'Is who about? What are you talking about? Have you been drinking?'

'Sheila. Who do you think! I've got a present for her but I don't want her to see it.'

'She's out somewhere. What did you get her?'

But he was away, out rapping the driver's window and Catherine saw Anthony Stewart and his cap appear.

'Hiya Catherine. Not a bad day.'

Men never failed to amaze her. This was an occasional, just an occasional, drinking companion of her husband's. Years ago Peter had been labouring on new housing sites in and around Newtownards, work which had actually lasted almost a year, and when extra labourers were needed he got Anthony started. She couldn't recall where they knew each other from — probably some betting shop — though she had a vague recollection that like Peter he had attended Slate Street primary school but had been in a different class. It was difficult to keep track when at least two dozen people and several old teachers had been pointed out to her over twenty-five years, some perhaps ten or twelve times, as 'having been in my class' or 'he was a real, wicked bastard.' Case-hardened by such reminiscences, the next two dozen schoolyard acquaintances thrown her and her husband's way through weddings, and, as they got older, increasingly through funerals, hardly commanded her riveted attention. To her the owners of the bald heads, the paunches, the shining suits, never looked qualified to have once been young-faced. To her husband they hadn't changed a bit.

God only knows where he found Stewart, she thought.

Anthony opened the back of the van into which he disappeared and Peter spat into the palm of one hand and then the other, as if sparring for a fight. A bag of cement had to be removed and placed on the footpath to allow a comfortable negotiation. Catherine's first thought was to raise objections to 'that heirloom' coming into the house, but the dusty, dirty object, which resembled a small upright piano, held a certain fascination and Peter was exuberant, even though he was puffing as they carried the desk — he called it a Davenport — through the house and out the back into the yard. She could see by his monosyllabic responses to Anthony's drawling questions about the whereabouts of old acquaintances which Anthony then went on to answer himself, that Peter was growing impatient. He was even more agitated when Anthony stayed for a cup of tea. She knew Peter was anxious for his old friend to disappear and so she indirectly teased him.

'Now which one was Nipper Henderson?' she asked the visitor who munched at his fourth biscuit, driving her husband to distraction.

When Anthony eventually left, his van had hardly turned the corner of the next street before Peter had removed a hinge and with three screws attached to his lips repeated to his somewhat ashamed wife that 'the heirloom' was an old, but solid desk, and was meant for a present for Sheila. On the previous Saturday her O-Level examination results had arrived through the post. She had passed in all her subjects, with distinctions in English, French and Geography, and though she had been restless all summer her mother and father wanted to encourage her to go back to school, just as Jimmy had done, to take her A-Levels. She had agreed to this, uplifted no doubt, by her results.

By dinner-time he had sanded down the drawers and left the hinges and other metal strips and plates to soak in some stripping fluid overnight. Before hiding the parts underneath old sacking he realised that surgery was required to a large portion of gangrenous panelling at the back.

'Where's Jimmy?' he asked. 'I need him to go to McDonnell's wood yard.'

'Don't you remember, he and Mary Ann are away up to the Kesh to see John.' Peter tutted and headed off on the errand himself.

The next morning after Sheila left to go down town with some friends, Peter was once again covered in sawdust.

Through the kitchen window Catherine watched him. Like a craftsman he used a small chisel on one or two knots for about half-an-hour. She came out to the yard and handed him a cup of tea.

'Ah, that's great!' he said. 'Thank you. Well?'

'It looks nothin' now but I'm lookin' forward to seeing it finished.'

'I must say woman, you're looking well today!'

'Catch you yourself on!' Catherine looked up to the sky, ignoring the compliment. She continued: 'Have you seen our Sheila's boyfriend? He looks far too old for her . . . God, in our day your mother would have killed you if you held a fellah's hand.'

'Ho! Listen to you. The cow forgets she was a calf! Come here and give's a kiss . . . '

She started to smile: 'Leave off. Anyway, Jimmy's come in. He stayed in Micky Conlon's last night. He's upstairs in his bedroom. Probably heard every word you've said! He's going out again if there's anything you want him to get.'

'No. I'm okay. Right, break's over. Back to work.'

For four hours Peter worked unremittingly, grinding the remaining surfaces to a glass finish with first rough, then smooth, sandpaper. He shook himself down and cleared up the shavings, brushed the sawdust into a shovel, and stared at the sky. The afternoon was dull, the air cool and still, but he imagined the yard was teeming with small flies, and although few houses had their fires lit he swore that atoms of soot were falling so slowly as to deceive the eye. He ran a damp cloth, free from detergent, over the wood which he, with his own hands, had meticulously brought to light: as it dried he scratched his head as if that would help him decide whether to stay put or make room indoors for the varnishing of the desk. He spotted Catherine who was washing fish at the sink and asked for her advice. She said she would prefer if he used the yard. She watched him thinning down scumble oil in a jar and with a little brush and a little love he accentuated the contours of the grain before giving a depth of contrast to the lines of nature.

There was a song on the radio in the living room and Catherine found herself day-dreaming. These glimpses of the past were immensely satisfying, especially since the predominant present tended to be full of troubles and disappointments. She enjoyed this harmless activity which was almost always provoked by music. Standing hanging clothes on the line, or at the washing machine the familiar airs of an old number from the 1940s came from the loudspeaker. If she concentrated really hard, her mind, with a trick, would suddenly roll over on itself and for an instant she would experience the past with a rush of pleasure. These feasts lasted only a split second each but they were all the richer because of having tasted the same fruit, the innocent passion, the good times, a second time around. Sometimes she would even cry for the past or for lost youth, then she would chastise herself and think of Peter, think of the kids, and think of Jimmy. She thought of her seventeen-year-old son, her favourite child, though she felt ashamed to admit it. She knew that God saw into her mind, and saw this intense love which she swore didn't diminish her affections for the others.

The varnishing over, she watched as Peter surveyed from all angles the body of the desk, and lying separately, the top which had to be once again attached to the hinges, and the drawers. He smiled at her.

'What do you think?'

'It's lovely. Beautiful. She'll be very pleased . . . There's someone at the door. Could you get it, my hands are wet.'

Yes, he thought to himself, slightly grumpy because he was tired. And mine are covered in varnish, but I'll go anyway.

\* \* \*

They were there but neither of them could believe it. Jimmy's mouth was in a snarl such as one sees on the face of a dead dog whose guts have been scattered by a passing car. Tubes were in his mouth, wires were running from his bare chest. His tiny nipples sat like small buttons on his hairless chest. He had never shaved. His left eye was black, his head was scored and scratched. From the colour of his body the blood in his veins had given up. But he was alive. There was a faint pulse. A doctor came every five minutes. The priest had been. At the bedside vigil Catherine and Peter sat, accompanied alternately by Raymond, Sheila or Monica, and occasionally by one of Jimmy's grandparents.

The dinner had been abandoned, the desk left in the rain which had suddenly started after six. Sheila had heard about a shooting when she was coming up the road and then she was stopped by a neighbour and she knew by his tone that something was wrong. She was in tears in the corridor outside and threw her arms around Mary Ann when she came running through the casualty entrance.

Peter took his wife towards the lavatory. She gripped his arm. She was cried-dry. Her husband was almost insensate. The smell of chloroform created a small, concentrated terror at the back of his mind. He could observe nothing around him and simply kept praying for his son to live, to survive this calamity, to come out of it. He thought of his own faults and moodiness, how only yesterday he had been short tempered when he couldn't find him, and he cried out loud and bit his fingers to suppress a total breakdown. Catherine came out of the toilet a few minutes later, her cardigan unbuttoned. She was ashen-faced and stern.

'We've lost him Peter!' she screamed. 'I felt him go!'

They ran into the ward. Mary Ann was stretched over her boyfriend's body, placing a farewell kiss on his cheek and wiping her tears from his face. Other relatives had formed a group at the bottom of the bed and were sobbing. The doctors expressed their sorrow.

*   *   *

In the corridor their huddled group moved with the slowness of refugees in shock and had the look of a funeral cortege. Catherine stopped.

'Oh Peter — ah Jesus! . . . He was the most beautiful soul I ever knew,' and her husband understood what she was saying. He began blubbering uncontrollably and his head felt as if it had been smashed open like the shell of an egg and his scrambled senses were flying in every direction, off the walls, onto the floor. Wave after wave of Jimmy's image flooded through his mind, the smiling face, his humour and youthful innocence. A wave of guilt overpowered his senses and all he could think about were the things he had denied his son or the times when he punished him as a child. The acoustics of their small house was such that every little noise from above was amplified through the floor boards. When the kids were younger and diving in and out of each others' beds he shouted to them to keep quiet. When they continued he would race upstairs to chastise them. He would tell them to shut up but Jimmy would continue to giggle. He would hit him and warn him that if he found it funny he'd get hit again. Jimmy would snigger and he'd hit him again and he'd giggle again with that infectious laugh of his until Peter could maintain his seriousness no longer and would burst out laughing and they would all give each other 'a huggle', which was their description for a cross between a hug and a cuddle.

The couple stood clutching each other, sobbing violently, squeezing hard the reality of their being which only emphasised his passing. Catherine knew that part of her soul, not just her own flesh and blood, had been wrenched from her by something diabolical. Of the five children she had carried inside her there had been a special, glowing feeling during his pregnancy. She recalled excitedly waking up her husband when life was first felt. For him the novelty appeared to soon wear off and sleep became a preference over this entertainment. She was tickled and fascinated at the shape of his tiny knuckles and heels knocking on the wall of her womb or punching it. Some of her others had almost put their feet through her kidneys and had her constantly running to the toilet with the pressure on her bladder. When John had stretched so hard she felt as if his feet would come out her mouth! But Jimmy had been playing a game with her and moved about as if for her comfort. If she talked to her navel he was listening. Are you quite finished, she would ask. I'm tired. She swore she felt a sign and then he would retire to peaceful repose. He had helped her decide upon dinners or to make up her mind on a whole range of matters. Undoubtedly, as a child, a boy, and a young man, he had got up to much mischief, but nothing evil, she knew. And despite her possessiveness, she was happy when he was happy, and wasn't the slightest bit jealous when he looked into the eyes of girls his own age or when he brought Mary Ann into their home.

She knew there would be no recovery for her from this crime committed by someone against her son and her family. Life would go on, but every hour of every day she would cherish his picture in her mind and would drive back the brimming tears, hemmed in by sheer composure. Oh the treadmill would go on okay, but life was . . . She became hysterical, tore lumps of hair from her temples and was overpowered by a madness, into the depths of which her mind desperately ran, seeking to reverse time, hoping to find sanity, hoping to awaken from the nightmare.

She violently punched her husband in a spurt of an attack, and, before her eyes rolled in their sockets, her body crumpled to the ground in a fit. With a ferocity beyond her normal capability she flung off those who bent down to her aid and kept shrieking, 'No, No, No! It's not true! It's not true! Jesusssss! Jesus! It's not true!'

Peter was distraught: his own facial muscles were locked into a twisted expression which aged him, putting on years in minutes. He hugged her. He begged her. He lied to her. He kept saying, it's okay, it's okay, as she sat on the floor, upright like a toddler, her fists flaying. Eventually they restrained her and a doctor gave her an injection which sedated her.

She woke up, drugged, lying on her own bed, hating everything, every person, the wrinkled face of her mother before her, the ugly, masculine hairs from a hive on her mother's chin which had never bothered her before, the hand with its bony, transparent skin stroking hers, their wedding rings rubbing, the useless gold. This attention and the wails of her other sons and daughters were of no comfort. What right had they to cry? They who stole his sweets, pushed him around. They never loved him the way she did, had. A convulsion, like a shadow, darkened her and made her shiver. If they want to help me, she thought, then make Jimmy walk through the door.

Suddenly, she leaped out of bed in a panic and ran downstairs, past her family who were confused and on edge. She went straight to the bathroom and desperately pulled at the soiled clothes in the laundry basket, scattering them over the floor.

'Oh no! No!' she cried. Then she found the shirt Jimmy had worn yesterday. She pressed the fabric against her lips and nostrils and breathed through it, getting some relief from the attack that seized her. She wrapped up the shirt in a cellophane bag and went back upstairs, saying nothing, and locked it in a wardrobe before returning to bed

Then she began crying and grabbed her mother in an embrace, begging for some solace, for some respite from the black, unending chasm inside her.

'Oh mammy, mammy, mammy; why, why, why?'

'Come on Catherine,' sobbed Mrs Stewart as she sniffled back a rheumy nose, which was sore and flaked at the nostrils from constant blowing. 'Let's say a prayer.'

\*   \*   \*

John applied for parole and was permitted four hours, unaccompanied. It was accepted that Republicans kept their word and honoured parole: besides, if the convention was abused it was comrades in similar circumstances who would be penalised. John returned to the jail in a deep depression. When he was still walking around the perimeter of the Cage, fifteen minutes after the time for lock-up had been repeatedly called, the other internees knew it was best to leave him alone and even the warders had made no attempt to approach him.

It was Fitzy, his cage O/C who came over to him and told him he would have to go in. He sharply withdrew his shoulder from the friendly hand, turned on his heels and stomped into the hut where he sat on the edge of his bed. Attempts were made by some of the others to break the silence or involve him in some distracting conversation but he sat impassive. Then he suddenly apologised and several men crowded around him for comfort, gave him a mug of tea and started a game of cards.

The therapy lifted him out of his despondency but only for a short time.

In bed, when the lights were out, he cried into his pillow and his head became sore through repeated bombardment with the same thoughts of his brother, whose life paraded before his closed eyes. Schooldays, holidays, Christmases. What they were doing together — pulling crackers, fighting with the girls, swimming. Their re-unions when he would return from sea.

At certain points he would just burst into tears thinking about his naive young brother, and now his broken-hearted mother and father. There were times when, even though the sense of loss still prevailed, he seemed to be drifting into a light sleep but the words 'he's dead' would travel slickly like a hormone from his head to his heart triggering off thudding palpitations.

At about six in the morning, before the warders unlocked the creaking doors, he rose and dressed and sat with his head in his hands.

Not only was his sleep affected but his appetite was also a victim of his morbidness. He would feel hungry, would sit down to some potatoes, meat and gravy, which was, despite being reconstituted from a food parcel, more appetising than prison fare. He would have two spoonfuls and would then rush off to the toilet and be sick. He knew he had to pull himself together and he knew that were it someone else in mourning in similar circumstances he would be extravagant with advice and remedies. But that approach, he could see now, bore absolutely no relation to the reality of such grief.

On the Tuesday he had a traumatic visit with his parents and Monica. He sat next to his mother. His sister across the table fidgeted in the plastic chair, and the three of them held hands. There were more tears and his father, his old, greying father, swayed in agitation, the thick fingers of his joined hands dancing with nerves.

John had several other visits with his family over the next few weeks. Each member was slowly coming to terms with the death. Nobody mentioned to him the arguments in the house, the cruel words slung at each other — the furious rows which would lead to Peter walking out, slamming the door and coming in drunk in the early hours. Or Peter's attempts on other occasions to meet Catherine three-quarters of the way, only for her to lie on the sofa, suffocating the atmosphere. Or her refusal to come out of the gloom, to communicate with any of them. Her days on end lying in bed.

Things eased, but very slowly. Sheila never went back to school again. Peter moderated his drinking. Catherine went shopping and made sense in conversation but when she walked home, heavily burdened by the lightest of messages, she would look up to the sky and for her the clouds would form his face and she would say, I love you Jimmy, I love you. This deal with life, this arrangement, kept her sane and gave her time to put meaning into her existence. He was always there.

Memories long since forgotten kept surfacing.

She recalled her fortieth birthday when Peter and even her own mother had forgotten to send her a card and she felt a bit neglected. It was the afternoon before her husband discovered the reason for her sullenness. He apologised and said he would go and get her a card immediately, and a cake, and flowers, but belated patronage was no use to her and she shouted at him and then burst out crying. The kids cleared out and then Peter stormed out, muttering that he would never understand women.

Half-an-hour later she was peeling potatoes when Jimmy came in, his face beaming, hands behind his back as he circumnavigated the furniture rather than turn. Suddenly he declared, 'De Daaaaa!' and produced a birthday card — signed in his child's scrawl — which he had bought from the rewards of several errands he had solicited from neighbours. When she saw the five big Xs she burst out crying again and hugged him and when she saw he was confused she laughed to assuage his perplexity.

Then she remembered the cat.

One day she had answered the door to find Jimmy and his pals extremely agitated. Her son placed a kitten on the ground. It was too well-groomed to be a stray but from its mournful miaows it was clearly in agony. Jimmy was visibly upset.

'Mammy, mammy, mammy. A big dog bit the wee cat and it's crying. Can you help it?'

'By the looks of it it's dying,' she said as she bent down to examine the suffering creature. Its legs were stiffening and a stream of urine emerged from its back fur. Then it died.

Jimmy began crying, even in front of his friends, and she held him close to her.

'Ach son, come on now, it's better dead and was suffering too much. Don't be crying. What's wrong?'

'Theresa the cat's died on me.' He was choking back tears. 'I was going to call him Geraldine but I forgot its name so I called it Theresa.'

'There now, it's gone straight to heaven and is happy now.'

'You mean to say he went straight to heaven?'

'Yes, straight to heaven and is happy now.'

'But mammy he didn't bite. Theresa didn't know how to bite and he didn't scratch.'

His innocence gave her a lump in the throat. She wrapped the kitten in newspapers and then in a bag and sent the gang over the fields where they buried it and said prayers over the grave.

\*   \*   \*

John had begun eating again but still had troubled nights, though jail-associated dreams were once again beginning to dominate.

He was looking forward to seeing Big Stevie and was standing on his tiptoes at the fence, trying to catch a glimpse of the Belfast man. Two countrymen and three other city men were also in the prison hospital where it was routine for new prisoners to be held for a night after they had come out of the reception bay. The object of the procedure was to allow the government to demonstrate to human rights bodies and the Red Cross that there was a comprehensive monitoring process from the time of arrest, usually by the British army, to the handover for police interrogation, to the admission to the prison camp and into the hands of another authority. Regardless of the process, seriously injured prisoners ended up in the military wing of Musgrave hospital or in civilian hospitals. Less seriously bruised prisoners went to the prison hospital.

Six new men had been brought in during the night in the back of blacked-out minibuses. They appeared with their guards at the hospital gate and had a long look at the inside of Long Kesh, or the Lazy K as the warders called it. Their first sensation wasn't the smell of strange cooking steaming from the kitchens but an underlying smell of metal, an iron-greyness in the nostrils, followed by the dissonant noise of bolts on bolt-holes, keys in locks and the clanging of gates.

They felt extremely vulnerable. A helicopter, chopping at the air with a vehement power, was arriving at the British army base which was within the camp. Two British soldiers with alsations on leads crossed over a concrete road and pretended to set the dogs on the prisoners. The soldiers laughed as the frightened prisoners and the cursing warders tried to hide behind each other. The men carried their few possessions in large, heavy duty brown paper bags. As the reverberations from the rotor blades subsided shouts of recognition came from the directions of the several cages.

'You oul fuckin' eejit! Imagine gettin' caught!' their companions behind the wire shouted.

'What Cage are you going to? Hey zombie, what Cage is he going to?' The warder ignored the abuse and one of the country men shouted, 'I think I'm going to Cage Five. Is your Cage, Five?'

'Naw. This is Three. But sure you can get a transfer tomorrow or get a Cage visit.'

They walked along, separated by high fencing from their comrades whom they hadn't seen for some time.

'How's things going on the outside? Everything okay?'

'Sure I'll tell you when I see you!' shouted one of the novices, unable to get the feel of the place or a clear understanding of the authority of 'a screw'. The others repeatedly encouraged him to loiter at the fence.

'Fuck them 'ens. Stand here for a while. I haven't seen ya in a year!'

'Move on! Hurry up!'

John saw Stevie in the group of new arrivals and waved frantically, beckoning him. A broad grin appeared on Stevie's face and he ignored the warder ushering him onwards. They shook fingers through the wire. Stevie dropped his few belongings and his strong hands clawed at the fence. He was standing akimbo and his leg muscles stood out — those legs which had leaped walls and strode streets in bounds. The animal in him had been tethered at last.

'Well comrade.'

'Well comrade.'

'Fancy meeting you here!'

'I've just dropped in to say hello and then I'm off.'

John laughed for the first time in a long time. 'Where are you for? Do you know?

'Hey Wright! Where's he for . . . Donnelly's the name?'

'If he'd move on he'd find out. He's in with you lot.'

The prisoners were being dispersed. The large gate opened in front of Stevie and another young man from south Derry. A uniformed, non-political prisoner — a teenager doing a short-term sentence for burglary — pulled a trolley on pneumatic tyres loaded with mattresses, blankets, clean sheets and pillows behind them into the control area, a small square section in which all human traffic was halted and checked, and then locked behind them before the next gate was opened.

'Two from reception!'

'Two on!'

The log book was marked. The large, inner gate was then unlocked, bolts withdrawn, and the two men were met by many friends who took charge of them and their bedding material, and who were effusive in their hospitality. Other Falls men were anxious to hear the latest from Stevie but he ushered them away:

'We'll get a yarn later. I want to have a yarn with John first.'

'I'm sure you're sick of walking 'round the Crum. We walk around anti-clockwise here as well you'll be glad to hear!'

'I'm tellin' ya, Belfast Prison is something else. There's fellahs walking round the yard talking about just getting ten years if they recognise the court and sixteen if they don't and they're all obsessed with their own cases. "The solicitor says this", "The solicitor says that" . . .

'It would frighten you and they can't wait to get sentenced so as they can get settled. I'm telling you, I brought guys into this movement six months ago and told them it would be over before Christmas! The internees would be out, there'd be an amnesty and the Brits would be talking again. What's worse, I believed it myself!'

John laughed.

'What's things like in here?' asked Stevie.

'The usual. There's random screw searches and we get a heavy Brit raid about once a month. That can be nasty.'

'You know what I saw in the Crum' . . . the death cell in C Wing where Tom Williams was hung. I got into it one day and had a good look. It's swept and washed out at least once a week and is always prepared. I saw the trap door. It was kept behind a door like a wall cupboard, only when you opened it you were on a platform and above you was the gallows. The trap door opened into the basement.'

'I'll tell you better than that,' John interrupted. 'There was a screw, a Catholic, who took part in the execution and who gave Williams a rough time. Afterwards he left the jail and became a merchant seaman. I think he worked on coal boats. He was so remorseful, or sick of what he'd done, that he threw himself overboard and he was never found again.'

'Here, we'd some good times at sea,' Stevie reminisced as John smiled at the thought of the wild, free oceans of just a few short years back. They both knew that all of the talk was a preamble for the discussion which John wanted and needed.

'I'm very sorry about Jimmy.'

John shook his head.

'It was me that went to see your da. He hadn't a clue what we were talking about. We were out in the kitchen. It was just before the body came home. He told us to fuck off, that we must have got him killed and then he cooled down and apologised and agreed to a military funeral.'

'I had no idea he was connected, Stevie, and when I heard it I cursed myself. He was so quiet. I still can't get over it . . .'

John turned his head away and swallowed his tears.

'Was it my doing? Was it because of me, because I got put in the Kesh or sent him on messages for us?'

Stevie smiled, 'Naw, Nothing like that, though it all could have played a part. He was active for months, even lied about his age to get in. He was good, very courageous. He joined the First Batt so that nobody down the Road would know. I operated with him. I was too hot down the Road, a couple of Brits in particular were on to me, knew what I looked like, so I moved to Andytown and it was there I found out he was a Volunteer.

'The Brits messed him about for being your brother, okay, but no more messin' than anybody else is getting.'

John felt a glow of pride line the edge of his desolation. 'When the Brits arrived outside your house there was a panic. I had asked to be on the guard of honour. We got the berets, belts and gloves off okay, and we didn't think they'd raid the wake. But the bastards surrounded the place and came in, apologising — you know the shit. I suppose you heard all this when you got parole?'

'Only some. They didn't tell me everything.'

'There could have been uproar but your ma, the poor woman, was hysterical and screamed at everybody for no trouble. I had bum ID but a Brit who knew me came up to me laughing and I was hauled off to Mulhouse Street, then Castlereagh, then the Crum' and the Court. They dropped the charges — they actually gave me three berets when I was leaving the Crum'! Outside the jail they had the doors of the jeep opened and ready for me. Up to Castlereagh for round two and then here.

'I'll never forget your house so long as I live. The Brits were walking through your living room, nodding to each other to have a look at Jimmy. Their radios were crackling, the Saracens' engines were running in the street. Your oul dog was in the yard going mad. People were gathering outside but they were pushed away and Johnny Kelly, ya know Johnny with the bad leg, he must be near sixty, he was arrested for hitting a soldier.

'And through it all your da was sitting in the corner beside the coffin, crying like a big child, holding two broken pieces from an ashtray a Brit knocked off the mantelpiece. Somebody said Jimmy had made it at school.'

Stevie stopped talking, uncertain of the effect of the conversation on John, but feeling his own dander rise.

'Tell me this,' asked John, tight-lipped. 'What actually happened when Jimmy was killed? I've heard a couple of things.'

'Well, you know we were out on a snipe. Nobody had seen the Brit patrol. They must have spotted the comings and goings, moved in from behind, and as soon as Jimmy appeared at the corner with a weapon, they shot him . . .'

Now it was Stevie's voice which was broken.

'The Brits were dancing and whooping and a soldier held the captured rifle above his head like a scalp. Then another Brit, a fuckin' black bastard, lifted Jimmy's head by his hair and shook him. He was the one who was clocked. We were still in the area and one of the boys popped up from behind a garden wall and blew him away.'

There was a barely audible sniffle from Stevie. The uncharacteristic racist slip testified to his emotional state.

'Come on in,' said John quickly, 'and I'll show you where you are. You'll get a visit today so if you want to get washed and changed into some of my clothes, go ahead.'

# CHAPTER 13

# THE LETTER

---

'Close the bloody door!' someone up the hut shouted at the last one out. The imprints of boots and shoes were wettest around the inside of the entrance but tapered off as they vaporised further up the floor. Four blow-heaters were meant to service the concave, corrugated iron hut with its thirty-one inmates, but the icy December draughts criss-crossed one and other between broken windows and along the length of the hut between the two ill-fitting wooden doors at either end.

A number of men were still out on the afternoon's visits. For some this was their last before Christmas, though as many of the final visits as was administratively possible to handle had been booked for the following day. There had been a rush in smuggling for the past two weeks; indeed it began directly after what was deemed to be the main army raid for December was over. The contraband — mostly vodka but some whiskey: each concealed in two or three pendulous balloons — survived the frisking by warders with an ease suggesting that they were turning a blind eye.

Had the warders also been observant they would have noticed in the food parcels' inventories an unusual supply of jellies — orange, tangerine, blackcurrant, all laced with vodka which was the least odorous spirit — and an increase in bursting, fat apples — the main ingredient for jungle-juice, as the extremely rough, seven-to-ten-day-old cider was called. When the next raid was anticipated the brew was downed even if fermentation was incomplete. Initially it would be drunk quickly, without being seen or smelt, as the prisoner concentrated his attention elsewhere. But as it took effect on the senses the drinker became very affectionate towards the last drops. The hangover, more often than not, consisted of vomiting and diarrhoea but the drunkenness was considered worthwhile.

Stevie, John and McGurk had been walking around the yard for over a half hour and were talking about going in. McGurk, a swarthy man nearing thirty, came from south Tyrone. As was common he was in with a countrymen's food clique, which pooled food parcels, but over several months he and John had struck up a close friendship. Often they would sit together talking late into the night, or would take hut cleaning duties together for the day or, as now, would walk around the yard — bouwlin, it was called — for hours on end yarning about this and that aspect of history, IRA activities, books they had read, country traditions and recalling life before the troubles had resumed in 1968.

It was bitter cold and the weak light was retreating like a hatch over the dome above them. Currents of accelerating wind clashed as they squeezed through the coils of barbed wire on top of each fence. On the ground myriads of small, dark diamonds rippled quickly across each puddle.

'No, we'll do another few bouwls,' Stevie said.

McGurk drew on his pipe and drew comfort from its glowing bowl around which his fingers were locked. Stevie had also taken to the countryman, this new authority on Irish history, and they would put questions to each other in challenge and counter-challenge.

Hands now plunged into pockets, fingers turning over pocket dust, they were walking at a brisk pace, overtaking others every second or third lap.

Two fences away and below the wall was the catwalk — an inside perimeter link between the look-out towers. Blurred, uniformed figures in marching formation approached one of the posts and were called to a halt. One fell out and disappeared into the turret to relieve one of two colleagues who, seconds later, emerged to march off with the others in their regular routine. A group of prisoners shouted at the soldiers, questioning their prowess, reminding them of the latest IRA action. When they drew a response from one of the snapping privates, making his frustration boil over, they delighted in drawing this to the attention of the leader as a breach of discipline. Stevie laughed into the wind at the carry-on and the wind blew back into his lungs.

When the patrol disappeared out of sight the two sentries in the watch tower slid their window open and at first poked fun at the prisoners. But when the mutual abuse subsided the inmates struck up a conversation.

'How long are ya here for?'

'Faw months, then we're off to Germany.'

One inmate who suggested they were all internees of Long Kesh was clouted on the back of the head by a comrade who was not amused. The two soldiers smiled.

'Lass time we was ere we was in The Ahdoyne. Do you know et?'

'Know it. I was reared in it, ya bastard.'

'Niaw, niaw Paddy, what about discipline!'

'Well tell us this — I can hardly see ya from here: what age are you?'

'I'm twenty-eight. Why?'

'And what rank are you?'

'I'm a private, why. Why do you want to know?'

'A fuckin' private and you're twenty-eight! My mate here was a brigade commander and he's only twenty! A fuckin' private! Would you ever catch yourself on!'

'Catch meself on! You're the feckin' fools Paddy,' he shouted, as the dialogue trailed off into degenerate exchanges which both sides thoroughly enjoyed.

An army helicopter which they had heard lifting off about fifteen minutes earlier moved down from the top end of the camp and sat hovering several hundred yards overhead. Suddenly there was a blaring broadcast from its loudspeaker system and it played a tinny version of 'Good King Wenceslas' and then 'We wish you a merry Christmas!' Moving backwards it performed a large circle in the sky so that all the Cages received seasonal greetings. Stevie shook his head in bewilderment and the three men, warmed-up by their exercise, turned in for the evening.

John tossed and turned in bed. He looked at his watch. It was half-two. Somebody had a rattling cough. Half-a-dozen snores were competing. There was a rising smell of sour socks close by which the cold hadn't managed to freeze. The rats were scurrying in the timbers. From the bottom bed a glow from another insomniac's cigarette described a parabola and then there was a sigh of smoke, some of which became a wide, grey bar for a few seconds as it was caught in the sharp light filtering through from outside lamps. Water from the tank of one of the two latrines at the bottom of the hut continually trickled. At night the noise could become eerie and would tug at the slumbering mind and pull it back to consciousness. But even the trickle had frozen and was now silent.

John stared at the bunk above him: the flat wire spring which provided the suspension was embossed with little sags of mattress, and the discoloured sheets had become loose. A pair of trousers and an overcoat, used to compress the blankets and give additional warmth, were close to falling on the floor, so he sat up and tossed them back as best he could over the body in the bed above. One of the bed's spring-hooks was broken and was swinging to and fro every time the man above turned over. It was life. Even in here it was life. For some reason he thought about Angela McCann, where she would be now and what could have been between them. He even quietly laughed when he remembered her bitchiness and the incident over the love letter in the dance-hall which at the time had shattered his pride and morale. He recalled their first kiss and he felt warm inside for having known and loved her.

You still love her, you fool, half of him said to the other half. Oh, I know. I know, I know, I know, he answered.

So he lay with her again, snug, nestling up close to her in her Aunty Maureen's towelled dressing-gown, and a thousand miles away from fences of barbed ice, the frosted panes of glass and an all-male milieu.

Before he knew it he was sound asleep.

There was a sharp shriek from the thick metal hinges which needed oil. He was familiar with the first sound. Secondly, was that running? He heard no barking. He stirred. The doors being unlocked every morning was so routine to all but new inmates that they didn't wake. But when there was a raid the warders would steal up to the entrance of the three occupied huts in advance of the soldiers and, as silently as possible, unlock the doors so as to spring surprise and create fear, a fear which sent the alsations into a frenzy.

The doors burst open, the lights were switched on and a line of soldiers in riot helmets ran up the centre of John's hut banging their batons off the beds as they went. The reveille continued until an officer strolled up the aisle.

'This is a raid.'

There was a loud crack, a blow unmuffled even through the blankets. A prisoner who was heard to remark, 'You don't say,' was struck on the knee with a baton.

'You will do as you are told.'

'You will stay in your beds until told to get out. When told to arise you will indicate which are your clothes and which locker you own and you will identify yourself when asked. You will then be allowed to dress and will be taken to the canteen until the search is completed.

'Tell your mum I send my regards,' he smiled and the other soldiers quietly laughed as they all shared the same sense of humour.

'You ! Get out of bed!' screamed an NCO into the face of a scared teenager. He jumped to the floor, shivering. He was wearing an old, heavy, checked shirt, underpants and two pairs of socks.

'Get them pyjamas off! Let me see.'

He gave the soldier the shirt which was searched before being thrown back at him.

'Okay. You can put it back on. Now the socks.'

As if they were diseased he held them at arms' length and shook them. Others were searching lockers, taking no care with the neat piles of clothes, reading letters from wives and girlfriends, scrutinising family photographs, probing mattresses and shining torches up bed-ends for contraband.

Prisoners who were searched and processed were each escorted out by a soldier. There were scuffles at the door and the O/C of the Cage, Fitzy, who was half-dressed, pushed past a soldier and confronted a senior warder.

'We were told we were being taken to the canteen so why are we being put against the wire?'

The warder appeared embarrassed. Before he could explain an army officer stepped forward. He had no beret but had a cravat around his neck which smelt of cologne. He wore a wind-cheater — which didn't appear to be of British army issue. He tugged at the wrists of his leather gloves. He was quite tanned, given that it was winter; and spoke in polished tones:

'I am in charge here while the major is out and I say you go to the fence. We have to search the canteen.'

'But there's frig all in the canteen. It's empty.'

'Soldiers. Take this man out.'

Fitzy was led out of the hut, shirtless, his teeth chattering, two soldiers digging their grip into him and marking his arms.

Chilled by the winter's night the morning air made straight for the bones. Seventy-nine prisoners were spread-eagled against the fence. Stevie refused to tremble even though the grime-covered metal mesh was draining his palms white. He turned over in his mind the option of just refusing to continue with what he considered in part to be self-imposed humiliation. He would be batoned, the dogs would be set on him to get him to conform to the orders. But if he still refused he could only be beaten so far and would be removed to the punishment block or the hospital. If they all refused then the Brits would have a major problem. A general burning-down of the camp had often been talked about but, unfortunately, given the mix of the prisoners and the various levels of commitment, it was impossible to expect such disobedience. Besides he could start something and there was no guarantee that the Brits would concentrate their reprisal on him. One of the older, less able men could end up bearing the brunt of a bad beating.

There was a noise of collapse and then a groan.

An old man from Newry, who, talk had it, had suffered an injury during the IRA campaign of 1956-1962 which had deranged him, had fainted and fallen go the ground. A young soldier kicked him and told him to get up, suspecting that he was acting. Stevie turned on the soldier, fists knotted by his side.

'Kick him again and I'll knock you back to fucking Liverpool!'

The soldier grabbed him by the collar and forced him against the fence but Stevie pushed his throat against the soldier's grip so that for a second their faces met in hatred. A warder came between them and another soldier, clearly with some authority, ordered Stevie and the next prisoner to carry old Joe to the canteen.

They laid him down on the floor and a warder fetched a cup of water. When he left them alone in the canteen Joe winked out of one eye.

'You're definitely a countryman!' joked Stevie. 'Look at this. No search at all.' He surveyed the empty canteen. The door opened again and prisoners, two or three at a time, filtered in. The main points of concern among them were the survival of their Christmas alcohol and the extent of the damage to handicrafts — the wooden harps, jewellery boxes and minature spinning-wheels they had carved for friends and relatives or for the Green Cross — a Republican charity which sold the items to help raise funds for prisoners' dependants.

Some four hours after the raid had begun somebody watching from a window reported that the raiding party was pulling out, although a line of prisoners against the wire in the adjacent cage was plainly visible. It was a half-hour before they were allowed back into their huts. The place was in a mess. Bedding and clothes scattered everywhere, boot marks on sheets. A bottle of ink had been spilled over a shirt. Most handicrafts were smashed. Photographs were torn or missing. Christmas cards had been scrawled on by Petes and Mikes and Bobs. Sugar had been poured over cheese and meats: salt over sweet things. Lighter fuel had been sprayed into the water container.

The place reeked of vodka and the floors were soaking from overturned creamery cans which normally contained milk but had been pilfered for the brews. Fitzy went immediately to a spare locker which was in a no-man's-land between two beds, the exact position it had been in earlier. He smiled and was joined by two others. They tilted the locker and the grins fell off their faces. Splinters of wood from a false panelling indicated that the pair of bolt cutters and the camera which had been wrapped in cloths had been found in the secret compartment.

'Well frig that,' said Fitzy. 'Back to the drawing board.'

Some prisoners were called for visits. They had no time to fuss about their dress or about being unshaven and while they were away the others cleaned up the huts. The only food which had been spared was a large home-baked Christmas cake covered in icing and marzipan which had been thoroughly probed for the proverbial file and hacksaw when it had been handed in to the parcels' office.

'To Pat and his comrades. XXX Pauline,' the icing read.

Later that night, after lock-up, John's hut decided to have their party. They were taking no more chances. Some of the lost stock of spirits had been replenished on that day's visits but the shortfall in jungle juice would make an appreciative difference. John called the hut to attention. He stood on a bed and wrapped in a blanket, toga-style, began a speech: 'Friends, Roman Catholics and Countrymen,' he winked at McGurk and the South Derry men. 'Lend me your ears.

'Stevie!'

Stevie stepped forward. He had two large red fire extinguishers under either arm. No one knew what to expect next. There was no sign of smoke.

'Stevie, open the champers.'

He twisted off the valve top of one of the extinguishers and began pouring jungle juice into large, dirty mugs, filling them to the brim as the queue of cheering and clapping men lined up.

'You see, comrades. This simple demonstration of Irish ingenuity, this clear example of humanity prevailing over . . .'

'Ah shut up and get pouring!'

'Anyway,' John continued, as all enjoyed the banter. 'I think it is quite obvious that the Brits are not as smart as they think they are. And so, comrades, the drinks are on us!

'To Freedom!'

'Freedom!'

'To Victory!'

'Victory!'

The cake, crumbling at the circumference, was laid out for Pat's food clique, and sliced. Inside two minutes three-quarters of it had been devoured.

Pat crossed the hut and offered the last piece to be divided between John, Stevie and McGurk. They were sitting on beds in deep conversation in an area partitioned off by blankets draped between lockers and bunks which offered some privacy. Stevie thought the weather had turned mild or else the alcohol was beginning to take effect because no one any longer complained of the cold.

To the right of Stevie's head, pinned to a locker, was a large newspaper advertisement which contained the names of all the internees, reminding them that they were not forgotten and wishing them a Merry Christmas and a peaceful New Year. It was quite an impressive list and helped buoy morale by making them feel important. They were an element in the political crisis who could not be ignored.

Less than five hundred yards from where they were, however, in other cages further up the Camp, were convicted Republican prisoners, equally entitled to attention but whom even the internees neglected. Some of them were serving life sentences.

'Hold it!' Stevie shouted at McGurk as he was about to sink his teeth into his slice of the cake. Stevie's finger and thumb handcuffed him at the wrist and forced his hand back from his mouth. John stared on, perplexed. Using his fingers carefully, Stevie revealed a razor blade which had been inserted by the soldiers length-wise into the cake. He had seen a glint of light reflect off it, just in time.

'The bastards!'

'Thank you, Mr Donnelly,' said McGurk.

'Not at all. You can buy the next round,' he said, pointing to the fire extinguisher.

Many different sessions were in progress within the hut: card games, sing songs, private concerts, discussions.

McGurk produced a big balloon, swollen with about half a pint of whiskey.

'Where the hell did you get that?' asked John.

McGurk tapped a finger against his right temple, indicating intelligence.

'I heard the Brits coming in this morning and had the stuff ready, just in case. As soon as the row started I dropped it into my trunks beside my balls. The Brit was either too flustered at the commotion to notice me or too embarrassed.'

'You can say that again.'

'This is going to be some night.'

'You can say that again.'

Their conversation covered a wide nature of topics. McGurk spoke affectionately about his wife and his three children and his resolution to see that the war would be over before they grew up so they would never have to go through what his generation were experiencing. He said his family in Tyrone were great and gave material and moral support to his wife. By now they were slightly drunk.

'Never hear you talk much about women, John, though I see plenty of different ones up on visits,' the countryman said.

'Well, I'll tell ya. I really fancied this one years and years ago. We went out a lot and I thought one day we'd end up married but we never got anywhere. Maybe I was too serious.'

In deference to some men who had turned in, half the lights were switched off.

Although match sticks were banned McGurk produced one from his jacket's top pocket and ran it along the floor. In the dim light the match hissed into flame and the splinter slowly shrivelled across the mouth of the pipe bowl. The tobacco lost its moistness, tensed and sparked.

\* \* \*

'Visit for O'Neill. J. O'Neill!' the warder shouted across the yard. Although it was only March he wore just a shirt and tie on top as if he was trying to impress everybody that he was impervious to the cold. The message was sent into the hut. John was already washed and dressed and ready to see his sister Sheila. Having been processed and searched he stood in the corridor of the prefab hut talking to a fellow inmate but was motioned on towards Box 7.

There was a latitude granted by the warders which often allowed one or two visitors of one prisoner to nip into the box of another prisoner to have a snatch of conversation. A large concourse of people — wives, children, girlfriends, parents, brothers and sisters, friends — passed up and down the visiting area. Amidst the exchanges of banter was another scene — a married couple clinging to each other, the woman in tears.

A warder knocked on the door of the visiting box opposite John. A young man, vaguely familiar, came out. 'Two minutes!' said the prison official. The young man suddenly acknowledged John with a loud 'Hello!' and within seconds his visitor, a woman in her twenties, came out from behind him.

'Lord, what are you doing here!' she said, with a trace of that old confidence. Though taken aback, John smiled at Angela. Despite his confusion he snapped up the attractive figure before him. He gazed at the soft bridge of her nose and noticed that the freckles had gone. She had kept her hair as he had remembered it, tucked behind her ears and long. She skipped her first remark which wasn't really a question and asked, 'How are you keeping, John?'

'I'm okay. How are you doing? How long have you been back?' He then realised that the other prisoner was her brother, Sean McCann. Sean made himself scarce and struck up a conversation with some friends further along the corridor.

'Ach, I've been back a while.' Just above her right eyebrow was a little pock-mark, probably a birth scar, which he had always found attractive. He was embarrassed at finding himself looking her up and down.

'It's been a long time,' he said at last.

'Over six years. A lot of water . . .'

'Yes.'

'You haven't changed a bit. Made a name for yourself too. Your case about being tortured was on the news. I read about you in England.' So she took an interest in me, he thought.

'Listen, John, I was sorry about Jimmy . . .' Her tone suddenly changed. 'It was terrible.'

'Yes,' he replied, hearing his name, being reminded of the heartbreak. 'He was going out with your sister, Mary Ann. She was up to see me once. Her and Jimmy. In fact, it was in this very box that I last saw him alive . . . Mary Ann's a nice girl.'

'Not like her older sister,' Angela added demurely, an expression which John had never seen in her before and which touched him. 'Are you really keeping okay?' she asked, intensely.

'Yes! I'm okay. What about you? Have you made your first million yet?'

'Huh, that nonsense,' she chuckled with some disgust at the thought.

One warder was growing impatient with Sean, ordering him to move on. Another was shuffling just a few feet away from the couple: 'You're well over the time. The visit was up five minutes ago.'

'I suppose I'll have to go,' she said, looking around. Sean came back and was kissed on the cheek and for an instant the barely audible smack caused John to sigh. She turned to leave and unexpectedly pressed John's arm with her hand. 'All the best,' she whispered gently. He didn't know what to say. She wore a black leather coat against the March weather. It was fastened by a slim belt in a simple knot and he would have loved to have grabbed and held her, despite the past.

He watched her walk down the corridor to the locked door, beyond which was freedom, through which only visitors and warders could pass. He finally called out, 'All the best, Angela!' The use of her name triggered off a feeling of awkwardness. The door was open but she suddenly stopped and looked back. By now his head was in a whirl of confusion. She gave him a meaningful glance and, in a flash from the past, winked at him. He began laughing and saw her smile back. Then the door was closed.

The next day John was still in a euphoric state but had kept telling himself to calm down, to measure his steps. He came into his hut that afternoon and saw a letter lying on his bed, her handwriting even familiar from a distance. He lifted it. Inside the serrated edges of the envelope — where it had been opened by the censor — was a letter. He lifted it to his nose and his heart thudded when he smelt the scent of the perfume, Youth Dew. He clenched his teeth but would be patient, very patient. He placed it under his pillow and went out to the yard for a walk. He wanted to relish the reading of it. He strolled over to Stevie's hut. Stevie had, surprisingly, moved out of John's hut about six weeks before. He hadn't been in any rows and John felt a bit aggrieved since he felt that there was a real bond of comradeship between them. Stevie was already out walking, so John joined him.

'I was looking for you!' he said.

'Ná bí ag caint i mBéarla!' [Don't be speaking in English!]

'What?' said John. 'What did you say!'

'Dúirt mé leat, ná bí ag caint i mBéarla! Tá mé ag foghlaim Gaeilge le mí anois.' [I said, don't be speaking in English! I have been learning Irish for over a month now.]

'Maith thú, ar fheabhas. Anois tá fhios agam cad chuige ar bhog tú amach. D'fhoghlaim tú i le háthas a chur orm!' [Very good, that's brilliant. Now I know why you moved out. It was to surprise me!].

'I'm sorry,' said Stevie, who was nervous about his use of Irish so far and had to break into English. 'I don't understand. What did you say?'

'Well,' replied John, enthusiastically, clapping him on the back. 'I said "Beidh lá eile ag na b'Paorach go fóill". There is hope for old Ireland yet. Beidh lá eile ag an b'Paorach go fóill!'

*   *   *

*Dear John*

*Once again, or should I say, at long last, I put pen to paper to write to you and ask your forgiveness. As I write I cannot help but cry both tears of sadness and of relief. I have been such a fool all these years, have squandered so much, hurt so many people and degraded myself through being conceited.*

*When you left Ireland my friends told me how much of a bitch I was and this hurt me. I wrote to you two or three times. I don't know whether you ever received those letters. I heard you were back in the Gulf but I wrote for the wrong reasons! I said I was sorry and apologised but if you read them you probably saw how hollow and hypocritical I was being. Maybe that's why there was no reply. I was just wanting you to get me off the hook for what I had done.*

*My Aunty Maureen used to keep talking about you and praising you. I was a little bit piqued one day and light-heartedly told her what happened between us at the dance. She was very angry and didn't speak to me for weeks! So, it was only slowly that I had an appreciation of my own cruelty.*

*In 1966 our family moved up to our present address in Andersonstown. But despite the move I still couldn't stick Belfast. In '67 I went to London and got involved in the whole flower power era for a few months. I was home for two years but then left again over an issue* which I now understand you know about and I since heard that you helped sort out. A belated thanks!

I had a good job in London for some time and eventually ended up owning my own house. Into property, at last! Some other time I'll tell you all about it but let me say John, dearest John, that I have never gotten over you.

Last August I was listening to the news one day when I heard that an IRA man and a soldier had been shot dead in West Belfast. My stomach turned over and I couldn't get out of my head the obsessive thought that it was you who had been killed. It was a crazy notion because, believe it or not, I had followed closely your goings-on from writing to Patricia and knew you were still interned in Long Kesh Camp. When the name Jimmy O'Neill was read out later that night I sobbed my heart out. Do you remember we brought him down town to the Wimpy Bar one day and he had us on the edge of our seats with laughter?

That night I tried to phone home but couldn't get an answer and when I did eventually get through it was only then that I learned that he had been going out with our Mary Ann and that my family had been down at the wake. John, nobody had ever told me about Jimmy and Mary Ann such was the gulf between my family and myself. I had become a complete outsider, a stranger. I spoke to my mammy on the phone and actually made up with her since the big argument we had had some time before. I decided to come home and by Sunday night I was in Belfast.

I stood watching the funeral on the Monday and I caught a glimpse of you for the first time in all those empty years. You looked wretched and I felt so sorry for you and your family because of what you had come through. I knew then that my home and heart lay in Belfast. I went back to England and sorted out myself and eventually sold up my house and came back to Andersonstown. Then four weeks ago our Sean got interned.

I suppose I should finish off now but I just can't help pouring my soul out to you. John, have we really changed that much? I can understand life having made you harder but I feel that I have really sorted out myself at long last. Throughout all those years I have thought of you. Do you remember that afternoon at Maureen's? They were the most wonderful moments of my life.

I have to confess that there is still a bit of the schemer in me. It was no accident that we met in the visiting boxes. I was out with your Sheila two weeks ago for a drink and she told me how we could try and get the visits to coincide. I was panicking when the warder said that the visit would be over in two minutes. And we thought you still hadn't come out. Our Sean had been up and down getting a light, asking the warder what time was it, were the visits on on St Patrick's Day, were his letters through the censor yet, was he allowed raw meat in parcels. I'm sure the warder thought that jail was cracking him up. And then Sean nodded to me that you were through. That's when I got up to leave. God, I was really nervous even though I may have appeared self-confident.

It was wonderful seeing you again and that is why I have been so relieved and full of hope. At the risk of completely offending you I would like to repeat the warmest, most sincere words I have ever come across. A love letter from you to me: 'Let me know through a shooting star, or the draw of the plucked petals, or the buttercup yellowing my throat, or through that crack in the pavement which my feet may cross, if you are for me!'

I hope upon being reminded of that night that you have not torn this up. After you left the dance I retrieved your letter from the stage. I always carried it around with me. There were times, really, really hard times when I took it out and read it to myself, and absorbed from it the courage and love behind it.

John, I wasn't all bad, I was just lost.

I would like to see you again, or, at least, to hear from you. But if you don't wish to see me I will understand, it is perfectly understandable. But please write to me, at least, and let me know.

Love
Angela,
XXX

P.S. I now have a view of the world which, you'll be glad to hear, includes more than myself!

— Angela

# CHAPTER 14

# DIARIES

Extracts from the diaries of Jimmy O'Neill saved by Sheila from a British army search

## 1968

**January 1st:** I do not think I shall write things of privacy in this diary. Of those things I have, this is private. Later I suppose I shall write madly but until then I pray that it should come.

**Friday 5th:** Didn't go to Mass or library as usually do. Look before you leap — must remember that.

**Sunday 7th:** St Louisa's start back tomorrow. I'm glad. I'll see somebody I like.

**Monday 8th:** This morning it snowed and settled. Seen Margaret McGorrian this morning but was too nervous to say hello. Got two Victorian pennies. That's ten I have, plus eight Edward the Sevenths and two George the Fifths silver thrupenny bits. Did eckers early. Have a geog test tomorrow and I have no idea about mining in Durham and industry in the north of England. O God help me tomorrow.

**February 12th:** Sheila if you ever read this I'll kill you, yes you!

**February 29th:** Jimmy Saville on *Top of the Pops* was great.

**March 2nd:** Radio Caroline went off the air.

**March 9th:** Handball is back.

**March 19th:** In butcher's for mammy after school getting sausages. There was an argument about England. I joined in. Jimmy, the butcher, backed me up. Very interesting, even though I was laughed at.

**April 5th:** Martin Luther King, king of the downtrodden negroes, has been assassinated.

**April 23rd:** New decimal coins came out today. Five new penny equals a shilling, ten new penny equals two shillings. Trolleys are going off the Road soon. Thinking of joining weight-lifting to build up my biceps.

**April 28th:** Louis Armstrong — 'What a wonderful world'.

**May 6th:** Britain's first heart operation took place the other nite. Donor an Irishman. First heart op took place, I think, on the 2nd of December.

**May 12th:** The trolleys went off the Road today, very sad.

**May 13th:** Dirty, stinkin, smelly diesels on the road.

**May 14th:** Cousin Tony can get BBC 2 on their TV.

**June 5th:** TODAY SENATOR ROBERT KENNEDY WAS SHOT THRU THE HEAD. HE IS CRITICALLY ILL. TOOK BULLET OUT.

**June 6th:** TODAY SENATOR ROBERT KENNEDY DIED OF YESTERDAY'S GUNSHOT.

**June 7th:** I went to the library and got a book called *Farewell Flying Saucers*. The man who shot R. Kennedy was arrested.

**June 8th:** Somebody was arrested in London in connection with the assassination of Martin Luther King. Daddy didn't come in until 5 this morning.

**June 25th:** Tony Hancock committed suicide today.

**June 29th:** Our John gave me a pound after he won the races. Lester Piggot won the Irish Sweepstakes Derby. Sir Ivor came second but I don't know who was riding him.

**August 8th:** My mate Noel and I cycled to Helen's Bay. Noel's cat caught his second bird yesterday. UTV is still on strike.

**August 15th:** We had a great bonfire and Noel got off with Deirdre Masterson. He said she's a dirty baste and put her tongue right into his mouth. He said he felt like throwing up. Swapping spittle, ugh!

**August 21st:** Russia invaded Checkyslovakia and they're still there. Practising self-hypnosis.

**Saturday October 5th:** Derry civil rights march today. Gerry Fitt, our MP, got hurt and we prayed that he would be okay.

**October 6th:** Fighting broke out in Derry today again. Police were appalling during the fighting. A petrol bomb was thrown at police in Derry. Blood boils. Feel awful.

**October 7th:** I was made a prefect in class today because my work has improved.

**October 8th:** The cabinet support police action in Derry.

**October 9th:** Queen's University students march today. Also Paisley in Shaftsbury Square. Last night a petrol bomb was thrown at the Protestant church on the Falls Road, up at Broadway.

No clash between Paisley and the students.

**October 11th:** Biafra reduced to small size. Got a book on E.S.P. and after read it lent it to Micky Conlon. We are to do an experiment.

**October 14th:** This morning I was told to take Jackie Hunter to the head master to be slapped. But instead I took him for a walk around the school for twenty minutes. This afternoon my form master sent for me and slapped me and I lost my prefect badge.

**October 25th:** Studied Conlon in sleep and got results. Asked him did he dream of a girl, yes. Did he sleep on his left side, yes. Was the song, *Wheels on Fire* but it was *Those were the days.* 66 out of a 100, not bad.

**December 24th:** Came sixth in class, highest in class at English.

## 1969

**January 2nd:** Peoples Democracy march set out for Derry. Major Ronald Bunting, a friend of Paisley's, was waiting for them and there was some fighting. Started back to school. A OK. Got out at 2. Went up to the chippy tonight and stood at corner.

**January 4th:** Snow expected. Fighting in Derry. 59 injured. Bunting's car was burned.

**January 13th:** Master Armstrong kept Doke, Dick and me in after school. I had to count in thousands all the people in Norway, but when I was half-way through he told me to go on home and that would teach me not to be 'facetitious'. He's used that word about fifty times this week.

**January 28th:** Late for school. Paisley got 12 stitches in his arm today. Did English test.

**February 4th:** Late for school. There is to be a general election this month. Unionists unstable. We went to St Clement's Retreat House. Seen films on the Holy Shroud of Turin. Having a great time. From my bedroom window, room 86, I can see across the Lough and the lights of County Down opposite. My mate Kieran tells me all his worries and I listen. He is troubled.

**February 24th:** Tonight is election night and at Bannside the Rev Ian Paisley got very closely to Captain Terry O'Neill.

**April 22nd:** Got hair cut. Micky Conlon and myself kidnapped Linda Gormley and brought her down town then over to the museum. I think she fancies him. Bernadette Devlin made a historic maiden speech in Westminster today. More fighting tonight. No 1 Beatles. 'Get back to where you don't belong'.

**July 1st:** Do not try to find fault in God's plan. There are none. Evil and sin do not exist on earth but in the mind.

The nights are warm and we spend them playing handball and later standing at the corners. There is a light mist in the evening and sometimes a heavy smell from the dry drains and sewers.

**August 10th:** Having a brilliant time in Donegal. Our family is the best family in the world, okay!

**August 13th:** There is fighting in Derry. A huge riot and the fellahs have hoisted the tricolour over Rossville Flats. Tonight at about 12.30 gunfire broke out in Falls Road. Fighting in Belfast, Derry, Dungiven, Newry, Omagh, Enniskillen, Lurgan, Coalisland.

**August 14th/15th:** B Specials went mad tonite shooting all night. Snipers all over the place and gunmen in a blue mini. Saw petrol bombs being made. Our John was to go away but stayed because of the troubles. Conway Street was burned to the ground. Troops moved in. I helped the men lift flagstones and put up barricades at the top of the road. Remember 1916!

**August 17th:** Latest news at 5.30. Troops to stay as long as the P.M. says so.

**September 3rd:** Our John secretly brought me into Radio Free Belfast in Leeson Street. An *Irish News* man photographed our John operating the station.

**September 20th:** Barricades came down today at about 3.30.

**September 27th:** Our John came in and said Loyalists burned down five houses in Coates Street and the British army didn't do anything. The barricades were put up again.

**October 10th/11th:** Hunt Report came out.

Heard shooting at 11.30. Continued all night. Protestant sniping on Shankill Road at cops and army. Constable Arbuckle shot dead and two civilians dead. About 100 injured. Civilians were Protestants.

**December 19th:** The Scottish soldier at the billet told us to F- off and called us Paddies. On Thursday night Noel Cassidy and I had bunched together and bought him five cigarettes as a present.

## 1970

**December 1970:** I have decided to begin a diary again. It is almost a year since I wrote and a lot has happened since then. There was big trouble on the weekend of June 27th and many people were killed, including an IRA man defending St Matthew's Chapel in the Short Strand. A week later was the Falls Curfew when more were killed and I got caught in CS gas. You can hear bombs plenty of times now. At school you are either an Official or a Provie. I'm not in anything. Go to the youth club on Tuesdays.

**December 3rd:** Had bad dream last nite. Dreamt that the soldiers were chasing me down our entry as I had a .303 rifle.

We are collecting groceries for the old age pensioners at Christmas and I had to make a speech in the Assembly Hall. Was a bit nervous. Went up to mate's house in Whiterock and walked home over the football pitches. Behind me was our mountain and I looked over our beautiful city which at that time was clear with just a few lights being switched on.

**Tuesday December 8th:** This morning was awoke for 'school' at eight but managed to fight off my ma to explain it was a Holy Day of Obligation. It's not like her to forget.

### When I have fears by John Keats

When I have fears that I may cease to be
Before my pen has gleaned my teeming brain,
Before high-piled books, in charactery,
Hold like rich-garners the full-ripened grain;
When I behold, upon the night's starred face,
Huge cloudy symbols of a high romance,
And think that I may never live to trace
Their shadows, with the magic hand of chance,
And when I feel, fair creature of an hour,
That I shall never look upon thee more,
Never have relish in the faery power
Of unreflecting love; — then on the shore
Of the wide world I stand alone, and think
Till love and fame to nothingness do sink.

## 1971

**Wednesday February 3rd:** Called over to Mickey's and heard that soldiers were raiding the Kashmir Road area for guns. We walked up to see what was going on. Eileen Austin who goes to our youth club, and her sister and other girls were fighting the Brits with hurleys. Feelings were very high.

**February 4th:** There was more trouble again, also with a few gunners taking pot shots at the army. Nail bombs, acid bombs, jelly bombs, hand grenades at the duck patrols. There were a hundred arrests.

**February 6th:** 1/4 to 2 am (Sunday morning): Tonight's trouble is bad with 3 civilians dead and one British soldier. I counted at least 25 explosions and the number of shots couldn't be counted. This trouble really annoyed me. Our John came in late and I heard my mammy say that he had blood on his hands and she abhorred hate. Our Monica shouted, 'You have no right to say that to him!' and there was a big row which ended in tears all round and John asking did she want him to leave the house and she shouted back 'do you want me to leave the house!' Anyway, when my daddy came it was all kept from him.

**February 7th:** Went to Mass with the lads. During Fr Murray's sermon, which was against the jelly bombers, a man stood up and condemned him for being one-sided. He then left Mass and the woman behind us (who was really well-dressed) shouted out that she agreed with the man and she then left with many others and if anyone else had left so would we have. Everybody was later talking about what happened and somebody said the same thing happened in another chapel up the road. Later we went to the youth club. After this week I would say that my sympathies lie with activist Republicans. (This is nothing to do with our John.)

**Tuesday February 9th:** Went to school early and came home and heard news. First time ever I cried for my twisted country and the complicated situation. It seems solutionless and this time I was realistic. Last night a child of five was knocked down and killed by an army jeep and hence the riots commenced with guns out again. Today brought news of five civilians blown up at Brougher Mountain in County Tyrone. They are all dead and I don't know the circumstances surrounding it but when I listened to it on the BBC I cursed the English announcer but then I blessed him and thought, 'Let he who is without sin cast the first stone'. Everything is wrong. I too. And I also prayed that God would show the people which way to go and for him to direct me.

Later went down the road from school and spent the afternoon until 5 at the IRA funeral. Crowds of about 3,000 were there.

**February 13th:** School was terrible and I couldn't study. In the afternoon I was determined to work. There is 17 weeks to my exams and that doesn't give me much time.

**February 24th:** Got our ashes and then Noel and I again visited oul Willie in Slate Street and Mr McCarthy in McDonnell Street. A friend of my daddy's, a chiropodist he knows, had called in as arranged and did Willie's feet. We were also able to present Willie with a second-hand TV, which we had got repaired. I am reading a book by Robert Graves. It is called *King Jesus.*

**February 26th:** Heard at one o'clock that forty-eight women were arrested in Chichester Street protesting against the prosecution of a fellah who had marched in the IRA-style funerals. Later had an argument with my Uncle Harry over the troubles. He adopted the real Christian attitude and he was right and I know it but I was arguing from the passion angle. At about 12 midnight, at the height of the shooting, two policemen were shot dead and again I was stunned by the actions of men. Shooting has continued, especially in Ardoyne and in Cromac Square which up to now had been quiet. There was plenty of places set on fire and also nail and gelignite bombs were thrown. Later on the British army said that they had shot two civilians dead but tomorrow will tell the truth.

**March 1st:** The news this morning was of a soldier being killed. It happened in Derry. An army landrover was patrolling part of the Bogside area when it came under an attack of ten petrol bombs. The jeep went on fire and ran out of control crashing into a wall. The soldier, an 18-year-old youth, was thus killed. Although this was terrible we became used to it. Life, which originally was precious, loses its value after the first dozen or so killings . . . Mother shouts in, 'Kids, did you hear that?' She is referring to an explosion which took place thirty seconds ago. 'Yes, I heard it.' I shout back, and I think, God help us.

**Thursday March 4th:** Went to the youth club to see *Top of the Pops* in colour.

**March 5th:** Heard of trouble in Leeson Street so left school at 3 and went to observe. The soldiers baton-charged the people and my rage built up. Our John came along and ordered me home. Have since heard that the rioters have hijacked a 2,000 gallon petrol tanker. Petrol bombs galore. The riot started when the soldiers raided the Long Bar. (There goes another explosion. And another one.) Whilst at the top of Leeson Street I heard three nail bombs go off. Have heard on news that one civilian was shot down by the army. Our John is not in yet and I am down on my knees praying. Please Jesus, it's not him. I can hear more machine-gun fire.

**March 9th:** We were all at the corner and heard two very loud explosions and then we heard of the shootings. The IRA were fighting each other in Leeson Street and Cyprus Street. One fellah was shot dead. Others were wounded. Fell asleep about two o'clock.

**March 10th:** 10.15 p.m. After some studying was called for my supper and on *News at Ten* there came a newsflash. Three men were shot dead tonight. They were found in Ligoneil and they had been shot thru the head.

10.25 p.m. Mother has just shouted up that the news announced that they had an unconfirmed report that the three men were British soldiers in civilian clothes.

10.45 p.m. Went downstairs again and heard the news. The three men were British soldiers — they were from a Scottish regiment. I again felt like crying. This is wrong and I am moved for the man who thinks this right. This brings the total number of soldiers killed to six.

When our John came in I asked him could he shoot somebody thru the head and he said what was I talking about, there's a war going on. I think he could but it's okay for him, he knows his mind and what he's doing. I wanted to press him further but didn't because I know he's got a lot on his mind and anyway I admire him and I didn't want to upset or annoy him.

**March 12th:** Was coming down the Antrim Road in a bus today and there were two girls sitting in front of me. They were laughing and one turned around to me and said to her friend: 'Well, what do you think?' She replied, 'Umm, seven out of ten.' The first one said: 'No, ten out of ten. He's real sweet.'

I tried to say something mature but was spellbound with admiration for this one and I followed every turn of her head and was excited by her hearty laughter. I was with her for five minutes and was so happy.

I got off at Carlisle Circus and said: 'Cheerio now!' and touched her on the shoulder. She turned around, as if real feeling had passed between us. She had the most luscious eyes and lips and said: 'Bye, bye now.' And I will probably never see her again.

**March 28th:** Had more talks with father — these on the troubles and Republicans. He being a moderate, and right, cut me to ribbons. But can I help it if at this age I am caught up and have these ideals which I know to be a natural quality of my time. Is it my fault that I like to think that I cherish this land, that I love this place?

Later: Sooner or later I asked this girl, Patricia, home and sooner or later she said yes. So I left her home to Cawnpore Street. She told me she was sixteen and worked in Boots chemist (and had muscles to prove it!). I walked her up from the club at 11 and didn't get home until 1/4 past 12. We stood lumbering in Dunmore Street entry and she wore a maxi coat like Anna Karenina. When we got to her door she said: 'By the way, I'm only 14 and in your Sheila's class.' I was mortified but I ran the whole way home and let the rain wash my face. I'll be arrested for baby-snatching.

No. 1. *Hot love — T-Rex.*

**Easter Saturday:** Came home to an argument between mother and father and John over the display of the tricolour from our house. I think John was right. But he was told in no uncertain terms that the flag wasn't flying.

**Easter Sunday:** Me and my mates went to watch the IRA parades from Beechmount Avenue which turned out to be brilliant. The British army were taking photographs from the roof of Broadway picture house but some fellahs spoilt their film by shining mirrors using the sun at them.

**Saturday April 17th:** Sheila brought me the *Irish News* in bed and sure enough they had printed my letter. I was really pleased!

**Friday April 23rd:** I thought I was limited but more comes up from below and there must be a reservoir in me. It is damp and I look out upon the wet roof across the way. I think I should try to leave school and become a library assistant. Whilst working there I could do A-Level English, then I could write about life and what I feel. It is truly frustrating being imprisoned by ignorance.

**Wednesday May 5th:** Today an immersion heater was installed in the house and everybody was trying it but the electrician put the switch round the wrong way so that it's on when it's up and off when it's down, but that's only being bitchy.

**May 21st:** There was trouble in the New Lodge Road involving Scottish soldiers. On *News at Ten* I saw brutality. Four Scotch soldiers beat and kicked one Catholic man from one side of the street to the other. The regiment involved was that which lost three soldiers in the killings a while back. My feelings were ones of crying at the lostlessness or else of anger and future retaliation. I again was tempted to sign up. Help this country, God.

**June 24th:** After *Top of the Pops* we went to Noel's bedroom and yarned. At about 1/4 to 10 the drizzle had stopped and we went to the corner where we viewed the world. Offered hankies to the girls coming out of the Broadway pictures crying having seen the film *Madam X*. Some more were walking past, talking about something and one said to her mates: '. . . so say a wee prayer for me . . .' and as quick as lightning we all said in unison: 'Our Father who art in heaven . . .' They started laughing. The night was great and urgeful. Got the habitual fish and bottle of milk.

**June 29th:** Gave pint of blood in Durham Street. The nurse said: 'You've a very young face,' and I said back, cheekily: 'You've beautiful, bursting blue eyes.' And I think I embarrassed her but didn't mean to.

**July 5th, 1.15 a.m.:** As I write now I hear an explosion — the cause. What of the justice? The rights and wrongs are torturous. Frustration in belief. I think those violent on our side (technically non-Catholic) may bring about an end to this. Is God in liaison? 1/4 to 2: Two explosions, one after the other, have raked the land. I have got a summer job in Fleming's groceries. Start when I come back from my holidays.

**July 7th:** I was lying in the yard enjoying the sun when Splaasshhh! our Sheila upstairs threw a cup of water around me.

**July 11th:** Went hitching with Noel. We got a lift to Dungannon and from there to Bundoran, then Salt Hill but went back into Galway and bedded down on benches in the city square.

Now outside Oughterard. It is very bare and lonely countryside. The sun is out and the wind high in the sky is whistling.

**July 14th:** We got into Bundoran and Noel went off drinking. I told him I'd see him in the morning. I left the bar and wandered down the town. Went on to the beach. Listen, I am lost. I need somebody's help. There was a snake in my gut, twisting my bowels into knots, and I wandered with this pain in me and took myself up the cliff path beside the golf course. I bedded in a small shelter on this path and have just woken and walked to the top, looking out over the Atlantic. I became detached yet I thought, why am I always *here*. A unique happiness came over me. I have ended up here alone. Because Nature is here I come close to God. I wanted company earlier: I am now content. I know that when I leave this place I will have happy associations with it. The wind and the sea imbue the growing man. White foam shivers. I sit at the edge of the world. Miles out a lone beam travels to the water. I feel related. There is something *rare* about me. Before I had doubts but now I know.

I am cold — it doesn't matter. A stream of happiness bursts its banks into my soul and I cry to God for experiencing the long thrill of life.

**July 26th:** Mr Fleming was not at work today because he got a kicking by the British army last night so I was more or less in charge of the grocery section.

**August 7th:** Was out doing deliveries around Springview Street and there was still badness in the air. A man in a car was driving past Springfield Road barracks when his car backfired. A soldier shot and killed him. This is terrible and tragic. I wonder whether all this trouble is worth the life?

**August 9th:** The news is awful, really awful. My brother John has been arrested and nobody knows where he is. I'll begin at the beginning.

I was minding granny's house and had Noel Cassidy with me. We woke early, very early, and could hear screaming and Saracens. We went down to the bottom of Clonard Street and the people were out banging bin lids, building barricades. We stopped a fellah and asked him what was going on. He said: 'They've introduced internment; we're all gonna go to jail. It's internment!'

The place was black with people and everytime the Saracens raced down the road everybody scattered into the side streets and hid behind cars and the fellahs fought them with stones and petrol bombs. The community is like a chicken with no head. I was glad that our John hadn't been staying at home. We went back to my granny's and didn't know what to do though Noel says he's definitely joining. On the five to eight news we heard that one soldier is dead and that there is rioting in all Nationalist parts of Belfast, in Omagh, Derry, Newry and other places. The barricades are going up again, on my own doorstep and I thought — this is my country.

I went home through the crowds which were milling about with stones and bottles, even women, and just knew before I saw the people around our door that something was up. It was one of the Walshe's told me, 'they got your John in your house'.

The Brits sledge-hammered the front and back doors at around four o'clock and John for some reason had gone home last night. They kicked him down the stairs and put a rope around his neck and bound his hands. They wouldn't say what they were doing with him. When my mammy saw me she ran over and clutched me and held me so tight. My daddy phoned an SDLP councillor and he said they've rounded up hundreds, civil righters, the students as well as Republicans. We heard that in Andersonstown they took away a son when the father wasn't at home.

Later: My ma would hardly let me out of the house at all but I promised her I'd be round in Noel's and anyway she said she knows I'm sensible but she said she doesn't know what she would do if anything ever happened me. I told her she could buy a new one and she sorta smiled.

The pirate radio stations have returned and it is back to Radio Free Belfast days. I spent the anxious evening running about listening to news' bulletins, mostly RTE which has good coverage.

**August 10th:** Still no word about John but Faulkner has announced the introduction of internment. I hate that man. I put on the news and broke down. Fourteen shot dead, rioting in many towns and many people have been wounded. The soldiers have been trying to take the barricades down and they have met with resistance. Jesus! The fuckin' place won't let me live in peace. I'm shattered.

Later: I have done it. I lifted stones and fought the Brits. I was out at the Springfield and then Beechmount and at Broadway. At first I ran with the crowds protesting by occupying and filling our streets. Then I stayed with the rioters. My stone was with a thousand others and I thought, *we're all in this together*, and I asked God's forgiveness.

We were out in great numbers and it seemed very successful until the soldiers started shooting live bullets. Their first plunged into the wall at the corner of the chemist's. Later they stopped at the Avenue and were out on foot. We replied with bottles and stones and I was against the right-hand wall in the Drive when a bullet lifted a lump of masonry above my head. Two seconds later another bullet ricocheted off the ground into the sky two yards from where I stood. Eventually they got us pinned down in the side streets but a Republican sniper opened fire along the Avenue and the Brits returned the fire everywhere. I fell to the ground with my arms around my head and lay crumpled till the shooting stopped. It is worse than '69 and there is a real war-time feeling. Yesterday Noel and I speedied up one of the telegraph poles and erected the tricolour. Swanzey, who was arrested, was released from the barracks. The soldiers cut his long hair off with a dagger. He said the screams in Girdwood made him nearly mess himself. Our house is like a morgue and ma and da haven't slept. Monica's looking after everything. Raymond phoned from England to find out what's happening as it's all on the news over there. I caught our Sheila making petrol bombs in the entry and told her to get home as this wasn't for wee girls.

**August 11th:** Seventy people have been released and two hundred and thirty interned. We are waiting to find out where John is. In Ballymurphy Fr Hugh Mullan was shot dead by the British army when he went to administer the last rites to an injured man.

**August 13th:** I haven't eaten. I'm sick with worry and I've prayed every minute. My mammy's been crying non-stop. The RUC and British army have both denied having our John in custody. They said he must have been released if he was arrested at all. All of those arrested last Monday have either been interned in Crumlin Road jail or in the prison ship *Maidstone* or released. My daddy and Uncle Harry began visiting the morgues to see if he had been released and perhaps killed in crossfire. Twenty-three people have been shot this week and some of them haven't been identified.

**August 18th:** Jubilation at home! John has been found to be in Crumlin Road Jail. He and a number of other men were separated from the rest. My mammy was so relieved when she found out. They saw him this afternoon and after the visit she was still crying. She said to us all. 'They tortured your brother. They tortured him,' and then she cried again. But we bucked her spirits up by thanking God that he'd been found. My daddy then gave me £5 for doing well in my O-Level results which came on Monday amid the crisis. Tomorrow I'm going down to buy *The Irish Republic* by Dorothy Macardle and *I'm still waiting* by Diana Ross.

**Saturday August 19th:** The mystery of the night has been discovered.

Earlier walked up from town through the Loney and up Leeson Street and I thought of what the people are going *to rise* to. Britain, this is where your power in Ireland will be broken. This is the barrio that will break you!

Tonight my mammy made me swear I would never join the IRA and I swore for her. Tonight also I met a very old friend. It was very funny. I used to knock about with my cousin Tony

O'Neill and knew Mary Ann McCann from then. She's since moved up the road. She was in the White Ford Inn wearing a jumper, zipped up at the front and I'm sure she wasn't wearing a bra. She's got really nice. I said to her in my usual stupid goat-way: 'Do you fancy going fishing?' and she replied, tuned-in right away, 'Naw, you'd only catch ammonia,' and we laughed. I walked her home, held her hand and kissed her at her corner against the hedge. I told her that my brother was one of those arrested and interned and she said that she has an older sister in England whom she thinks used to go out with him way, way back. So there you have it, not a coincidence but a real connection. I believe in connections. I think I remember her too. She's agreed to go out with me again and had actually thought it was her friend Paula I was trying to get off with. I'm on top of the world. Yes! Life is presenting itself. And there I was searching for a bed in which to rest this mind. I was nearly skundered though, in front of her, when the barman queried my age but then dropped the subject.

**August 27th:** The Provos have now admitted responsibility for the explosion at the Electricity headquarters on the Malone Road in which a man died and 35 people were injured. I know all about our John and those other men and what happened but I cannot agree with them.

**August 29th:** More people walked out of Mass tonight when a priest condemned the IRA.

**Tuesday the 31st, the last day of August, 1971:** This month has been the fastest one so far in my life. It went like a flash. Our John was arrested, tortured and interned. I used violence and I have fallen for Mary Ann. But I am left holding the same problem. This country and I may survive together and see bright days when we can lead others in the arts and in fact every aspect of life.

**September 2nd:** More city centre explosions and 42 people hurt. If that was the IRA there is no justification and any support will consequently diminish.

**September 7th:** Saw our John in the Crum' today and he is fine. What spirits he and his friends have! A hundred people have now died in the troubles since August 1969. Noel got a loan of his da's car and he and his girl and me and Mary Ann went for a spin over to the Floral Hall up by Cave Hill. The two of us went for a short walk and kissed and cuddled and I felt her right breast and she looked so longingly into my eyes that my heart was fit to burst with joy. I put my arms around her and we looked at the lights from Holywood shimmering on Belfast Lough.

It is interesting to note how memories are formed. Last week, for example, has not solidified yet. But internment week and the July holiday have set and they shall remain the same forever, never to change.

**September 15th:** There was near riots and then a man in a combat jacket and wearing a small mask asked us to clear the corner. He had a gun. Mary Ann whispered to me that she knew him and I so admired him. It was him okay, Cuchullain reincarnate. I once saved him in a fight on Black Mountain when we were kids! It's a long story.

Faulkner signed 219 internment orders this morning. Curse that man. But God loves him as much as he loves *you*.

4 a.m. I can't sleep. I can't get over seeing him blaze away at the Brits. He was prepared to die. And he roared: 'Up the IRA!' at them when he emptied his gun before running into the entry.

**September 16th:** Is he to be left on his own? What happens if he dies or goes to jail? I admire the Republicans but there are just certain things I am not capable of doing.

Mary Ann and I have talked about it. She at first laughed at me but apologised when she saw the look on my face and says it's up to me. But the morals of it wreck me.

**September 24:** Was asked to accompany my great Aunt Rita to England this weekend, all expenses paid! She is going to see her brother for a few months before they both die. He left Ireland in the early 1920s because of the troubles. So we got the Ulsterbus coach to Aldergrove and we passed the burned-out ruins of Squire's Hill Tavern where the three Scottish soldiers were killed back in March. The skies were clear and Belfast glinted preciously below us.

8.25 p.m. From observation the Irishman is highly emotional and not as materialistic as the English. The standard of living here is very high. The people are not like us, no sense of community, of togetherness, of having shared strife. Their priorities are different. For us a day is twenty-four hours and bedtime is anytime you choose. In some of our minutes there are seventy seconds!

**Sunday, September 26th:** Am heading home, thank God. Changed trains at Guildford for Woking. And then there was this lovely bridge (for blowing up). There isn't even a house burnt out and the Protestants and Catholics in Belfast have more in common than do the people over here. And then they are shocked to hear that a man you know can kill. And all *their* fathers were in the British army. I hear a loud backfire and I smile. I love everybody but I move with a few. I had an argument with this old man in the station who maintained that the world is mad, especially the Irish because of our fight. Yet, he too *fought* in the war.

So the thinker having taken himself off misses his land. I am rooted to this sad land and its people as much as I am devoted to the flesh and blood which gives me life, as much as I am bonded to the truthful-happy soul I attempt to keep faith with. I sit and think. I remove all distractions and distortions and I wish the self away into the self. Travel deep. Touch the point of life. Into the core. Communicate with the red hot core of life! Once you touch it you are moved. The soul moves. The experience is heaven on earth.

**September 29th:** Left Mary Ann home and walked down the road hearing shots. Got in and heard bad news. In Shankill Road pub there was an explosion which killed two and injured many more.

**October 5th:** I never blame anyone. I exonerate most and think that people are never ultimately responsible. Because of this I cannot be extremist. If only I could in my mind fix properly the idea that there are evil people then I could learn to hate. Listen, I don't want to kill. I must though make a stand for what is right. We have gone through an awful lot.

Made contact with the *Tatler* newssheet, Ballymurphy, and wrote an article for it. It's either write or shoot. I am really confused. I want to do that which agrees with me.

**October 16th:** On news heard of a large arms haul in Amsterdam. Four tons of arms bought by the Provo IRA and destined for here were seized. No matter how I reject violence this frightens me. Our guns.

**October 19th:** There was a big fire in a large building in Great Victoria Street. I stood watching the flames eat up the statelet of N.I.

Later, coming down Malcolmson Street, the soldiers stopped us and a Scotch captain told us we had thirty seconds to 'fuckin' get home'. We nervously took our time. No wonder less patient people react with guns.

We have six centuries of history and present day oppression. If soldiers are prepared to kill innocent people as well as the IRA then the justification of the IRA killing them is present. Played Sean Ó Riada records and found part of me in his music.

**October 23rd:** Two women were shot dead by the army in Omar Street.

Steeped in this country I feel at times for extreme violence. No. Not yet. It has not got far enough yet. I am soaked in centuries of blood.

**October 24th:** The British army shot dead three young men for the simple civilian crime of theft. The soldiers have now licence to murder.

Statistics for October: 27 people died, 150 wounded and there were 150 explosions.

It is a disappointment, a great disappointment that violence will change the situation. It is the only way.

Mary Ann introduced me to her people who are nice. It appears they had a lot of trouble with the eldest one, Angela, who now lives in England.

The country is almost everything.

I once wrote that we were becoming immune to the deaths. That was a lie.

**December 5th:** Shocking news this day. Catholic pub, McGurk's bar, on New Lodge Road, was blown up last night. Fifteen men, women and children were killed. My God. It must be Loyalist revenge.

**December 10th:** Our John has been moved from Crumlin Road Jail to Long Kesh Internment Camp.

**December 24th:** Many houses have candles in their front windows in solidarity with the internees. I put one in ours. I don't know what to do. What should I do?

**December 30th/January 1st:** Before I write the following words their meaning has died a thousand doubts this day. Perhaps by putting them down I hope to reinforce their meaning.

Anyway, Christ has become country. I have been demented for months, agitated, and Mary Ann says she has got to know me so well she can see my torture. I went into town and got a bus to Dundonald. I had a lot of thinking to do and wanted to be on my own. I walked down the Newtownards Road. I stopped outside the gates of Stormont and had a good, long look at the place and what it represents. I then walked on into town, looking at some of the swanky houses, then other ghetto areas just like ours and at Goliath crane in the Shipyard, a place where our people never knew work. I crossed the Lagan and made my way across the city centre to the west of the city. Looking up in the cold December sunny light I saw the Royal Victoria Hospital and behind it Black Mountain. The day was reminiscent of other cold and sunny December mornings but I felt a change coming on. One of totally bending my life to the cause. I suppose it was only a matter of time. There is nothing left to do but enter into sacrifice and war. I feel so relieved.

Later: Went out tonight with Mary Ann and told her of my decision. She squeezed my arm and told me to be always careful. We went to the dance, had a few drinks and I kissed her at the stroke of midnight when the group announced the New Year. Some girls cried because their brothers or boyfriends were in jail.

I am home now and it is almost 3 am. I shall make my mark in this world and I hope I am worthy of it.

I don't know how 1972 will take me but I shall make this my year of years. Your health! To my pledge, to the Republic!

Tonight I felt for the first time that I could justly stand for the Soldier's Song.

## 1972

### January
Armoured cars and tanks and guns
Came to take away our sons,
But every man will stand behind
The men behind the wire!

\* \* \*

We never could get over August '69. I remember after seeing the destruction, the burned-out homes, walking up Divis Street and the Falls kicking stones and trying to discover reason.

\* \* \*

To die fighting is to cling to real life.

\* \* \*

The years surpass the day, the hours, the moment. Time itself can become a history. A particular time. I shall make times into a particular history. What value my life?

Came home for tea and heard the start of the evening's horrible news. The First Battalion Parachute Regiment went mad in Derry and shot dead 13 unarmed civilians. This was after the civil rights march.

\*   \*   \*

It snowed and we walked the streets, all collected in unity. Clearly, I cannot continue with my studying.

\*   \*   \*

Yesterday was horrible. It was Derry's Bloody Sunday. John Hume of the SDLP has changed the call from civil rights to a united Ireland or nothing.

\*   \*   \*

Rioting broke out and the people fought the soldiers in the snow.

**February**
The British embassy in Dublin was besieged and has been burned to the ground! Three cheers! Dublin is redeemed. It was great to hear the crowds singing *Four Green Fields* outside the embassy. Support like never before: '"What have I now," said the fine old woman . . .'

\*   \*   \*

FLESH
Her low-cut bra
Set her breasts
Out like bubbles.

Ah! Mary Ann!

KISS
That little split
Middle of her lower lip
Doubled pleasure.

## March
The Provisional IRA have called a three-day truce whilst they put forward peace proposals.

\* \* \*

The truce ends in one minute's time. One explosion now as the news comes on.

\* \* \*

Walking up the Grosvenor I heard explosions and a fleet of ambulances passed me. Six people dead and 149 injured in Donegall Street. Terrible.

\* \* \*

Heard of the announcement of 'Direct Rule' from Westminster. Faulkner and his government will resign soon. A slight victory for the Nationalist people.

\* \* \*

Loyalist power cuts against D R.

\* \* \*

## April
I was walking past St Dominic's School whistling and an old man stopped me and said: 'Son, it's good to hear you whistling. Years ago you would have heard many people, nearly every other fellah on this road, whistling, but recently I have heard no one. It is good to see someone happy.'

\* \* \*

## May
I walk around wearing a grey cardigan, a clean shirt, denims, an anorak and Dr Marten's boots. The anorak, jeans and boots are part of the image!

\* \* \*

There is a hunger-strike until death by the prisoners in Crumlin Road Jail for political status.

\* \* \*

Have completely given up studying but mother and father have no idea. One of the lads (married) says: 'We are on our way out, we're finished,' and so he's pulled out. It's up to him.

\* \* \*

## June
We collected signatures in petitions in support of the men on hunger-strike in Crumlin Road Jail demanding political status.

\* \* \*

Many internees have been released and my ma's hopes have been raised but John told me that the only time he'll get out is when the war is over, in a year or two.

Saw the lads in our local. It is just like the French Revolution the way they met in pubs and held their meetings and had endless political discussions.

\* \* \*

The swallows and the swifts have returned. They conquer the evening sky over Belfast. Their elegant swoops and risings are great to watch.

\* \* \*

The IRA offered to the British a chance of peace talks but they refused. The Loyalist paramilitary UDA postponed for two weeks their permanent no-go areas.

Had for one minute a great suicidal tendency for Ireland. Felt like assassinating Ted Heath or Reginald Maudling.

\* \* \*

I'll give credit where credit is due. God, you made a beautiful evening, a masterpiece — the sun feeding us its glorious light, the

sky a blue dress with a white hem, and children, streets of
raucous, lively children, each of their destinies a slow sprouting
mystery.

*   *   *

A ceasefire has been announced.

*   *   *

Loyalists have a pirate station — Radio Nick. Why can't they
become socialists instead of following the blind alley of
conservatism and imperialism.

**July**

11.40 p.m. You want to hear the shooting that is going on now!
I'm changing into dirty clothes and going out.

And the truce is over.

*   *   *

Last night there was a big gun battle around the Road
involving 2,000 rounds of ammunition. Two soldiers and three
civilians were shot dead. Every night somebody dies.

*   *   *

Tonight I was arrested and brought to Broadway army post. It
was obviously just a routine arrest but I was transferred by
Saracen to Springfield Road Barracks. I was determined not to let
the side down and though terrified I only gave the barest of
details and refused to talk about neighbours who they said were
connected. They also said I must be in the IRA because all IRA
men they arrested had the Prayer to St Joseph on them like me.

I also had a photograph of Mary Ann in my pocket and they
burnt her eyes out with cigarette ends. The place was full of
English accents which is really amazing when you think that in
every house, in every street around the place are Belfast accents.
That's how foreign they are. It was only when I was up against
the wall in the courtyard that I realised quite a few others were

also inside. Hughie O'Neill from round our way got a bad beating. They had his head in a tank of water which must be used for puncture repairs and I could hear him drowning and then his head would be lifted out. But he didn't talk.

Before I went in for interrogation they told me I had to have a medical and I was sent into a room to strip. I took my clothes off and then this man came in wearing a white coat and he told me he was the doctor and told me to take off my underpants. Then the door opened and he laughed along with a lot of other soldiers and two RUC men. He wasn't a doctor at all. When I was being interrogated a soldier banged the table and shouted was I not going to open my mouth. There was a lost Johnny Long Legs dancing on the wall, demented and claustrophobic. The soldier grabbed it by the wings and rubbed it against my sealed lips, killing the poor thing, but I never moved. They then whacked me around the head, said I would end up dead or with my brother John in jail. They threw me out after about four hours. How I held on to myself I'll never ever know.

* * *

At around three there were many explosions caused by the IRA and there is no escaping the moral responsibility — through association — of today's bloodshed which has so far taken nine lives, four of them civilians. Reaction of supporters is mostly one of two. Some outspoken ones, privately but to your face, criticise you. But most rush to your aid and nurse your morale. 'Bloody Friday' has been well-named.

* * *

Free Derry has been invaded and there have been many internment swoops again. The Brits are calling it 'Operation Motorman'.

## August

Soldiers are out in strength and it is back to porridge. There were explosions, shootings and robberies and then came the *ninth* and they had interned us for a year.

500 people have died so far.

'Well we got no choice
'And we got no innocence.'
— Alice Cooper, 'School's Out'

\*   \*   \*

Mary Ann and I went up the mountains today. I said, pointing to a field, this is where we fought the big boys back in '63 or '64, and she said I was wrong, it was over there. I helped her up the steep parts and held her hand and we stood on one of the banks at the Hatchet Field beside the now deserted cottage and looked out across our tortured city. It was quite emotional. Like myself she is a Republican. We went on up to the trickling stream which she had fallen into and she insisted it was me who fell in! She said, 'God help us when we're together twenty years, what will your memory be like then!' I thought this very sweet and touching, a statement of our togetherness and we lay down on the dry grass and, for the first time, a magnificent dreamy time, we made love. On the mountain top above West Belfast. I love her so much.

\*   \*   \*

Everytime we get the chance we make love. Everytime their backs are turned, or we can get babysitting, we make glorious love! We're crazy!

\*   \*   \*

Mary Ann and I visited our John today in Long Kesh. I told him to keep his eyes off her! Her family are going on holidays and I shall spend tonight, all night with her.

\*   \*   \*

I called up at half-seven and later we went down the Shaws Road for a walk. The light was dwindling but it was a hot summer's night and the very tar on the road was as alive as the lawns of Greenan basking in the final warmth of dusk. Before we left her house we heard some Proms' music — Strauss, I think —

and Mary Ann wore a long, patterned dress beneath which were her bare breasts, her teenage body into which I fit like a bee's tongue combing the flower's honey. She broke into a waltz on the Andersonstown Road, opposite the applauding poplars in St Joseph's training college, and in reply I whistled one of my favourite songs. She asked what it was and I told her, *Leila* by Derek and the Dominoes, and, filled with the night, we publicly hugged and kissed and made eejits of ourselves. Anybody who looked at us could see that it was just so much *Nature!*

Afterwards we went home and slept in her parents' double bed and made love, and made love, and made love. As I fell asleep she was still tickling my back! I asked her to set the alarm because today I would be very busy. I didn't even hear it going off but when I awoke there she was with a tray and on it a glass of milk and toasted soda bread which I ate in bed! She stroked my cheek and kissed my bloodshot eyes and from the Shaws Road I saw her wave from the back window and I blew her a kiss which I will recapture from the atmosphere and deliver myself tonight.

Went to the place for the business and discovered that we were delayed. Had a few hours to kill and with the okay of a friend, my big friend, I came down the Falls and called into our house. From the window of my bedroom where I am now writing I see my da working hard down below at an old desk which is a secret present for our Sheila. I love that old man, he is a good father. My mammy hands him a cup of tea and they share some joke or other and they smile together . . .

I have just sat for a few minutes and thought about last night, about my life and the times we live in and the decisions each of us — Republican, Loyalist, British soldier — make. We can be motivated by love, by noble passions, by fate, by adventurism or by selfishness, and despite our intellects many of us ultimately fall for our feelings. I don't have the answers, I know, and I admit that I am a victim of my version of the truth which matured under this sky, in these streets, as I grew up amidst family and friends, in the currents of our small history.

However, I know this much and it's as simple a declaration as I can make, looking down from mine and my brother's bedroom upon the man and woman below who brought me into this world through their own declaration of love.

I look at them with gratitude.

It is great to be alive and I thank God Almighty for having given me a mind of my own, for allowing me to have touched and savoured the beautiful mysteries and quandaries surrounding our existence on this earth, and for allowing me to have seen these years in West Belfast . . .

THE END